Boss From Hell

Georgia Le Carre

Boss From Hell
Published by Georgia Le Carre

Chapter 1
Lillian

"I don't understand why he won't just pop the damn question," Maggie complained in a frustrated voice. "I mean, I'm not fussy. I don't need anything fancy. Hell, he could ask me to marry him on a freaking bus and I'd happily say yes."

Maggie and I have been friends forever, okay, not forever, but since we met in third grade so I knew her well enough to know that assertion was an outright lie. She'd be totally horrified if her boyfriend actually proposed to her on a bus. I almost laughed at that impossible image popping into my mind, but I made a great effort not to.

Maggie's pain was real.

I covered her beautifully manicured hand with mine. "He's probably just taking his time. Aren't you the one who is always complaining about him rushing into decisions?"

It was the wrong thing to say. Her features became pinched. "Rushing into decisions? We've known each other for seven years!"

"Maybe he has a plan," I soothed. "Maybe... he just wants it to be perfect. Why not relax and enjoy the ride?"

"Easy for you to say," she grumbled.

"If you feel that strongly, why don't you propose to him?"

"I can't do that. I'll look desperate."

"You are desperate," I pointed out.

"I'm not," she denied vehemently, then spoiled it by draining half her cocktail in a single gulp.

I sighed. "Come on, Maggie. It's me you're talking to. Be honest. You can't wait to start your own home and have a family, can you?"

If I was honest, that had been my dream too, once upon a time. But life had flipped things around for me, and now I was just focused on surviving day to day. There was no time for dreams, not when real life was so tough and demanding.

Maggie nodded. "Fine, I'll give you that, but there's just no way I'm ever proposing to a man. Anyway, enough about me." She leaned forward, her eyes shining. "Tell me what's going on with you."

Maggie had a talent for flipping her mood around in an instant. She could be down and out one moment and the next, she could be laughing uproariously as if she didn't have a care in the world.

"Well..." I started and paused. "Where to start with the mess my life is in?"

"Start with the job hunt. How's that going?" she prompted.

"It's not going," I admitted and sipped my chardonnay.

"Why is that then?"

"I don't know. I've sent several resumés, but so far... nothing. Sometimes it feels as if I'm sending them into the ether to languish forever."

Maggie frowned. "That's strange. You're good at your job, and you have excellent references."

"Actually, I'm getting a little worried," I confessed. "I have savings, of course, but my monthly expenses are high, and could eat through them in no time. I need a job sooner rather than later."

"Hmmm... let me think if I've got anything that I could hook you up with." She frowned. "I have an opening at the agency that pays really well."

I brightened. "You have?"

She thought for an instant, then made an apologetic face while shaking her head. "Nah, cancel that. What am I thinking of? That job's not for you. Forget it."

"Hang on. How about letting me decide what's for me?"

"Trust me, the job is more trouble than it's worth."

"Let me decide," I insisted.

"Well, I suppose, it *is* a very well-paid job with awesome bonuses, and if you're really, really desperate..."

"I'm really, really desperate," I said quickly.

She sighed. "Alright. Don't say I didn't warn you."

"Yeah, yeah, get on with it."

"You'll be the PA of a ghastly man called Maximus Frost who owns Frost Investments."

"Okay. Tell me more about this ghastly man," I invited.

"He comes from a ridiculously wealthy family, but decided to build his own multi-billion-dollar company from scratch. His investment company is one of the leading investment firms in the country. Which is why his attitude puzzles me. He behaves like a spoiled brat which he can't be, not if you consider how hard he must have worked to get to where he is."

"How much does the job pay?"

She quoted a figure and I gasped.

"Yeah," she said, nodding sagely. "That's how much no one wants to work for him. It's more of a bribe than a salary. The man is a terrible tyrant. An absolute monster. I swear he's been through more secretaries than any CEO in the past 100 years. I keep sending my girls to him and he keeps sending them back in tears."

I sat back and stared at her. "Wow."

"Yeah, he has a reputation of being a complete asshole. The phrase, 'boss from hell' was invented to describe him. No PA has lasted a full month."

Now, I was intrigued. "Yeah?"

"Yeah," she stated emphatically.

"Maybe I would."

She stared back at me. "Maybe, but I wouldn't bet on it. We've sent him our best talent and every single one has left in the first or second week."

"I think I'd like to give it a try," I said slowly.

Her eyes widened. "You would?"

"I certainly could do with the money."

Suddenly her eyes twinkled like blue stars in her face. "If you want to give it a shot, be my guest. In fact, I'll even make it a bit more interesting and throw in a hundred dollars if you can last more than a month."

I laughed in disbelief. "You want to bet on me not lasting a month?"

"That's right."

I looked at her with narrowed eyes. "You're serious?"

"Dead serious. The job is yours. I'll be happy to lose a hundred bucks if I can send someone to him who can last longer than a month."

"You're on," I said. "One hundred bucks says I stay the whole month."

She laughed. "You never could resist a bet, could you?"

"It's more the salary," I quipped.

She grinned and drowned the rest of her cocktail. "Looks like I just won myself a hundred dollars. I'll email you the details in the morning.

I sipped my wine, enjoyed the feeling of the cold liquid going down my throat, and cautioned, "Don't count your chickens before they're laid, Maggie."

"Oh, I'm pretty sure these chicks are getting laid," she claimed confidently.

I squared my shoulders. "I think I'll be able to handle Mr. Frost."

"Just don't be shocked if you're out of there in a week," she warned darkly. "You won't be the first or the last."

I raised my glass. "That is not going to happen. I've had my share of difficult bosses... and I have a way with them."

She clinked her empty glass with mine, then summoned the waiter for another round. I wasn't worried about Mr. Frost. My situation made it irrelevant how my boss behaved. The bottom line was what mattered and that was being able to make my mother's mortgage payments on time.

Maggie ordered another round of drinks, then turned back to me. Her eyes were gleaming mischievously. "Oh, by the way, I forgot to mention. Maximus Frost, by all accounts, is also sex on a stick."

She laughed gaily at my shocked expression. "Good luck winning the bet."

Chapter 2
Lillian

The next morning, as I did most Sundays, I went over to my mother's house to help with the weekly cleaning. As I polished a small bird figurine, and not for the first time, I thought it was time for her to sell the house and buy something smaller.

There was simply no reason for her to live alone in a five-bedroom house. To start with she didn't need all this space, but more importantly, she couldn't afford the mortgage payments without significant help from me. If she sold it, she could buy something smaller outright.

Maybe today was the day I would broach the thorny subject.

I watched her dust a picture frame of my dad resting on the night table. Ever since Henry, my stepfather, passed on, my father's photographs had begun to appear all over the house. As if she wanted to forget she'd ever had a second husband. I couldn't blame her. Henry messed up her life big time.

I hated him for the mess he had left for my mother to

clean up. It had been his dream to own a sports bar and grill and he had convinced my mom to join him on the enterprise. Just like that she left her job, remortgaged the house, and took out a loan at the bank.

It had seemed to work at first, but it soon became apparent that the ship was sinking. After the initial excitement of a new restaurant, the dinner crowd had thinned and Mom had taken another loan without our knowledge, to service the other loan. Madness.

"Um… how are your finances, sweetheart?" Mom threw over her shoulder. She had tried to make the question sound casual, but I heard the worry in her voice.

"Not too bad," I replied, my voice equally nonchalant.

"Hmmm… I was thinking…" She straightened to look at me. "Why don't you move back home?"

I couldn't help the expression of dismay on my face.

"Lillian, it will help you cut down on expenses. Besides, you should be here. After all, you shoulder most of the mortgage burden."

"It's no big deal, Mom."

"It is a big deal. A very big deal. Don't think I don't know how hard you have to work to do that," she cried. Her lower lip started trembling and she bit down on it. "I don't know what I'd do without you."

I sighed. It looked like today probably wasn't the best time to bring up selling the house and moving to a smaller place. Never mind. Helping her with the mortgage payments was nothing compared to the horror I had watched her live through when the restaurant was gone, the receivers had turned up at her door and I had to empty my bank account to pay them off.

I shook my head free of those memories. I was determined to forge ahead with life and not focus on the things that had gone wrong. Moving back home was a recurring nightmare that I had no intention of making into a reality.

"It's fine, honestly. You know I'm happy to do it. Plus, I'm starting a job on Monday."

"Really?" she asked, perking up.

"It's only temporary, but..."

"Oh well, the offer still stands."

"Thanks, Mom, but you know me. I love my space."

"I know," she said and patted my hand with affection. "You've always been so independent. Much more than Rose." She frowned. "Have you spoken to your sister lately? How is she?"

"I spoke to her yesterday. She's fine."

She looked sideways at me. "And Dylan and the girls?"

"Fine too."

We moved our cleaning stuff to the next room.

"Did she say anything about getting a job?"

"You know the answer to that," I told her gently as I wiped down a lamp. This was a big bone of contention between my mother and sister. Their conversations frequently ended in shouting matches with Rose accusing Mom of making her out to be lazy. Rose and Dylan had decided that she would stay home until the twins went to school. That didn't sit well with Mom, but I was with Rose on this one.

"A woman should have something of her own," Mom grumbled. "You never know when things can change. Dylan earns enough now, but he could lose his job."

Mom had always been an optimistic person. It was the

reason why Henry had managed to convince her to hop onto his dream. But these days, she saw the glass as half-empty, and who could blame her after the financial wringing she had gone through?

"He's not going to lose his job," I said. "And even if he did, dentists are in high demand in New York, everyone wants to have a brilliant smile."

"That is true," she conceded. "So tell me about this temporary job."

I told her about Maximus Frost and how he had built his enterprise from scratch. I'd have told my "old mom" about how horrible he was and the bet, and she would probably have wanted in on the fun, but not now. It would probably piss her off that we were taking life so casually by betting on something as important as a job.

Life had become precarious for her. It saddened me to see her worry about everything, but there was nothing I could do about it.

After spending the morning cleaning the house, I made a salad and we sat down to eat lunch together. She regaled me with harmless gossip from the doctor's office where she worked as an assistant. More than helping with the mortgage, the job kept her busy enough so that when she came home in the evenings, she didn't dwell too much on what she had lost.

I left after lunch and headed to the farmer's market to buy veggies for the next week as I'd be at work... working for Maximus Frost.

Chapter 3
Max

"Your coffee, Sir," the waiter said, placing a cup of steaming black liquid before me.

I grunted a response and took a sip. It was my third cup of the day and it was only nine in the morning. Next week, the plan was to reduce it to a maximum of two cups a day.

Chris, my best friend and second in command joined me, and we briefly discussed the three new companies we were trying to acquire for the next twenty minutes.

Afterwards, we took the short walk back to our offices. Chris got off on his floor and I carried on up to mine. As I got out of the elevator, the security guard who manned my floor called out a morning greeting. Ignoring him I headed straight towards my office. After all this time, he still didn't get it. His job was not to brown-nose me. His job was to guard the damn premises.

I ground to a halt at the sight of a woman sitting at the desk in my outer office.

"Who the fuck are you?" I barked.

She looked up, her wide blue eyes as calm as a blue lake on a hot summer day and... fucking smiled at me. Standing up, she straightened her pencil skirt as if I had all day to wait for her. She grated on me before she even opened her mouth to speak.

"Good morning, Mr. Frost. My name is—"

"I didn't ask your name. I asked you what the fuck you're doing here." I snapped, cutting her off. I wasn't interested in what her name was.

"I'm your new personal assistant," she said, that eerily calm smile never leaving her face.

Robotically calm women gave me the creeps. I narrowed my eyes as I jogged my memory. I didn't remember the temp agency emailing to let me know that they would send someone. I was just getting used to the peace and quiet.

Coldly, I stared her up and down. She was quite something in the looks department, but if she thought her sex appeal would cut it here, she had another thing coming. True I had a thing for women in tight pencil skirts, but only in totally different circumstances.

When I was at work, I was purely and totally in work mode. Oh well, maybe it was a good thing she was here. Work was starting to pile up.

"Fine. Get me a coffee. Black, no sugar." I turned to go to my office before I remembered: I was cutting down on coffee. "No, don't," I said irritably. "Get me some water. None of that plastic stuff, make sure it's in a glass bottle. I have a running account at the deli down the street."

I entered my office, and even before the door had shut behind me, I had already turned on my computer. I logged onto my email account. Hell, without a personal assistant, my inbox was flooded with emails. I scrolled through, opening important ones and responding with brief replies where necessary. I was completely lost in my work when a knock sounded on my door, I looked up impatiently. A crack sounded from the back of my neck. I'd been sitting in the same position for too long.

"Come in," I thundered.

The door swung open and Miss what's-her-name strolled in. Her lack of briskness annoyed me.

"Your water, Mr. Frost."

I massaged the back of my neck and looked at my new PA properly for the first time. She was surprisingly quite ravishing, with lustrous long blonde hair tightly held back in a ponytail.

A heart-shaped face and plump lips, all good things on my list of wants, but those eerily blank blue eyes. Imagine fucking that! My gaze dropped down to her slim-fitting skirt. She had curves, if you liked that sort of thing.

I did, but not at work.

I made a mental guess of how long she would last. Probably less than a week. Despite her nice packaging, she was probably like all the others. Inefficient snowflakes. All with no exceptions expected special treatment as if it was my job to make it nice and comfortable for them when they fucked up.

I raised my gaze and met her cool one, staring right back at me. Another woman would have reacted to my shameless examination in two ways. Red-faced embarrassment, or the disgusted feminist's chin upturned pose.

My new PA did neither.

She waited for me to finish my inspection. Her non-reaction, and those eyes that should have creeped me out, did something completely unexpected. They made me want to fuck her. Right there on my desk. I wanted to bend her over my desk, bunch that pencil skirt around her waist, and give her the riding she deserved. I wanted to see those calm blue lakes ripple with unbridled lust.

Heat whipped through me and rushed to my cock.

What the-?

I'd never had such a violent reaction to any of my assistants. I preferred my women to be willing, anonymous hookups.

"What's your name?"

"Lillian Hudson," she answered calmly.

"Once you leave here, take a trip to HR and get them to sort out an email for you," I said, and opening the top drawer of my desk pulled out a file. I'd had so many assistants over the last two years I'd made a special binder to give them a crash course in what they needed to know to work for me.

You'd think that being handed all the instructions in one place would make it a breeze, but of course, it didn't. I had the misfortune of getting saddled with fools and idiots.

"Read that," I said, sliding the folder towards her.

Silently, she picked up the folder.

Then I pulled out another folder that contained some projected numbers and calculations for some of my projects and handed it to her. "Feed the info in these files into the relevant databases. I want it done before you leave the office today."

Okay. Maybe I didn't need the whole thing done by

today, but I was curious to see how calm and collected Lillian Hudson would be after hours of heavy, monotonous work.

Would she think she was too big for data entry and quit today? If she was a quitter, better still. I didn't quite like that she was so distracting anyway. I'd rather she left so I could get back to things the way they were before she arrived. I wanted to go back to thinking with my brain.

I told her briefly what to do and curtly dismissed her.

She didn't make a move to leave, but she did flip through the folder. A frown pulled at her very kissable lips.

"All this?" she asked quietly. "You want it *all* done today?"

I swung a black look at her. "Is that a problem?"

Her facial muscles moved and produced that supercilious smile again. "Not at all, Mr. Frost."

My cock swelled even more when she called me Mr. Frost. Damn, the woman. My only consolation was she would almost certainly be gone by the end of the week. Which, by the way things were shaping up, would be a good outcome. Might as well guarantee and help hasten her departure with a few well-chosen unreasonable requests.

"Anything else I can help you with?" I asked sarcastically.

"No, Sir," she said crisply and left.

For some reason, I felt a pull of something approaching curiosity about her. Something I'd not experienced in a long time for any woman and never for one of my staff. Angrily, I pushed the feeling away and focused on my work. I only had an hour to clear my inbox before I had meetings back-to-back, then lunch with a potential client.

The next few hours were blissfully quiet as I had re-routed all calls to her extension. It gave me the peace to get on with my work. I read through some proposals from our managers and made some notes on what sounded potentially interesting.

My cell phone broke the delightful silence in the room. I glanced at the screen and swore. It was my mother. Was she in town? I hoped not. I swiped the screen.

"Hello, Mother," I greeted, barely able to contain my impatience. My mother was one of the reasons I'd been eager to leave Connecticut. She was needy and clingy and it drove me crazy. It wasn't quite as grating on the phone as in person.

"Hello, Maximus," she replied gaily. She was the only one who insisted on using my tediously pretentious full name. "You haven't called in almost two weeks. Don't you miss your parents?"

My mother had a selective memory when she wanted to. I quelled the rising irritation. "Mother, we spoke a week ago."

"I miss my only child," she cooed.

Ah, one of those calls. Might as well get it over with. With a sigh, I settled back and scrolled through a business proposal while she prattled through a list of complaints. They started with things I had, or hadn't done, then moved on to my long-suffering father and how he wasn't being attentive to her needs.

"By the way, I arrived in New York last night, and I've booked a table at the Four Seasons for the three of us at eight o'clock," she said.

I stopped reading as my head jerked up. Shit. All that

time, she had been working up to tell me that. It was just like her to just show up without any advance warning.

"You're in New York?"

"Yes, but don't fall over yourself with excitement."

The next worst thing after her neediness was her sarcasm.

"You should have let me know you were coming," I muttered, barely able to keep the temper out of my voice.

"I will next time," she lied breezily.

"You said you made reservations for three. Who's joining us?"

"Bring your girlfriend. You can't tell me there's no one in your life, Maximus."

"There isn't," I said through gritted teeth. My mother meddling in my love life was the third reason she was so annoying.

"Fine. Come alone, but if you change your mind..."

"See you later," I said and cut the connection.

I had five minutes to spare before my client meeting. Needing to stretch, I got up and left my office. Lillian was at her desk, her brow faintly creased as she concentrated on something that didn't look like the work I'd given her to do.

"Have you started inputting the numbers I gave you?"

She looked up. "No, Sir, I haven't. I thought it wiser to read the other file you gave me first."

"Why do I always get the lazy ones?" I grumbled, exasperated. At this rate, it will be days before the database gets populated.

She gazed back, completely unruffled by my comment.

"Show the clients in when they come," I ordered, and walked away in disgust.

"Yes, Sir."

My clients arrived a few minutes later and Lillian showed them in. She offered and served us all refreshments. She had taken the initiative to order delicious dim sum canapes which went down well with everyone. I had to admit she was so cool and professional, no one would have guessed it was her first day.

In the afternoon, she knocked on my door and when I barked at her to enter, she did so with that annoyingly tranquil smile still fixed on her face.

I found my eyes raking over her body. What the fuck was wrong with me? Sure, she had a smoking hot body, but I didn't hit on employees. Ever. It was a hard rule. No negotiations.

"All done," she announced maddeningly.

"What is all done?" I snapped.

"The data you gave me to enter into your database. It's done."

Impossible. I frowned darkly at her. "All of it?"

The deliberately blank smile widened slightly. I recognized it. She was feeling victorious.

"Yes, all of it. I found a way to do it in batch form."

I had to see that for myself. I clicked on the mouse until it took me to the custom-made program which enabled me to see all the numbers at a glance. She wasn't lying. She *had* done it.

A new respect for her came over me.

Maybe she wasn't as pathetic as the rest of them. This new development made my earlier decision to hasten her departure irrational, but she was too distracting to keep. I looked up, nodded curtly, and dismissed her with a wave of my hand. Dismissing her from my mind was a bit harder as I continued trying to read a report by one of my managers. She had to go. Definitely.

I came out of my office at half past five and Lillian was still at her desk.

"Good night, Sir."

"I need you to accompany me to dinner," I said brusquely.

"Sorry?"

"You didn't think this was a nine-to-five job, did you?"

"No, Sir," she said serenely. "What file do I need to take with me?"

"The White Water one."

She could keep my mother company while I worked on that file.

Chapter 4
Lillian

As I looked for the file he'd asked for, my mind was abuzz.

Gosh, he had come so close my skin tingled.

I know Maggie had warned me he was sex on a stick, but freaking hell! She had not prepared me for the gale force ten sexual magnetism that blasted out of that icy man. I mean, he really lived up to his name. Frost. Even his eyes were so light they shone like dangerous shards of gray ice in his tanned face.

Even though he was undeniably and devilishly attractive and at least six-four inches tall, (tall men, I had a thing for), he was a hard pass for me. Nothing could make up for his lack of manners. Rude didn't even begin to describe his character. The insolence was simply out of this world. The man was downright awful; it was almost as if he got a special thrill from making his PAs feel like crap.

Never in my life had I ever come across such a grumpy, disagreeable ogre. He never smiled, not even when his clients were around. I noticed he wasn't horrible to them though.

Just me.

As I sifted through the files, I tried to regain my composure. I don't think I'd ever had a boss ask me to go out for dinner with him, even if it was meeting clients. From behind me, I could actually feel him brimming with impatience. To my great relief, I found the file in the next few seconds and pulled it out.

Grabbing my handbag, I followed him to the door.

As I hurried behind him, my eyes took in his physique from the back. Wide strong shoulders, slim waist, and narrow hips. I found my gaze drifting downwards towards his ass. It was covered by the jacket of his suit, of course, but I was willing to bet it was tight and firm. For some reason I couldn't fathom, I found myself wondering what it would feel like to cup his ass and yank him to me so I could feel his hard, hot erection.

Shocked by my insane train of thoughts, I shifted my gaze away from him and stared at the elevator doors as we waited for them to open.

I didn't understand myself.

He was supposed to be a hard no.

Why would I even have such crazy thoughts about such a rude asshole? True, he was handsome—in that hard, frighteningly cold sort of way—but he DEFINITELY wasn't the kind of man I gravitated towards. I liked gentle, caring, highly cultured men. He was clearly none of those things.

My heart was pounding like crazy when the doors

swished open. Brusquely he gestured for me to enter. I swallowed hard and walked in.

It was just the two of us in the elevator, and tension grew with every passing second. I couldn't wait for it to come to a stop and for the doors to slide open. Being in an enclosed mirrored space with Maximus Frost invoked all sorts of weird feelings inside me, as if the space was too small for both of us.

A memory came to mind of a movie I'd watched years ago where the hero and heroine stopped the elevator and had sex in it. The scene stayed with me and made me question whether I could ever do something like that. I thought no, but today... Jesus.

What the hell was wrong with me?

An image so vivid and so real rushed into my head.

Maximus Frost pinning me to the cold walls, his hot breath on my neck as he peppered burning kisses down my throat. His hands running over my hips and ass then, in one fluid rough movement, he pulls up my skirt and yanks down my panties before thrusting deep into me. No warning, no asking for permission. Pure caveman stuff.

The elevator came to a halt, bringing me back to reality. My panties were wet and the urge to squeeze my thighs was so strong shame gripped me. I tried not to fidget as I recalled the insane fantasy I'd just indulged in. What would he think if he read my mind?

When the elevator doors slid open, Mr. Frost stood aside to let me out first. That old-fashioned gesture amazed me; I never expected him to be so gentlemanly after the way he had treated me all day in the office.

Saying nothing, I walked out into the basement, before stopping and turning to face him. And. Wow. The overhead light caught his eyes and turned them translucent. They would have been freakishly beautiful if there wasn't so much frost in them.

"We'll take my car and I'll drop you off. You can take a cab to work tomorrow morning. Put it under expenses." Without waiting for an answer, he turned on his heel and walked away, taking big strides that carried him away swiftly.

Seething at his impervious attitude, I hurried to catch up with him, wanting to tell him that no, I wasn't going to go in his car, and there was no way I was taking a cab in the morning whether the company was paying for it or not. The problem was, by the time I caught up, Mr. Frost was already inside his car, a gleaming SUV that was as dark as his personality.

I had no choice but to enter.

"Shut the door. I haven't got all day," he barked, without looking at me. He was staring straight ahead, gripping the steering wheel tightly. He was obviously used to giving orders and having them instantly obeyed or he saw red. Even before the door had shut properly, the engine had roared to life and the car was moving.

The arrogance of the man was unbelievable.

What an asshole. He didn't bother to tell me anything about the client we were meeting, nor had he taken the time to check if I had any other plans for the evening. No wonder he never kept an assistant longer than a few days.

It was tempting, really tempting, to tell him where he

could shove his stupid job, but of course, I kept my mouth tightly shut. It was not just losing the bet with Maggie, but also my bank account balance that bought my silence. Everything wasn't only about me, my mother needed help with her mortgage until I could convince her to sell her house and buy a smaller one.

In the meantime, she depended on me.

Gritting my teeth, I stayed stiffly silent.

As I usually did when I was feeling down, I searched for a memory that would make me smile. In this case, the one that came was Mr. Frost's face when I told him I'd finished inputting the data into the system. The way he had looked at me in stunned disbelief before clicking on his computer to check for himself.

That moment was pure gold.

And when he confirmed I wasn't lying, he looked up at me with a grudging respect in his eyes. It hadn't lasted though, and he had gone right back to his impossibly rude self. Still, my little triumph had carried me through the rest of the day... until he demanded I accompany him for dinner while looking down at me like I was a piece of gum stuck to the bottom of one of his expensive shoes.

I made myself breathe in and out evenly and promised myself that I wouldn't be Mr. Frost's assistant for long. I'd keep applying for jobs until I found the perfect one. In the meantime, I was going to take all the crap that he was going to dish out - as long as it was just words. After all, words had never hurt anybody.

Or so they said.

When we reached the restaurant entrance, he tossed his car keys to the valet. I noticed he didn't bother to say thank you or even acknowledge the man. It wasn't much of a comfort, but I found myself relieved to see I wasn't the only one he was rude to. It wasn't personal. I stood behind him while he barked something at the hostess. Silently, we followed her across the restaurant to a corner table.

To my surprise, an older woman dressed in pastel-colored, clearly expensive clothes, and a pearl necklace was already at the table.

"Maximus," she cried, staring at him as if he were the most precious object she'd ever laid eyes on. This odd reaction led me to believe she must be his mother. Only his mother could look at *him* like that. Also, she had the same silver eyes, the only difference was his were hostile and hers were haughty. He bent his face and allowed her to kiss both his cheeks, but I could feel his impatience even from where I was standing.

"Mother," he noted and stepped back.

His mother turned her regal attention to me. Her gaze was thorough, my face, my hair, my clothes, down to my shoes. When her regard returned to my face again, there was a vaguely puzzled expression in them, as if she couldn't understand how everything fit together.

"This is Lillian." He didn't say anything else after that, and his mother didn't seem to expect anything else either.

She smiled at me. "I'm Marilyn, Maximus's mother, as you may have figured out."

Maximus, huh? "It's a pleasure to meet you, Mrs. Frost."

She leaned forward as if what she was going to say next was confidential. "Please, call me Marilyn. Mrs. Frost makes me feel so ancient." She drew back and chuckled.

"Let's all sit down," Mr. Frost said impatiently.

We sat down and his mother proceeded to ask him personal questions, the kind a mother would ask. I was now thoroughly confused. This was obviously a family dinner, so why had he asked me to come with him?

He didn't seem to care that I was present. In fact, they spoke as if I wasn't there at all. From their conversation, I gleaned that Mrs. Frost lived in Connecticut and was here in New York just visiting for a few days.

It was all very weird and the file felt heavy on my lap. One question kept running through my mind: Why on earth had he asked me out for dinner with his mother?

"I hope we're not boring you, my dear." His mother smiled at me and condescendingly patted my hand. "We like to catch up on gossip when we meet."

The waiter came and took our order for dinner.

"Pass me the file," Mr. Frost instructed as soon as the waiter left.

Wordlessly I handed him the file and he eagerly opened it and began to look intently through it.

"Tell me about your family, Lillian," Mrs. Frost invited, her cold eyes curious.

I was taken aback. Why on earth did my boss's mother want to know about my family? I looked at him, but his gaze was firmly on the pages of the file.

I took a deep steadying breath and smiled politely. "Well, my family consists of my widowed mother and my older sister who is married with children."

"Oh, do they live here in New York?"

"Yes, we're dyed-in-the-wool New Yorkers."

"Maybe one day you and Maximus will come back to Connecticut and raise a family there," she said.

My jaw almost dropped from shock, but before I could attempt to correct the error of her impression, Mr. Frost spoke up.

"Mother, leave Lillian alone. We barely know each other. You'll scare her off." Then he went back to his file.

I blinked with amazement. What the hell was going on?

Then I understood, or at least, I thought I did. He was quite happy for his mother to think we were romantically involved. Maybe she pestered him about getting married and having a family, or for being a workaholic with no intention of setting up a home any time soon. I could see that being the case, but...

A burning fury grew inside me.

Mr. Frost was using me! And that was not the worst of it, he had let me believe that this was a business meeting. What he really wanted was for me to keep his mother entertained and lie to her while he got on with his file.

I bit my lower lip to stop myself from saying anything rude and fisted my hands under the table. The horrible man could have been polite about it and asked me nicely if it was something that I wanted to do as it was not part of my job description.

The food came, smelling delicious. Mrs. Frost's manicured fingers tore at the leaves of her artichoke with great appreciation, but I simply couldn't enjoy my meal.

I was seething.

All I could think about was the arrogance with which he'd told me to accompany him to dinner when all along he just wanted me to sit around appeasing his mother while he worked.

I couldn't wait for dinner to be over so that I could give

him a piece of my mind. And then I remembered – I was supposed to last a whole month, not get fired on my first day.

Bite your tongue, Lillian.

Bite your wayward tongue.

Chapter 5
Max

When my mother excused herself and got up to go to the bathroom, I grunted and carried on reading.

A waiter came to our table and spoke to Lillian, "Is there something wrong with your dish, Miss?"

I looked up curiously. She had hardly eaten.

She raised her gaze to him. "The food is fine, thank you. It's the company that's a problem."

The waiter's eyebrows flew upwards. He glanced at me, then very wisely withdrew, without comment.

I was incensed.

Lillian turned her expressionless gaze to me as if daring me to say anything to her. I couldn't believe her arrogance. I was so pissed off I was of the mind to fire her right then and there, but something stopped me.

Nobody had ever stood up to me before, and it was a new feeling that I wasn't sure how I felt about.

I'd met all sorts of women and to be honest, they were all the fucking same. They ran after me, sucked up to me, and generally offered everything on a plate in the hope there would be a ring coming in the near future. There was no challenge or fun. They were just willing bodies in my bed. And afterwards, I couldn't wait to throw them out of the door.

My mother returned at that moment. On her face was the smile she used when trying to be friendly to people she thought were not up to her standard.

"Do you want dessert, mother?" I asked.

"Just coffee for me," my mother replied.

I turned to Lillian, my face impassive. "Dessert?"

Her eyes flashed with some hidden emotion. Then she smiled, an odd smile and I knew. It was payback time.

"No, thank you, Sir."

Laughter threatened to burst out of me. Sassy. Very sassy, but two could play this game. "Lillian," I chided gently, indulgently. "How many times must I tell you? Don't call me Sir outside the bedroom."

My mother's eyes nearly dropped out of her face, and hot color rushed into Lillian's cheeks as I coolly summoned the waiter.

"You're quite different from the women Maximus has dated in the past," my mother commented into the awkward silence.

I spoke up fast, my voice hard. "Mother, we talked about this before. Leave it alone."

I had a feeling that Lillian had reached her limit, and if my mother said one more thing about us being in a relationship, she was going to blurt out the truth, and it kinda suited me to let my mother think I was in a relationship. One less thing for her to nag me about. She had recently gotten it into her head that she was ready for grandchildren. As if it fucking worked that way. I'd never met a woman who had tempted me to take things beyond the bedroom.

"Can't I even have a conversation with your girlfriend?" my mother insisted.

"I think we're done here," I said, suddenly fed up with the whole situation.

"But we haven't even finished the wine yet, Maximus! You're always in such a rush!" my mother scolded.

I noticed Lillian had a slight smirk on her face, and that irritated me to no end. At that moment, I wanted to reach out, grab her by the back of the neck, and kiss her savagely—so savagely that she would come to work the following day with swollen, bruised lips, and each time she looked at me she'd remember the brutality of my kiss. And never dare provoke me again.

My cock stirred and grew hard.

Hell, why couldn't I stop thinking about how it would feel to fuck her? Lust burned in my brain. I was like a man possessed. I tried to rationalize it out; she was fine alright, but there were many women in the city who were as fine, if not finer.

I didn't understand why I was so obsessed with the idea of having sex with her. Maybe it was the way she had thrust her chin out and stood up to me. She wasn't a doormat like all the other assistants I'd had. You had to admire a woman who could stand up to a tyrant, one who was used to getting his own way all the time.

I shut the file and called for the bill.

My mother looked a bit miffed, but she said nothing.

Her driver was waiting for her at the front of the restaurant and I was glad to close the door after her.

While Lillian and I waited for my car to be brought around, she never spoke to me or even looked at me, keeping her gaze firmly on her phone's screen. It shouldn't have bothered me, but it did. I wanted to snatch that phone and violently smash it to the ground.

That would force her to look at me.

Once we were in the car I asked her to input her address into the GPS. As she did so, I noticed her fingers were slim and long, and her nails were well-manicured. I could imagine them scraping my back and digging into my shoulders as I fucked her hard.

My gaze moved from her hands to her thighs. That was the thing about pencil skirts. They ride up. In the heat of the car, I was hit by a fresh wave of her scent. Honey and lavender mingled with something else, something more... musky. At that moment, I would have given a lot for a touch or a lick.

She stared straight in front of her, bristling with suppressed anger.

"What is wrong with you?" I asked.

"Nothing is wrong with me. However, you led me to believe this was a business dinner. I don't think keeping your mother company and letting her think I'm your girlfriend counts as one."

"Got a problem with it?"

"No, but some advance notice would be helpful... so I can better play the part of your girlfriend."

I frowned. I certainly didn't expect that answer. My pulse quickened with forbidden longing. I gripped the steering wheel and was glad for the darkness in the car because she couldn't see how hard I was.

I felt like a fucking pervert getting turned on by my assistant subtly scolding me. The irony of it did not escape me. I was the one usually doing the scolding.

I didn't have anything to say in response. It pissed me off that she was right, but I wasn't going to admit it. I stopped in front of a nondescript apartment building and waited for her to get out, but she didn't. I turned to face her, and I was hit by the blueness of her eyes. Fuck, this was insane.

"Well, what are you waiting for?"

In the light of the streetlamp, her blue eyes sparkled with anger, but her voice was cool. "Thanks for dinner."

Then she was gone.

I wanted to watch her walk to her door, but I forced myself to turn away. This obsession with my PA was becoming downright unhealthy, not to mention terribly inconvenient. I was behaving completely out of character. I was more like a clueless teen with a raging hard-on, but I couldn't seem to stop myself.

I got home without knowing how I got there. My mind was so obsessed with the thought of Lillian and that crazy-hot body of hers. I pressed a button and the gates slid open.

As I drove into my driveway the usual sense of relief and relaxation washed over me. I enjoyed the fortress I had built for myself. It gave me the complete privacy I wanted. The faceless, nameless people who worked around the clock to keep everything running smoothly for me made themselves scarce when I was home.

The garage door opened remotely and I drove in. When

I opened my door, Tomo and Tyson, my two Dobermans, ran silently up to me. I rubbed their shiny heads in greeting. They flanked me on either side, their nails clicking on the granite, as I made my way up to the master bedroom on the second floor, taking the stairs three at a time. As soon as they got into the bedroom, they took their places on either side of the door, their eyes fierce, their demeanor watchful.

I needed a shower really badly.

I stripped off, dumping my suit and shirt on the bed then walked butt-naked to the bathroom. I turned on the shower, set it to cold, and stepped into the freezing waterfall. It worked. My hard-on died instantly. I set the temperature back to warm and filled my mind with thoughts of work and all the pending possible issues that could go wrong.

I loved success and I loved closing deals, but not for the money. I already had enough of that. What I craved was the thrill that came from winning. Despite trying to fill my thoughts with work, Lillian's face, staring at me with fury blazing in her eyes popped back into my head. Giving up, I grabbed a bottle of shower gel and scooped a generous dollop into the palm of my hand.

Working quickly, I spread the thick liquid all over my cock and proceeded to stroke myself. I remembered the scent of her. In my mind, I was fucking my PA, my cock in her sweet pussy.

I imagined the angry passion on her face as I fucked her.

I imagined her pressing her heavy breasts against my chest, her mouth sucking my tongue. My body convulsed and my dick began to fill and throb. I stroked it faster, sliding my hands up and down the shaft violently. I let out a groan as I felt my balls tighten and my cock began to spasm. Bursts of hot cum shot out.

Fuck me! I'd just jerked off to fantasies of my new PA.

I leaned my forearms against the cold tiles, bent my head, and let out a long sigh. This was so fucked up. I didn't need this distraction in my life. Most definitely not now. Not when I had to focus on getting my business to the next level.

Maybe... I should find a new way to encourage Miss Hudson to leave a little sooner than the others had done. Maybe that was the best solution.

Chapter 6
Lillian

I was shaking with fury. I was so full of explosive anger I couldn't even wait for the elevator. I ran up the ten flights of dank-smelling stairs to my fifth-floor apartment. I was panting by the time I reached my door. God, I'd never wanted to slap anyone before, but how my hand had itched to slap his arrogant face.

How dare he?

Never. Never had I ever encountered such an uncouth man.

Fuck the bet.

As for my mom's mortgage, well, I still had some savings left. There was enough there to pay for the next couple of months. Surely, I would have found another job by then. Even one I didn't like too much. Anything would be better than putting up with that bastard's shit.

I closed my door and, leaning against it, took my phone out and opened my banking app.

What?

There was $3400.00 less. I quickly navigated to the

statement screen. Slowly my body slid down to the floor. I closed my eyes and took a deep breath. Damn, I'd forgotten about my mother's house insurance direct debit. I'd set it up to be taken yearly instead of monthly to save some money and now it had come to slap me in the face when I was most unprepared to pay it.

I took deep calming breaths. *God doesn't close a door without opening a window.* I could do this. There was a way around this.

"Okay," I whispered. "Okay, you can do this."

Two options.

One: Tell the bastard to shove his job up his fine ass and concentrate harder on finding another job.

Two: Carry on working for him until I find something better.

With option one, there was a possibility I could come unstuck and put Mom's house and finances, not to mention mine, in jeopardy.

No, option one was not worth considering. There was really only option two for me.

I could put up with him until I found something else. I would train myself to become immune to his abuse and insults. Like water off a duck's back, they would slide off me.

In the end, I would be stronger for the experience. All I had to do was redouble my ability to stay calm in the face of any provocation from an unhinged maniac. I could do it. I know I could.

The sound of my phone ringing startled me. It was Maggie. It was almost like the universe was confirming I'd made the right decision. I clicked the green circle.

"How was your first day?" she asked cheerfully.

"Fine. It was fine," I replied evenly.

"Fine? What do you mean?" she demanded, her voice bristling with surprise.

I crossed my fingers. "It went well."

For a couple of seconds, a shocked silence ensued. Then...

"Oh my God. You're lying," she squealed happily. "You always were a terrible liar."

I winced. Damn her for knowing me so well. "I'm not lying. It *was* fine. He even invited me to have dinner with him and his mother."

"What?" she screamed.

I pulled the phone away from my ear and put her on speaker.

"Yeah, I met his mom," I said casually.

"Why would he take his temporary PA to meet his mother?" she asked suspiciously.

"I think he wanted me to entertain her while he read through a file."

"Oh." There was a small pause. "So you... um...like working for him?"

I cleared my throat. "Like is a bit strong, but I plan to win our bet."

"I see. Er... what's he like?"

"A bit rude but fine, I guess."

She began to laugh. "A bit rude but fine, I guess. What the hell, Lillian? You sound like you're describing a sitcom. Hang on... unless. Holy shit! You're attracted to him, aren't you?"

I froze. "No," I almost shouted. "I am not attracted to him. He's not my type at all."

"He's everybody's type. Stop lying to yourself. You want to have sex with him."

I sighed. "Believe what you want. I'm tired and I'm going to bed."

"Oh wow! You don't even want to discuss it. You must have it really bad for him."

"Goodnight, Maggie."

Her mocking laughter was still ringing in my ears when I killed the connection.

Chapter 7
Max
https://www.youtube.com/watch?v=Bqmrwx0W4k4

The first thing that floated into my head when I opened my eyes was Lillian. Her unruffled, calm face was blazing with undisguised, pure lust. What the fuck? That was the last thing I should be thinking about first thing in the morning. Self-disgust filled my gut and I vaulted out of bed.

I had to get rid of her, and fast.

She was death and destruction to my concentration.

Together with my dogs, I went for my usual run in the park behind my house. The air was cold and crisp, and I was glad to note how easy it was to keep my mind busy with business matters. But as soon as I got into the shower, dirty thoughts of her came flooding back. In the rising steam, I grabbed her flaring hips and fucked her so hard, she begged for mercy.

I gave her none.

I left the house and had breakfast with a semi-legitimate ex-hacker who kept me up to date with the goings on in the financial market. Sometimes he had valuable inside knowledge. Today he had none.

By the time I got to work, it was 9.30. Lillian was already at her desk with headphones over her ears. I assumed she was transcribing the voice notes I sent her earlier. She was wearing a white top that showed off her every delectable curve.

"Good morning, Mr. Frost," she said, taking her headphones off. Her face remained impassive.

I felt my blood pressure go up. Here I was, on fire for her body, and there she was, proud ice queen herself.

"Why are you dressed like that?" I asked curtly.

She looked down at herself, then back up at me. Her voice was even. "Like what?"

"Attire more suitable for a stripper."

Her eyes widened, but her voice was calm. "I'm wearing a turtleneck top," she said slowly.

"Yes, but it's at least one size too small. It leaves nothing to the imagination. You're going to distract the rest of my staff. Dress appropriately in future."

"I'll adhere to your... dress code in future," she said softly.

I grunted bad-temperedly and strode into my office.

For a second, I stood in the middle of my office, angry and resentful. Then I caught myself. Right. Time to begin Operation Get Rid of Ice Queen. I went to my computer and brought up the surveillance feed for the front entrance of the building.

I watched it for a few minutes and what I saw made me smile. I picked up the phone and summoned Lillian in. She came in with her notepad and a file. I noticed she had put on a black jacket and buttoned it. She put the file on the desk. "Here are the finished transcripts."

I leaned back against my swivel chair and stared at her.

"Were you late to work this morning?"

"No." Her voice was cool.

"Are you sure?"

"Yes. Yes, I'm very sure."

"Are you aware you're supposed to start work at nine a.m.?"

"Yes, I am. I was in the building by nine."

I took a deep breath. "Either you're lying, or the million-dollar, state-of-the-art surveillance system I've installed in this building is a total waste of money, and I should fire the firm and find a replacement contract."

She frowned. "I was here at nine."

I turned my monitor screen to face her. Then I walked over to stand next to her. I could smell her shampoo. Lemon. It was intoxicating.

"Is that you coming into the building?"

"Yes," she whispered.

"Do you see the timestamp?"

"9.02," she said slowly.

I walked back around the desk and sat down. "In fact, you were two minutes and thirty-seven seconds late."

"It would seem so."

"So you *were* lying before."

She pulled her eyes away from the screen, her face blank of all expression. "I wasn't lying. I made a mistake. I was under the mistaken impression I came in at nine. I didn't realize it was two minutes thirty-seven seconds past.

I'm so sorry. I will make up for the lost time tonight and it will never happen again."

I stared at her. How the hell did she so effortlessly manage to make me sound like the pettiest guy on earth?

"Make sure it doesn't," I muttered grumpily.

"Of course. Is there anything else I can do for you, Mr. Frost?" she asked with unshakeable politeness.

I waved my hand at her with irritation. "No. No. Go back to work."

She turned to go and I found myself watching her ass. That skirt, long as it was, was way too tight for a workplace.

"Wait," I heard myself say.

She turned around. "Yes."

"I need you to go to my house today and pick up some dirty laundry."

Her eyes flared, reminding me of the expression in them last night. That flash of something. Was that fury or lust? My cock jerked to life in my pants and I dipped my hand in my pocket to hide the evidence of her drastic effect on me.

"You want me to take your dirty clothes to the laundry?"

"I did say that in English, didn't I?"

A muscle ticked in her jaw. "Don't you have a housekeeper for that?"

I stood and took a few steps closer to her. She was so close I could just reach out and touch her. This was becoming a disease with me. This crazy desire for her.

I thought about the empire I had built. I built it over the best years of my life, giving it single-minded concentration. While all my friends were out playing, I was working. Always working. Without this... this... insane distraction.

Well, here was my chance to kill it forever. Goodbye,

Miss Hudson. But even as I said the words, I felt terrible. The words were like ashes in my mouth. "Do you have a problem with doing that?"

She stared at me for a few seconds, her eyes giving nothing away. Then she shook her head slightly. "No."

I was shocked at the relief running through my body. What the damnation was going on with me? I wanted her gone. Of course, I did. So why the relief that she didn't quit right then? Whatever that momentary relief was, I planned to kill it stone dead. I needed her gone. One way or another she had to go.

"I'll text you my address," I said and quickly turned away from her provoking presence. "Leave here after 2.00 pm," I threw over my shoulder. That was when Mrs. Timmins, my housekeeper, and her staff left, and the house would be empty.

I heard the door shut quietly behind me. I opened the file she had brought and quickly scanned her work. I couldn't find a single error.

I went to the window and looked down at the street below. She didn't deserve this. What I was doing was not right. I'd never sent a personal assistant to my house to pick up my dirty laundry before. True, I was horrible to them, but only because they were terrible at their jobs.

A surge of guilt filled me.

Then another instinct seeped in. Self-preservation. There was no room for pity here. She was poison for me. Pure, unadulterated poison. The faster I got rid of her the better.

Chapter 8
Lillian

Wow! He lived in a beautiful area. The garage doors opened remotely and I drove in. I looked at the plan of the house again, before I got out of the car. Choosing the right key from the ring, I opened the side door that led into the house and jumped back with fear and shock.

With my hand on my heart, I stared at two massive Dobermans standing behind the grill gate. They were both as still as statues but were snarling and growling so ferociously, they were frothing. One was even salivating. With their black lips pulled far back to show their sharp white teeth, they looked like demons from the pits of hell. They were truly frightening.

I didn't know what to do.

Their stance was crystal clear: I was completely safe while I was on this side of the grill gate, but any attempt to breach it and they would have no hesitation to eat me alive.

What now?

I frowned. Should I phone Mr. Frost? Then... quite

suddenly I knew exactly what to do. Mr. Frost knew the dogs would be here. He deliberately wanted to frighten me, which meant the sadistic monster was in all probability watching... I looked upwards at the corners of the ceiling and quickly spotted the video camera. I made certain to keep my face deliberately expressionless. I wouldn't give him the satisfaction of seeing just how much he had frightened and shaken me.

"What would you like me to do now, Mr. Frost?" I asked coldly.

From the other side of the grill gate, I heard his voice come through some sort of intercom or speaker.

"Back down. Stay," he ordered.

Instantly, both dogs moved. In unison and almost mechanically. They backed away and sat down, but never took their fierce eyes off me. I didn't look at the video camera again. Even though my brain knew I had nothing to fear, these dogs were so well-trained that they were almost robotic, my hand was shaking as I put the key in the gate.

Show no fear, I told myself. Not to him, or the dogs.

Taking a deep breath, I opened the gate and stepped into the house. The dogs moved not one inch. Breathing slightly easier, but always listening for movement behind me, I moved deeper into the house. Once I got to the bottom of the stairs, I started to feel safe again, and I began to notice my surroundings.

Wow! What a truly beautiful house.

I walked up the majestic curving staircase and made my way to his dressing room. It was accessed through his bedroom. When I opened the door, I couldn't believe my eyes.

Oh my God!

There it was, my dream bed!

The Icon. The luxury bespoke bed from Savoir, made in a time-honored centuries-old tradition and filled with millions of natural micro springs and swathes of teased horse tail hair and wool. All of it hand-made. I couldn't help myself. I had to stop and stare in fascination at the master-class in craftsmanship and style.

I'd only ever seen this beauty in a magazine. Here was the king-size version and it was even more regal and beautiful in real life. Maybe the day would come when I could afford to treat myself to the smaller, less expensive version.

So this is where he slept.

I took one last look and moved towards the dressing room. Heck, his dressing room was nearly the same size as my apartment. Everything was meticulously clean and tidy. I saw the laundry bag instantly. It was neatly bagged and even tagged with the name and address of the dry cleaners.

At that moment, I knew that taking his laundry to the dry cleaners was a job that his housekeeper normally did, but he thought asking me to do such a menial thing would humiliate me.

There was a mirror in front of me.

I looked at my reflection. I looked more like a stuffy school teacher than a stripper. My hair was tightly pulled back into a ponytail high on my head. I was wearing a buttoned-up jacket and underneath it a turtleneck top that was not tight by anybody's standards. Anyone in their right mind, that was. Perhaps a strict religious puritan could find objection to my modest attire.

Mr. Frost was in his right mind and no religious puritan. I could tell just by looking into his eyes that he was as dirty in bed as they came. He just enjoyed chastening and shaming me. I felt anger churn up inside me.

Look at him.

He had everything: looks, brains, success, money. He lived in this beautiful mansion, and he owned that wonderful bed, and yet the ungrateful man never smiled. Never showed any appreciation for anything. He was rude and awful to almost everyone. And frightening me with his black dogs, that... that was unforgivable.

Fuck him.

I unbuttoned my jacket, took it off and draped it over my arm. If I was a waitress I would spit in his food, but I was not. The PA equivalent would be...

Then I had it. I knew exactly what the PA equivalent was.

I snatched up the laundry bag and walked back to the bedroom. No doubt there were video cameras everywhere. Rich people always had them. And because he knew I was coming he probably had them all switched on.

Good!

I walked towards the gorgeous bed, put the laundry bag down on the floor, and my jacket on the bed. Quickly, I slipped out of my shoes, unzipped my skirt and shimmied out of it.

Then...I lay on his bed... my dream bed.

Wow! It was like lying on a cloud. The sheets were cool under my naked skin. Hooking my fingers inside the waistband of my panties I pulled them down my hips and legs.

I knew he was watching. I could feel his regard.

Wantonly, I spread my legs and began to play with myself. Little circles around my clit. I was already soaking wet. I didn't do what I usually did in private. Instead, I turned it into a magnificent show. Just like a stripper. I kept my eyes open and exaggerated the arch of my body as I slipped my fingers into me. I moaned and made little kitten noises as I finger-fucked myself.

I imagined him opening the door, coming in, and watching me. His icy eyes started to burn with lust.

Lust for me.

Mr. Frost begged me to let him fuck me, but I refused. Instead, I ordered him to eat me. Instantly, and meekly he buried his face between my thighs and sucked me obediently until I was ready to climax.

After I'd come, I sat up and deliberately made sure I left a wet patch on the bed. Leisurely, as if I had all the time in the world, I put on my skirt and zipped it up, but stuffed my panties into my jacket pocket. Then I slipped on my shoes, and smoothed the bed and pillows. Taking one last look at the delightful bed, I picked up the laundry bag and left.

Hope you enjoyed the show, Mr. Frost.

Chapter 9
Max

What the...?

I couldn't believe my eyes!

She had just masturbated on MY bed.

I watched the feed again to make sure my eyes were not deceiving me. No, they weren't.

She did masturbate on MY bed.

My cock was hard and hot for her, and my breaths came out of me fast and furious. I had a meeting in one hour and I still had some stuff to read up on before I went to it. I opened the report, but I couldn't concentrate. The words swam in front of me. All I saw was her. She with her silky legs wide open and her fingers busy.

What the hell was happening to me?

I stood and paced the floor of my office. This whole thing was mad. I stopped abruptly. I was becoming unhinged. Lust for her was turning me into a lunatic. How long had it been since I had sex with a woman? A month? Right. That was the solution. I needed a body. Any body would do. I went to my phone and scrolled through it.

Vivian. Nope.

Teresa. Nope.

Alison. Nope.

Nope. Nope. Nope.

Finally, Madeline. Yeah. She had roughly the same build and coloring as Lillian. I called her.

"Hey you," she cooed.

"Want to hook up tonight?" My voice was strangely guttural. Watching a grainy video of Lillian on my bed had turned me into a hot mess.

"I sure do," she agreed instantly.

"*Sans Frontieres*. Eight. Don't be late."

"Eight it is," she whispered.

I killed the connection and stared out of the window. Lillian was out there walking around without her panties. I should confront her. No! She had just declared war. And war it was going to be. I looked at my watch. I wanted to wait and see how brazenly she would face me, but I had a meeting across town I had to attend in an hour.

As I left my office, I sent her a message.

Book my usual table for two, *Sans Frontieres*, 8 p.m. and the Mimosa suite for one night.

Two minutes later my phone pinged.

Your table and suite are reserved.

* * *

The meeting was a bore, and I found my mind relentlessly wandering back to the surveillance feed from my bedroom.

At the end of the meeting, I decided I had missed great chunks of the presentation. I went to see Ralph's PA. She visibly shrunk when she saw me approaching her, which irritated me to no end. Why the fuck was she frightened of me? She had no reason to be. I'd hardly exchanged two words with her in the last three years.

"Can you send me a copy of the minutes of the meeting?" I asked, controlling my annoyance.

She swallowed. "Yes, Sir."

I turned away, then turned back to look at her half-curious, half-mystified. She was practically quaking with fear of me. Like all the others. How come Lillian was not afraid of me?

"Are you scared of me?" I asked.

Her eyes bulged. "I beg your pardon."

I had no time for this. "You heard."

She looked around her nervously, as if looking for someone to come to her assistance.

"It's an easy yes or no answer," I prompted.

She chewed her bottom lip. "Can you assure me that my answer will not affect my job?"

I looked at her with exasperation. "What have I got to do with your job? You work for Ralph. You have nothing to fear from me."

She straightened her shoulders. "In that case, yes, I am afraid of you."

"Why?"

She took a deep breath, then let it rip. "Because you are rude, aggressive, demanding, hostile, impossible to please, and completely lacking any kind of empathy towards your fellow humans."

I considered her response. "That's it?"

She nodded. "That's it."

"Okay, thanks. Get me those minutes a.s.a.p."

I turned away from her, my mind already churning with thoughts. So that was what my PAs thought of me. And that was probably what Lillian thought too, only she was a master of hiding it.

My phone pinged. It was Lillian.

If there's nothing else, I'm leaving.

I glanced at the time. Three minutes after five. I couldn't help the message my fingers typed out.

Yes, leave. I'm pretty sure it's been a very exhausting day for you.

Afterwards, I had a couple of drinks with an old college friend at the bar in Sans Frontiers until Madeline arrived at five minutes to eight. My friend made his excuses and left, and Madeline ordered herself a Vodka Martini.

She wasn't as I remembered her.

Basically, she looked nothing like Lillian. Not only was there no ponytail, she had also dyed her hair a completely different color. And her voice! It was so fake and shrill with affectation that it went right through me. What I wanted to hear was Lillian saying, 'Yes, Mr. Frost' in that husky sexy voice of hers.

I leaned back and took a swig of my whiskey. I didn't want to fuck Madeline. Not one bit.

She pushed her breasts forward. "I'm so glad you called," she said gratingly.

No point in putting off the inevitable.

"I've booked my usual suite for the night," I said.

"You're welcome to call a friend, have dinner with him, then stay the night and perhaps use the spa in the morning, but I'm out of here."

Her eyebrows flew upwards. She was so surprised she actually dropped her fake accent. "You mean you want to leave now?"

I nodded, put the room key card on the table and stood. "Enjoy your night."

She was still saying something when I walked away. I got into my car and drove like a madman back to my house. I greeted my dogs, flew up the stairs, and headed straight for the bed. I found the exact place she had sat on and I brought my nose close to the silky material and sniffed deeply.

Ah...

Her scent was faint, but I caught it... and instantly recognized it. I had encountered the same scent yesterday when she sat ramrod straight in the car with me.

I sat back on my heels and marveled at the way things were working out. It would seem Miss Lillian Hudson wanted me as much as I wanted her.

Chapter 10
Lillian

The first call I had that morning was from Maggie, but, to my surprise, she had not called my cell phone, but came through the switchboard.

"Hi, Maggie," I said.

"Hello, Lillian. I'm not calling as your friend, but as the owner of the agency," she said.

"Okay," I said warily.

"Now that you've had a couple of days to assess the situation, how is everything going?"

The day before played out like a video in my head—from Mr. Frost's demon dogs to my outrageous 'show' on his bed.

"It's going good," I replied.

"Are you sure? You can tell me if there are any... er... problems and I'll try to fix them."

"No, no problems at all."

"Not even teething problems?"

"Nope. Not even teething problems," I said cheerfully.

"Oh! Anyway, I've been thinking..."

"What about?"

"Well, our bet doesn't seem very ethical, does it? As the owner of the agency and your friend, I shouldn't have pushed you into it. It was wrong. It could place you in a position where you end up putting up with things that you wouldn't normally tolerate."

I didn't buy her bullshit for a second. "Weasel," I whispered.

"What did you say?"

"Nothing."

"You said something."

"I was wondering if you were trying to wriggle out of our bet."

"Of course not. I was only thinking of you."

"That's very kind of you, Maggie, but I'm happy to report that I'm fine."

"Well, in that case, the bet stands."

"Good," I cooed. "I've seen a lovely pair of shoes I want to buy with my winnings."

Maggie laughed suddenly. "You can't fool me, you know. I can hear the frustration in your voice. It won't be long before you're ready to quit; just be ready with my hundred dollars because I've seen a pair I like too."

"That is so not going to happen," I said.

"Come on, tell me the truth," Maggie's voice softened. "What's the beast really like?"

Honestly? He's a jerk of the highest order. I want to sock him in the jaw, but I also want to ride him hard from dusk to dawn. But of course, I didn't say that.

“He’s a workaholic and a perfectionist who expects the same of everyone around him.”

“But does he make you wet?”

“Are you asking this as the owner or the agency?” I asked innocently

Maggie sighed. "All I'm saying is, don't drive yourself to madness just to win a bet."

I chuckled. "It’s very sweet of you to worry about me so much, but like I said, I’ll be fine." At that moment, from the corner of my eye, I caught Mr. Frost striding into my office space.

“Thank you for the call, Miss Childs. I’ll be sure to keep you updated on my progress,” I said crisply and ended the call.

Mr. Frost stopped in front of my desk. His face was chiseled granite. Obviously, a night at the Mimosa suite with his booty call had done nothing to improve his mood.

“You were giggling,” he accused darkly. “Was that a personal call?”

“No, it was Mrs. Childs from the recruitment agency wanting a report of how I was faring.”

His eyes glittered. “And did you tell her how well you are... faring?”

Yup, he had watched me on his bed. I faced him dead on, my face expressing not an ounce of embarrassment or guilt. “The dogs were a bit of a low point, but I guess it really will be up to you to rate my... performance.”

A flash of emotion swept through those wintry eyes, but it blew by so fast I couldn’t tell what it had been.

He frowned. “I’m leaving in half an hour and I’ll be gone all day, but I’ve sent you work. Get me a coffee.”

"Yes, Sir," I said, watching his broad back. I knew I could handle his lack of social skills and his foul moods, the only thing I couldn't get a grip of was my weird, crazy physical attraction for him.

A funny thing happened later that morning. An attractive woman with injected lips and dressed in expensive clothes came through the lift. She had a phone to one ear, and in her hand, she carried a white box tied with a classy black ribbon. She seemed surprised and even amused to see me sitting at my desk.

"Good morning. Can I help you?" I asked civilly.

She held the phone away from her ear and her voice dripped with sarcasm. "I highly doubt it. You won't be here long enough."

Keeping my face politely expressionless, I stood. "That may be true, but for the moment I'm here to help."

She looked me up and down in the same proud way Mrs. Frost had at the restaurant, then dismissed me as unworthy.

"Thanks, but no thanks. I'm just going to pop into Max's office and leave this box of cookies for him," she said intending to sail past me.

"I'm sure he would appreciate knowing who brought the cookies," I insisted.

She looked at me as if she was speaking to an idiot. "There's a card."

I sighed and made a gesture with my hand. It was

simply not worth it. She was obviously a lover, and truth be told, they were perfect for each other. "Fine. Go ahead."

A couple of minutes later she came out, still talking to whoever it was on the phone with her. She didn't bother to speak to or even look at me. When the lift doors shut, I went into Max's office and looked at the card.

With love, Elizabeth

Chapter 11
Max

As much as I tried, I couldn't get Lillian out of my mind for any length of time. I'd never been attracted to an employee before and I was treading on dangerous grounds, but I couldn't stop thinking about her. The unpalatable fact was I didn't even want to stop.

There was something about her that fascinated me.

No, I wasn't worried it would last. I knew that as soon as I slept with her the obsession would end. So far, no woman had remained interesting beyond the bed. I didn't kid myself that Lillian would hold my attention for longer than a few weeks, but it would be a few very interesting weeks.

But for the moment, I felt like a man neither in control of his emotions nor his actions. Especially, when I cancelled a meeting so that I could get back to the office before five just to catch her. She was in my blood and she needed to be purged. A few weeks of fucking her day and night should do the trick.

As I walked through her office area, I could see that her desk was already cleared and she was ready to go home.

"Have you finished all the work I sent you?" I growled.

"Yes. It's all on your desk. A woman called Elizabeth came by with a box of cookies. It's on your desk."

I frowned. What the fuck was Elizabeth doing bringing me cookies? "I'll be leaving soon, so you may go now."

"Okay. See you tomorrow, Mr. Frost."

As if on cue, my cock jerked when she said 'Mr. Frost' in that husky voice. Obviously, it wasn't the first time a woman had referred to me as 'Mr. Frost', but when it came from Lillian it was one of the most erotic, suggestive things I'd ever heard.

I wanted to hear her call me 'Mr. Frost' as I pounded into her.

I went to my office, ignored the cookies, and quickly looked through Lillian's work. As I suspected, it was flawless. What a shame she came packaged like a sex bomb. If only she had been a dumpy middle-aged woman. She was the perfect PA.

I sat back and watched the clock, my hand relentlessly tapping on the surface of the desk as I gave her enough time to tidy up and take the lift down. When I couldn't wait any longer, I went down to my car and started driving it through the car park to where she was parked.

Even before I reached her, I could already see her standing outside her car talking on her cell phone. I stopped behind her car.

"Something wrong?" I called out.

"My car won't start. I'm trying to call AAA."

"What a shame. It'll take more than an hour at this time of the evening. Hop in, I'll give you a ride home and you can take a cab on the company tomorrow morning."

The hesitation was almost imperceptible, but it was there. She was reluctant to be in my car. Too bad. I wanted her in my car. I wanted her scent in my nostrils again.

She locked her car, got into mine, and closed the door. Whoa! And there it was. Stronger than the smell of her shampoo or deodorant or whatever perfume she used. And it was sweet. God, it was sweet. So sweet my mouth became dry.

"Thank you," she said softly.

I nodded and put the car in gear. I didn't try to make small talk and neither did she. I couldn't have even if I wanted to. Her scent had brought a storm of lust that refused to leave.

I stopped at a set of traffic lights and turned to her. "Did you know I was watching?"

Her cheeks colored. "Yes."

The lights changed. A car honked. I stared into her unrepentant eyes. More cars honked. I turned away from her and drove on. We were nearly at her block.

"Why?" I asked, my voice thick.

"Because it was my equivalent of spitting in your soup."

My brain whirled. That was her punishing me! Well, it fucking worked. I couldn't operate, I couldn't think, and I even stooped to vandalizing her car. I came to a stop in front of her building and turned to her.

"So what now?"

"Now you apologize..."

"For what?" I exploded.

"For scaring the hell out of me with your demon dogs."

I blinked with surprise. I couldn't remember the last time I had apologized to anyone or had anyone ask me to apologize.

"I'm waiting," she goaded, folding her arms across her chest.

I was so incensed by her impertinent taunt that my hand shot out and I did what I had been longing to do all evening: I gripped the back of her neck and pulled her to me.

A warning bell went off in my head as my lips crushed hers, but it was too late. An insane urge to possess her had already taken over. There was no going back. Her lips were soft and pliant beneath mine, and she tasted of grapes and heat.

She let out a soft, surprised moan when I thrust my tongue inside her mouth, but she didn't resist; instead, she tangled her tongue with mine, then sucked it. Hard.

Desire ripped through me and I wanted to taste every single bit of her skin. I could feel her heart racing against my chest. My hands ran across her back, brushing against her fragrant silky hair. The flow and ebb of the world disappeared as I drank her sweetness and longed to feel the fire of her body against mine.

Her hands crept around my neck.

I could feel her trembling. I wanted to take her up in my arms and never let go, but I could feel the moment passing like a gentle breeze—fleeting yet ever-present.

At that moment, common sense slammed back into me.

What the hell was I doing? I was in my fucking car in broad daylight. Lillian was not some bimbo I had hooked up with in a bar. She could lodge a sexual harassment complaint against me. And she would damn well win her case too. I could lose *everything* I'd worked so hard for.

This rough taking was not at all how I planned it.

I tore my mouth away from her and drew back staring at her. The look of unspoken longing and desire swimming in her eyes robbed me of breath. Then as if she was suddenly shaken out of her bubble of unthinking hunger, her eyes widened. She let out a little cry of horror and fumbled with the door. Pushing it open, she stumbled out.

I sat there staring at her as she ran to her entrance. I watched in a daze as she fished out her keys from her handbag, and fumbled with inserting them into the door a few times before she pushed it open and let it shut behind her. I wanted to follow her. The desire was so overwhelming, that I gripped the steering wheel hard enough to make my knuckles show white.

Jesus!

Taking a deep breath, I stepped on the gas and drove out of there, my mind awhirl with confusion, but after that initial shock and disappointment at my clumsy, reckless method, I remembered the video. I had the video. There was not a tribunal in the world who would decide against me after watching that.

Now that I knew I was safe, I couldn't stop replaying that savage kiss over and over as I drove home. Who would have thought that impossible-to-ruffle Miss Lillian had it in her to be so hot-blooded... so passionate?

I wanted more.

If she was that responsive to a mere kiss, how would she be in my bed with my cock buried deep inside her? How would she react if I grazed her nipples with my teeth?

Was she right now changing out of her wet panties? Or was she rubbing herself to ease the ache between her legs?

Chapter 12
Lillian

I burst into my apartment as if somebody was chasing me; my breath coming out in huge gasps. I leaned against the door and closed my eyes, trying to process what had just happened. I'd never done anything so impulsive before; I lifted a finger to touch my lips – they were swollen, but it was a delicious sensation.

My body quivered with arousal, and my panties were soaked.

I shouldn't have let Mr. Frost kiss me, let alone react like that. A tight slap would have been more appropriate. Why had I reacted that way, angling my body towards him and moaning like a complete slut? How was I going to face him tomorrow?

I thought of that kiss again and groaned aloud. At least, I hadn't made the first move, I comforted myself. Was he attracted to me the same way I was to him, or had it just been a jerk move on his part?

Either way, I shouldn't have reacted the way I did. But I couldn't seem to control myself around him. Truth be told,

Mr. Frost had an irresistible animal magnetism that drew me to him as no man had ever done—that was the only explanation I could come up with as to why I had reacted the way I did.

Any other man and I swear, I would have slapped him.

I groaned again and covered my face with my hands, embarrassed and horrified at what an idiot I'd been—a horny, stupid idiot. I made myself move to the bathroom, shedding my clothes as I walked. My nipples ached for his touch. After showering, I grabbed a towel and headed to my bedroom, just as my phone began ringing from somewhere inside my handbag.

Rummaging around I found it. It was Mom. The last person I wanted to talk to, but I answered just in case it was some emergency.

"Hey, Mom."

"Honey, I just got the letter from the Insurance Company to say the full yearly sum has been taken out of the account. Do you have enough?"

"It's okay, Mom. I set it up that way to take advantage of the discount."

"So... you're not short?"

"No, I'm not short."

The relief in her voice was evident. "Oh good. I just wondered."

"Everything is fine, Mom."

"You know, the offer to come live here with me still stands."

"Thanks. Who knows? I might take you up on it one of these days."

She laughed. "I'd love that."

"Mom, I just got out of the shower..."

"Oh right. Well, you better go get dressed then. Goodnight, darling."

"Night, Mom."

I finished the call, and after dressing in a pair of comfortable shorts and a T-shirt, I made myself a ham and cheese sandwich. I found I had no appetite. Eventually, I pulled the ham out, ate that, and discarded the rest. Then I grabbed a book and climbed into bed, but I couldn't concentrate. All I could think about was that kiss. Now that the shock was over, I could admit to myself that no one had ever kissed me like that before.

I remembered the firm hold of his hand at the back of my neck; the way he'd held me as if he knew I wouldn't resist...and I hadn't. I had parted my lips and allowed him to thrust his tongue inside my mouth. I wished I'd gone limp then, so I could have excused my behavior as shock; but no, I had given as good as I had gotten.

Ugh...

I tossed the book aside and slipped under the covers. The temptation to slip a hand between my legs was high, but I firmly told myself I wasn't going to masturbate to thoughts of him. No, that was just feeding blood to a vampire. I stayed awake for what seemed like hours before finally managing to drift off to sleep.

I was woken up by an erotic dream where I was fucking Mr. Frost in his car. Straddled atop him, I was in the midst of a wild ride on his dick unsure of how I got there, all I remembered was me telling him "You better make me cum like there is no tomorrow". Me, who never spoke dirty, even in my most erotic dreams.

My whole body felt hot and flushed.

I got up and headed straight to the shower. I decided I wasn't going to allow myself to think about him in that way. Why would I even want to? Yes, he was physically attractive, but his personality left a lot, really a lot, to be desired. I was usually attracted to a man's warm and caring personality, not his physical appearance.

I didn't know when I became so messed up that all I cared about was a man's physique.

Chapter 13
Lillian

I arrived at the office early, as I always did, except that day when I arrived two minutes and thirty-seven seconds late. I knew he had meetings across town this morning, so with any luck, I could put off meeting him until after lunch, but as soon as I entered my office space I smelled his aftershave.

His door was firmly shut though.

I walked to my desk, careful not to make too much noise. Only after I sat down did I question why I was tiptoeing. There was no putting off facing him. I was going to have to take in his coffee soon, anyway.

I powered up my computer and pretended to busy myself checking emails while my heart pounded so hard in my chest, that I could hear it. I kept glancing nervously at the time. It seemed as if time itself had speeded up and was flying. Before I knew it, it was time for me to take him his coffee. Agitatedly, I stood up and headed to the small kitchenette, telling myself that I could do this.

I had nothing to feel embarrassed about; after all, I

hadn't been the instigator of that kiss. In fact, I should be angry at his behavior. I allowed anger and indignation to replace my nervousness. By the time I knocked on his door, I was furious—he had crossed a line, no matter how I reacted. I was a normal, functioning woman. My body's reaction had been completely normal.

But my hands were trembling as I carried his coffee to him a few minutes later.

"Come in," he called.

I pushed the door open and entered. Without speaking, I set the mug on his desk. He didn't even bother to look up. Bastard. I stared at his bent head in disbelief. Was he going to pretend last night had not happened? No, I wasn't going to allow that. I cleared my throat and he looked up questioningly.

I met his gaze boldly. "You shouldn't have done that yesterday. Don't do it again." That was all I wanted to say, and I turned to leave.

His sneering voice stopped me cold. "I didn't hear you complain then."

I turned around, my mouth open in disbelief at his words, but before I could say anything, he spoke up again.

"In fact, I think you rather liked it. Judging by the way you're dressed today, I bet you're hoping for a repeat of what happened."

Anger churned in my chest. "How dare you?" I hissed.

He stood up abruptly, and a few seconds later he was standing in front of me, so close that I could inhale his scent. "In fact, I'm thinking that right now your panties are wet, and if I dipped my hand under that tight skirt of yours, my fingers will come out wet."

He closed the distance between us, and with one hand he pulled me hard against him. He angled his mouth over mine in a hot wet slide. Shame and desire mingled hot in my throat. I raised my hands to push him away but ended up caressing his shoulders.

I felt his hand underneath my skirt, moving up and then nudging my legs open. I wanted to pull his hand away, but I was frozen with pleasure. His finger hooked the edge of my panties and slipped into my wet folds. I should have stopped him, but I was caught up in a totally unfamiliar sexual frenzy.

Also, I was curious about how far he intended to go. I squirmed with pleasure. Everything in me demanded that I tell him to stop, but I kept getting distracted by what he was doing, and each time I opened my mouth, the words refused to come out. His fingers found my swollen clit and teased it mercilessly.

I moved my hips in tempo to his fingers rubbing back and forth, side to side, and in circles, against my clit. I moaned with pleasure while I wondered in semi-panic if someone suddenly came, but even that thought didn't make me draw away. My body was on fire; every inch of my skin was sensitive to the movement of his fingers.

His fingers slipped inside me and he began to fuck me with them. I couldn't think beyond the building tension between my legs and the need to orgasm. I was so close to the edge and desperate for release when he abruptly pulled away and stepped back.

He stared at me with an inscrutable expression.

"Shall we go over my schedule?" he asked in a calm,

collected voice. Turning away, he strolled back to his desk as if nothing had happened.

I felt as if ice-cold water had been poured over my head. Horribly humiliated did not even begin to describe the sensation I experienced as I made my feet step one in front of the other until I was out of his office. I went to my desk and picked up the iPad. I held it against my chest and stood there trembling.

After everything I had said to myself, I couldn't believe I had reacted to him in exactly the same way as I did yesterday. Was I that desperate for a man's touch that I was willing to let my boss push his fingers into me? My nipples hadn't gotten the message yet; they were hard peaks against my blouse and ached to be touched.

I could just walk out now, and forfeit my pay. I didn't care about the bet anyway. I was not like Maggie. Maggie hated to lose. When we were younger and used to play board games she would go crazy whenever she lost, but whenever I did, I just shrugged and said, "It's only a game. Maybe I'll win the next one."

The bet was no big deal, but I desperately needed the paycheck. That insurance payment had taken a bigger chunk than I had allowed for.

I made a decision.

I was going to go through with this. First of all, I needed this job. And secondly, I was to blame. I started it with my 'stupid show' on his bed. I steeled myself by inhaling deeply, filling my lungs with air, and made myself walk back to his office.

Anything he could dish out I could match.

I lifted my hand and made myself knock on the door.

He called for me to enter and I pushed the door open. His gaze immediately went to my chest and I knew he could see the outline of my nipples.

My face grew hot, but I lifted my chin proudly.

I walked towards him, trying to keep my composure. He was sitting behind his desk, staring at me with a smirk on his face. He knew how hot I still was for him.

"Have a seat," he said, keeping his eyes on me as I sat down. "Ready?"

I tapped on the iPad to the inbox.

For the next half-hour, we went through his emails, and then his schedule. When we were done, I made to stand up, but he spoke before I could flee.

"Do you want to finish what we started?" he asked. "You were so close to coming, weren't you, Miss Hudson?"

My heart was racing and I felt like I couldn't breathe. Then it hit me: he was toying with me. He expected me to say no and flee his office like I had done earlier. Well, two could play this game.

"Yes, to both questions," I said calmly.

He was momentarily taken aback, but he quickly recovered. "I like a woman who knows what she wants." Without another word, he stood up and went to the door. He turned the lock and my heart started thumping hard against my chest. What had I done? I cowered in my chair as he sauntered towards me.

He lifted me as if I weighed nothing and deposited me on his desk.

"Oh!" I exclaimed.

I wanted to protest; tell him that I'd been kidding, but my body craved his touch. He reached up to grip the hem of my panties and ripped it off in seconds. Then he pushed my legs apart. So wide apart that I had to rest my palms on his desk.

"Beauty," he said, staring greedily at the wet throbbing flesh between my legs.

Then he leaned in and kissed the lips of my pussy. My whole body trembled and I moaned with pleasure. He flattened his tongue and swiped across my slit; I felt my clit swell in anticipation, and my whole body tensed.

"Oh my God," I heard myself moan.

Mr. Frost licked my pussy with long, deliberate licks and my body bucked up against his mouth. I was growing wetter by the second and I knew that I couldn't hold out much longer. I reached down and tangled my fingers in his hair. He sucked my clit into his mouth, and I cried out, "Oh God!"

My heart was racing, and I was so close to coming, but suddenly, he stopped. I opened my eyes and stared down at him. He had a smirk on his face. "You *do* want me to suck you until you orgasm, don't you?"

"Yes," I said breathlessly.

"Beg me for it," he said, his smirk turning into a wicked smile.

"What?'

"Beg me to make you come," he repeated.

"Bastard," I hissed and tried to rearrange my clothes, but he gripped both my hands with one of his, stopping me.

"That's not how you beg," he murmured as he slipped his finger in and out of me.

I swallowed hard. I had my pride, but oh God! I wanted to come. I needed to climax. "Please, please," I whispered.

"That's better," he said and dipped his head between my legs again. He then proceeded to give me the most violent orgasm I'd ever experienced. It was so intense I cried out.

When it was over, and my senses came back, I realized what sort of position I was in. He'd stood up and was watching me, his eyes veiled. I glared at him. Indifferent to my hostility, he went around to his chair and sat down.

"If you want to keep your job," he said, "I suggest you get back to work and take these damn cookies with you."

"What do you want me to do with them?" I asked as I hopped off his desk. I could feel my pussy still dripping and my legs were unsteady. I had trouble catching my breath.

"Bin them."

That's how little he thought of the high and mighty Elizabeth and her expensive cookies. I snatched up the box of cookies and grabbed my panties from the floor. Then I rearranged my skirt and walked stiffly to the door.

I sensed he was looking at me. As I turned the handle he said, "You can come to my office for more anytime you like."

I don't know how I managed to walk out of his office.

Chapter 14
Max

I should have been ashamed of my behavior, but I wasn't. Not the slightest bit. It was worth it. I could still taste her in my mouth: a sweet nectar I could get drunk on. From the little I knew of Lillian she must be pissed as fuck. She'd never have believed she could come apart like that.

I, on the other hand, couldn't believe how hot it had been.

Hours later and my cock was still rock hard. I couldn't concentrate on anything apart from the woman who was in the next office. My phone rang and I answered it. Lillian's no-nonsense tone made my breath catch for a second. I could still hear her cry out as she climaxed. What would she say if I told her that she had been on my mind more or less the whole day?

"Chris is here to see you."

"Ok."

He didn't bother knocking, came straight in, shut the door behind him and said, "If I wasn't engaged, I'd be all over that." He jerked his head in the direction of my outer office.

"Have some respect," I said, irritated, then added. "I thought you were dating Jennifer."

"Relax, I'm just appreciating a beautiful woman." He sat down and drummed one hand on my desk as he contemplated me. "I've never heard you defend a woman before. Are you interested?"

Was I interested? Fuck, yes! I frowned. "I'm sure you didn't come by just to gossip about my new assistant."

Chris sat up straight in the chair. "Right. There is a luxury leather goods company which has come onto my radar. It's still very hush-hush, but they're looking for funding. It's not a start-up though.

"It's called La Zaire. They are bleeding heavily like the rest of the luxury sector, but I'm interested because it is bleeding more heavily than it should. Their current CEO has almost run it into the ground over the last couple of years. I've looked at the figures, and I believe we can turn it around very quickly with the right people and structures in place. Then we can use it as our base for our further acquisitions into this sector. I expect many more companies to go bust in the next few years and we can pick them up for a song. This will give us all the experience we need to manage all of them."

I was intrigued and listened intently as he gave me the background of the company. Even before he'd uttered the name of the company, I felt a sense of excitement. My blood pumped faster through my veins as enthusiasm filled me. Whenever I had this reaction over a potential deal, I knew not to pass it up.

We hashed it out for another hour, brainstorming ways in which we could get the company out of trouble. We had somebody in mind already. Recruitment would be expensive; i.e. luring him away from the current company where he was working. But he'd be well worth it—Jed Burner was a machine, a ruthless machine who knew exactly how to trim the fat off ailing companies.

I agreed in principle that we'd make a bid for the company after our team dug some more to verify Chris's information. I also undertook to get in contact with Jed Burner and get him on board so we'd have all our chips in place. Jed would be the hardest bit of the puzzle, but I had a good relationship with him and had worked on a deal with him once. We both respected each other.

I called Lillian and asked her to update my diary for Friday. Get a meeting with him. I would be flying to North Carolina to meet him.

Chris threaded his fingers through his hair and shifted in his chair as if all of a sudden, he couldn't find a comfortable position. Whatever it was that was on his mind was making him incredibly uncomfortable.

"Spit it out," I advised.

He grinned sheepishly. "It's about Jennifer. " He exhaled before continuing. "She's pregnant so we decided on a shotgun wedding, and well, I guess I want you to be my best man."

Whoa! Jennifer was pregnant and Chris was getting married. To be honest, I was shocked. Chris had always been the most commitment-phobic guy I knew. He'd always voiced very strong opinions against marriage or tying himself to one person for life.

I cocked my head to one side. "So... you're in love with her or just doing this for the baby?"

His face lit up. "Nah man, the baby's just the icing on the cake. I've always wanted to marry her. She's special. I know I'll never find anyone else like her again." He shook his head. "Sometimes I feel so stupid when I remember all the stuff I said about marriage, but I've seen the light. And it's a bright shining light. I'm actually eager to tie the knot. Shocking, I know, but I can't wait to make her mine."

A strange and totally unfamiliar feeling of envy came over me. I'd never envied anyone before. I didn't understand why I should feel that way. I certainly didn't want to be married. Maybe, I just admired the unshakeable conviction Chris had - that Jennifer was the woman for him.

I'd never met a woman I'd ever thought that way about. My mind shot to Lillian, but I quickly shook the illogical thought off. I knew nothing about her. She was a complete stranger - well, not so strange considering how greedily I sucked her off - but sex was no indicator. No one knew that better than me. Still, I found myself wanting to push her buttons further. She was intriguing.

"So, will you do it?" Chris asked.

"Of course, I will. In fact, I'd be offended if you asked anyone else." I meant it. Chris was the one person who had been a constant in my life. He was almost like a brother to me.

I stood up to shake his hand. "Congratulations! I'm so proud of you. At least one of us is going down the traditional route."

Chris stood up and grabbed my hand. "Thanks, Max,"

he said. “You’ll find your special person too. Just takes time and patience.”

I highly doubted that, but I didn’t bother contradicting him. "When's the wedding?"

"We want something very small and intimate, something that won't take months to plan. So, we're thinking about a month from now."

"What will your mother have to say about that?" I mocked. While Chris's mother and mine hadn't ever hit it off, they did have one thing in common: they both wanted us to get married in lavish style and give them grandchildren.

Chris shrugged. "She’ll just have to go along with it. What matters is what Jennifer and I want."

Chris left shortly after and I followed him out. There was an excitement inside me that I hadn't had in a long time as I stepped out of my office into Lillian’s space.

It was half after five, well past her official leaving time, but she was still at her desk. She stood when she saw us and picked up her purse. But when she met my gaze, her cheeks turned a rosy shade of pink. I knew exactly what was on her mind; she was remembering the way I’d buried my head in her sweet pussy and eaten her out like a starving man. Something I was desperate to do again... and again. It was risky business, but every lick and kiss was fucking worth it.

"I’ve finished the report you gave me, so I’ll be leaving now," she said awkwardly.

“Come on, you can ride the lift with me,” Chris offered with a grin.

“Sure,” she agreed.

Then she smiled at him. It was a smile that transformed

her face. Made her look like a beautiful angel. I stared at her in amazement. How come she never fucking smiled at me like that?

I knew Chris was in love with Jennifer and nothing was going to happen in that lift, but I felt jealousy like I'd never encountered before. It filled my gut with acid and burned my insides to think of them together in that confined space. He would be able to smell her. The way I had. Maybe, her smell would intoxicate him, and he wouldn't be able to help himself. The way I hadn't.

It took all I had not to make up some reason for me to go down to the foyer so that I could get in that lift with them. Instead, I gritted my teeth, turned away from the sight of them walking together and went back to my office.

Two minutes later, I couldn't stop myself. It was as if my body had a mind of its own. I called Chris. "Where are you?" I snapped.

"In the foyer. What's up?"

"Are you... alone?"

"Yeah. Why?"

"Nothing. Have a good evening."

Then my hand sent a text to Lillian's phone.

Don't wear any underwear tomorrow.

Chapter 15
Lillian

"How's the new job going?" my mother asked from the other end of the phone.

My phone was suspended between my ear and shoulder. One hand carried a bag of groceries and with the other, I struggled to insert the key into the door of my apartment. I should have let the call go to voicemail, except my mother had a tendency to worry if I didn't pick up my phone. It was easier to just answer, however inconvenient.

It couldn't be worse than the flurry of text messages that would follow asking me if something was wrong. She would even go as far as asking if I was still alive. Maggie said it would drive her crazy, but I had no real problem with it. I understood my mother had gone through a lot—from my father dying the way he did to getting married and losing a second, albeit useless, husband in quick succession. Then getting close to losing everything, and having to depend on her daughter to pay her mortgage.

It was a lot for anybody to take and probably made the world a very scary place for her. I got the door open, entered, and dumped my shopping bag and purse on the small kitchen counter.

"Sorry, Mom, what did you say?" I asked as I turned on the coffee machine.

"I asked how the new job is going?"

My body instantly stiffened as memories of the day came over me. And that unexpected text from him, and the way my hand shook as I sent him my reply.

As long as you understand that you can look but you cannot touch.

I was behaving so out of character I couldn't even recognize myself. I could just imagine my mother's reaction if I told her the truth of how my day really went. She had worked as a professional office support worker all her life, and if she knew how unprofessional her daughter had been, she'd have been horrified and probably disgusted too.

Thinking about it now made me shake my head.

I had sat on my boss's desk and let him eat me out. Who in their right mind did that? A voice in my head reminded me that it took two to tango. I reverted the accusation back to Mr. Frost. Which boss ordered his personal assistant to come to work without any underwear?

Heat and arousal whipped through me at the thought of obeying that text; it was wrong on all levels but my body craved him. Him eating me out on his desk had been the most exciting thing that had ever happened in my whole sheltered life. That orgasm almost made up for all the rudeness I'd endured at his hands.

"It went very well, Mom, better than I expected," I said, glad she couldn't see my face.

A sigh of relief came over the phone. "Oh, I am so glad to hear that. I was worried when you told me you weren't very hopeful about it."

I repeated the lie I used on Maggie, "Mr. Frost has a bit of a reputation for being a difficult boss, but he's not that bad. He's just a perfectionist who expects the same level of dedication from everyone around him, but he hasn't found fault with my work yet." That last bit, at least, was true.

"I am so proud of you, Lillian," my mother gushed. "You always were a clever little thing. Maybe you should consider going back to college. You're too smart and have too much potential to be working as someone's PA."

A sigh escaped my lips. We hadn't had that discussion in a long time. My mother couldn't understand why my ambitions didn't extend further than being a personal assistant. Maybe she did understand, but she just didn't want to acknowledge that I wasn't one of those women who were big on careers.

Once upon a time, I even dreamed of meeting Mr. Perfect, getting married, and filling a house with babies. Five to be exact. To many people, the idea was old-fashioned and daft, but to me, it was heaven on earth. There was nothing I wanted more.

And why not too? I had seen the kind of rock-solid marriage my mother and father had, and I wanted the same thing for myself. I wanted a man who would love me despite all my flaws. The way my father did my mother.

My mind stupidly went to Mr. Frost and I could have laughed at myself. He was the farthest thing from my dream husband. Mr. Frost was a lion—he'd eat you alive if you let him. That was one mistake I was not going to make. He could play with my body all he wanted, but that was all he was going to get—my body, not my heart or my devotion.

"Honey," my mother said, her voice tinged with caution. She was going where she knew not to. "I know how busy you are. Do you want me to get some prospectuses from a few colleges for you?"

I fought down my irritation. I'd told my mother countless times that I didn't want to go back to college. I loved my job, and all I needed was to settle into a PA role that I enjoyed. This one wasn't it, but it was a stepping stone to other jobs.

"Mom, I can do it myself if I want. I'm fine with things the way they are," I muttered, trying my best to hide my impatience.

"If you say so, sweetheart."

"I say so. Look, I've just walked through the door..."

"Oh! I should go get dinner ready too. Do you want to come over for some meatloaf?"

"Not today, Mom." Not in my state.

"All right, then. See you Sunday for the big clean."

"See you Sunday."

I hung up, part of me relieved, part of me filled with guilt. The logical side of me understood that my mom was still recovering from the loss and she needed me, yet I despised our reversed roles. I was the mother and she was the child.

* * *

The following morning, I woke up earlier than usual. Even though I should have been still very pissed at his domineering ways, I found myself incredibly excited to see him again.

I couldn't understand it.

On one hand, I detested his arrogance and rudeness with all my heart and soul, and he had also attempted to treat me as if I was his little servant, but he could also turn me to putty with just one loaded look, or a one-sentence text.

He was like my hottest fantasy come true.

I decided to comply with his text, but I had no intention of submitting to any other kind of request. I would dress as he had stipulated, but all he was doing was looking.

No touching.

He could look, he could even salivate, but no more.

I chose my outfit with more care than usual.

Mr. Frost clearly had an affinity for pencil skirts, so I chose one that clung to my curves and had a slit up one thigh. I considered wearing a blouse with a plunging neckline, but as I was rummaging through my clothes, I came across a sheer black top I had bought to wear on a night out. I'd never had the guts to wear it out even with a bra.

Without a bra, it would be...

I thought of Mr. Frost's wintery eyes as I pulled it off the hanger. I pulled on a pair of silky hold-up stockings. The stocking top showed through the slit of the skirt. I then searched for a long jacket to wear over it.

That way, at first glance, I would look completely decent, but when I took off the jacket, it would be downright scandalous. I slipped into a pair of black high heels and stood in front of the mirror. Through the almost transparent black blouse, I could clearly see the pink peaks of my nipples. I walked towards the mirror, my sheer stockinged leg sliding in and out of sight.

My outfit was totally outrageous, to say the least. It screamed fuck me in 107 different languages.

Yes, I was going to enjoy watching Mr. Frost squirm. It would be sweet revenge for the way he had tortured me the previous day.

I almost lost my nerve as I was leaving my apartment, but then I reminded myself of how greedily his tongue had moved between my legs.

I got into my car and drove to work.

I made sure my jacket was buttoned up before I got out of the car and made my way to my office. Inside I was a mess of emotions, but outside, I remained calm and collected.

"Morning," the security guard called out as I got out of the lift.

I smiled at him and returned the greeting. He had always been friendly to me and I appreciated that. I went to my desk and put my purse in my desk drawer.

I knew immediately that he was in the office. His bristling, inexhaustible energy was so pervasive that the place felt like a hollow shell when he was not around. There was usually no one around at this time of the morning. I took off my jacket and went to knock on his door.

"Enter."

He was dressed impeccably in an exquisitely cut suit with a crisp white shirt inside.

I felt almost dizzy with excitement as I waited for him

to raise his head from the file he was reading. He looked up and froze, his stunning eyes widening, then darkening.

That was when I knew my 'you can look, but can't touch' rule was simply not going to work at all. He was going to do whatever he wanted with me, and there was not a thing I could do about it.

Chapter 16
Max

"Shall I get you your coffee?" she asked.

I stared at her with amazement. I had plans for her. I had plans to torture her all day, but I'd failed to take into account her powerful effect on me.

Already, I was overwhelmed by a rush of heat and carnal need. I leaned back and let my eyes slowly take her in. She had gorgeous breasts, truly gorgeous. My gaze hungrily consumed their firm round shape. I wanted to massage those big, perfect tits with impunity, my fingers digging deep into her tender flesh making her writhe and twist uncontrollably with the same arousal I was feeling.

And her magnificent nipples; they protruded out like sharp pink rocks under the veil-like material of her top. I wanted to mercilessly rub and pinch the swollen, erect buds between my fingers until she totally lost it and helplessly trembled her surrender. Then I'd let my hungry mouth devour her. Suck her so hard and long my mouth left hickeys on every inch on her smooth milky-white skin.

"I can come back later," she mumbled, and half-turned.

"Don't go," I called.

She stopped in her tracks.

"You put on a show, I was enjoying it."

She turned back slowly, proudly. She was like a queen, waiting to be conquered. "Go ahead. Tell me when you're finished."

My cock throbbed for her. I knew I could have her right then, but not yet. She had to suffer first. I had a plan for her. A kinky one. I opened my desk drawer and took out the toy vibrator I picked up last night on my way back from work.

It looked just like a black thong, but cunningly, it had a remote-controlled vibrator in the shape of a small butterfly attached to the inside of it. I stood in front of her and held it out to her. Even from here, I could already smell her scent and it was driving me crazy.

"Put this on."

Her eyes were huge in her face. She had very beautiful eyes. You could drown in those calm lakes. I felt myself fall into their blue magic. For what seemed like an eternity her spell held me frozen, I couldn't look away, I couldn't move. I just wanted to taste her mouth again. Then she spoke, breaking the enchantment.

"Now?" the beautiful witch whispered.

"Now," I murmured in her ear. She smelled so good. The desire to lick her earlobe was unbelievable. I tried to hold myself back, but I couldn't control myself. The need was too strong. My tongue flicked out and I licked the warm curl of flesh.

She closed her eyes and whispered. "No touching, Mr. Frost."

I let the tip of my tongue run down the side of her neck

as she shivered. Then she took a deep breath, then stepped away from me.

"What are you waiting for Miss Hudson? Put it on."

Not looking at me, she took the thong and, bending down, carefully pulled it up her stockinged legs. I saw a flash of the delicate skin on the inside of her thigh. Soon... soon it will be full of bruises and love bites. My marks.

I walked to my desk and pressed the on button on the vibrator's remote control. Immediately, her hand shot out and tightly squeezed the back of the chair in front of her. I saw her fight to control her expression.

I smiled and turned the setting higher.

Her mouth opened in a silent gasp.

Good. It was working exactly as it said on the tin.

I turned it back down. This was not meant to be pleasure, but pure torture. By this evening, she would be begging me to put her out of her misery.

My voice was cool. "I need you to take a dictation."

She walked out wordlessly and came back with her iPad. While I dictated, I paced around her and played around with the remote. Testing it, seeing what level knocked her concentration completely off.

"Read it back to me," I ordered.

She read the letter out aloud, her voice strange and thick. Her work was full of mistakes.

"Good," I said. "You may go now."

* * *

The morning and afternoon passed in a strange flurry of distracted attempts to work and sexual excitement. The whole time I was aware of the remote in my pocket. I kept us both in a state of unsatiated lust.

Finally, it was time.

I called her in. Her cheeks were rosy and her eyes a little glazed. "Lock the door."

As she did, I pushed away the papers in front of me and wheeled my chair away from my desk. "Come here," I invited.

She came around my desk.

"Sit."

Obediently, she sat on my desk facing me. Her eyes were hooded, but she was trembling with basic instinct. I knew exactly what she wanted and how to give it to her.

"Open your legs," I ordered, my gaze never leaving her eyes. Her pupils were dilated to almost twice their ordinary size. Instantly, she widened her thighs. I curled my hands around her ankles, pulled them even further apart, and looked at her secret.

My cock surged. The thong was completely soaked, and her juices were smeared all over the creamy insides of her thighs. As I watched, even more liquid seeped out of the edges of the thong.

"Have you come yet?" I demanded.

"No." Her voice was barely a whisper.

"Do you want to?"

"Yes."

"Ask me for it... and nicely."

She bit her lower lip. "Can you let me come... please?"

"What's my name? Say my name."

"Mr. Frost. Please, Mr. Frost."

I slipped my finger under the thong and ripped it off. Her freshly shaven pussy was beautifully pink and glistening with need. Her clit was so swollen it was twice its size and it was pulsating like the tiniest drum in the world. When my fingers ran gently over it, she flinched and her thighs clenched reflexively. It was instinctive, a rejection, but it was no use.

This intruder could not be driven away.

This was only the beginning.

My fingers pressed tightly against her wet lips without any movement. I was enjoying the mere feel of her hot flesh, but her hips moved greedily and my fingers slapped her.

"Don't."

She stopped moving.

Steadily, gently I began to massage her sweet pussy. It flooded with more and more honey until they ran between my fingers and wet my shirt cuffs. With my other hand, I fondled her wonderful tits and felt her trembling as sexual ecstasy inexorably drew her in. My hands were shining with her juices as I tore open her blouse. She wasn't shocked. Instead, she jutted her naked chest out to me. Lewdly, I mauled at her beautiful tits. I even leaned forward and sucked on one.

I was incredibly excited by the way calm, collected Lillian Hudson began to shake and tremble. As her boundaries broke, she began to moan softly. Her orgasm was building. The dam was about to break and shock her consciousness with sensations she'd never dreamed of.

Her breathing was so shallow it was almost as if she was panting. All the while my touch was producing floods of sweet juices. I could see the tide of pleasure was overpowering her. She was no longer seeing me. Everything had disappeared except my touch and the pure sensations of pleasure between her legs.

She stood at the gates of her climax.

"Nearly there, Miss Hudson. Nearly there."

She whimpered restlessly as another shudder shook her body. With one decisive move, my fingers dug into the lips of her excited pussy, plunging into the heated interior. How wonderful my fingers felt inside her tight pussy.

My thumb gently massaged the swollen clit. I knew she would not be able to resist this invasion for long. The muscles inside her began to clench and spasm.

She cried out, suddenly, an animal sound. Then her pussy exploded with a burst of juices and she gave in, an orgasm that shook her body so violently, I had to hold her upright.

God, she was beautiful and I wanted her to be mine.

Her whole body shuddered uncontrollably as another thrill of pleasure overtook her. I could tell by the way her eyes had rolled, her vision was blurred, and she was lost to the pleasure that had overwhelmed every cell of her body and mind.

I didn't even exist.

She didn't see me stand and walk away from her.

I watched her recover. I witnessed her breathing calm down. Then, before she could turn her eyes and look at me as if I was a predator, I left.

As I walked to the elevator, I sent her a message.

You have three hours to pack before my driver picks you up. It's a working weekend for me, but you're mostly coming to get fucked.

Chapter 17
Max

I smiled as I pictured the look of fury on her face because I hadn't given her prior warning.

She hadn't said no, which meant she was coming.

I knew she wanted to fuck me as badly as I did her, and I knew it had been a hellish wait for her as well. I intended to bring this torture to an end for both of us.

I was going to teach her that you didn't play around with grown men and not expect consequences. What kept me going were thoughts of what I would do to her when I got her alone.

I found my mood greatly cheered and I couldn't wait for the weekend. I was going to enjoy myself. I was going to have her tonight, and the whole weekend. By the time we came back home on Sunday, she'd be out of my system. Then, of course, there would be the added advantage of meeting Jed and finding out face to face, whether he'd be up to a new challenge.

With half an hour to go before my driver picked me up,

I headed to the shower. I left the shower with a raging hard-on but refused to relieve myself by jerking off.

I was saving myself for tonight.

My weekend bag was always ready, and I grabbed it from the closet, said goodbye to my dogs, and left a note for my housekeeper that I would be back home on Sunday night.

I spotted Lillian standing in front of her apartment building, and a sliver of excitement went through me. When the car came to a stop, my driver stowed her luggage in the trunk and she climbed in.

I picked up her scent immediately.

She smelled of sex. She hadn't showered and I knew that was deliberate. I had the urge to grab her and take her right there and then, but I opened my laptop and pretended to read something. I'd never waited that long to have sex with a woman before.

The weekend was going to be perfect.

Lillian fished out her laptop from her bag and placed it on her lap. From the corner of my eye, I saw her turn it on and begin working on the document I'd given her to proofread.

The car had been moving for a good hour, and we hadn't exchanged a single word, but the air between us sizzled with sexual tension.

After my driver dropped us off we only had a short walk to my private jet. We sat next to each other. All the while, I was intensely aware of her beside me, feeling her body heat, even though we weren't touching.

In two hours and a bit, we were in Charlotte, North Carolina. Lillian, who had originally arranged the trip for me, had a driver waiting for us at the airport. He drove us to our hotel. The check-in was fast and smooth. A bell attendant escorted us to our room. We followed him down to the elevator, then to the third floor, and down a hallway to our room.

He opened the door to our suite.

"Where would you like these?" he asked.

"We'll take it from here," I said and slipped him a good tip.

He placed our bags on the floor, thanked me profusely, and left.

I turned to Lillian. "Do you want to freshen up before dinner?"

She walked slowly into the suite, looking around at the tall windows with stunning views of the city below us. Then her gaze returned to me. She contemplated me for a few seconds before she spoke.

"I thought you were having dinner with Klaus Minsky."

"I cancelled it."

"Why?" Her voice was soft, curious, but strangely distant.

"Because I'm taking you out to dinner instead."

She stared at me. "Why?"

"There's a saying, fuck around and find out. You fucked around on a grown-ass man's bed, Lillian. And now you're about to find out." I walked towards her and stopped very close to her, "The real question is, do you want to find out now or after dinner?"

"I'll freshen up for dinner," she murmured, taking a step back from me.

"And tomorrow... are you still meeting Jed Burner?"

"Of course. Tomorrow lunchtime. It'll give you time off to look around the city."

She chewed her bottom lip reflexively. "Which one is my room?"

"You can put your stuff over in that room, but you're sleeping in the master bedroom... with me."

Her cheeks flushed with color, but she said nothing as she grabbed her weekend bag and walked across the sitting room to the first door.

As it closed behind her, my muscles relaxed and I grinned like a fool. Everything was going according to plan. I took the opportunity to check my emails and respond to a few. When Lillian emerged from her room, she was dressed in a simple but elegant black dress which stopped just above her knees. Damn, she looked good enough to eat.

"Are you wearing panties?" I asked.

"Yes," she replied, her cheeks becoming rosy.

"Take them off and give them to me," I instructed, holding my hand out.

She wanted to say something, but she clamped her mouth shut instead and wordlessly pulled them off. Looking me in the eyes she dropped them into the palm of my hand. I stuffed them into my jacket pocket.

"Shall we?" I said, indicating we should leave.

We never spoke as we made our way to the restaurant. We were shown to a nice table in an alcove that looked out to a well-lit Japanese garden. I ordered a bottle of champagne. A waiter came back surprisingly fast. He carefully filled our flutes and withdrew.

I raised my glass to her.

“What are we celebrating?” she asked quietly.

I smiled slowly at her. “We’re celebrating us.”

She raised an eyebrow. “Us? Is there an us?”

I nodded. “There is an us. I’ll show you later.”

We clinked glasses.

“To us,” I murmured.

“To us,” she echoed.

I jerked my head towards the menu. "What are you having?"

She shrugged. "Maybe the Caesar salad.”

I shook my head. “No, you’re not having the Caesar Salad. You didn’t have lunch. You must eat something more substantial tonight.”

She frowned. “How do you know I didn’t have lunch?”

I took a sip of my champagne, feeling myself relax and enjoy the present. “I’ve had my evil eye on you all day, little Lillian. All day, I watched you go about your business with that little butterfly stuck to your pretty pussy.

She swallowed hard.

“Do you like steak?”

She nodded.

“Excellent. They do good steaks here.”

When the waiter returned, we gave him our order and he withdrew, finally leaving us alone.

"Tell me about you." Usually, when I was out on a date and I asked this question, I didn't really care for the answer. It was just a way to pass the time until we got to the main reason why we were having dinner together. This time though, I found myself interested in what Lillian had to say.

"There's not much to tell. I lost my father several years ago, but my mom is still alive and well, and my sister is married with twin girls."

"You've just told me about your family. Tell me about you, Lillian. What do you love?"

"I love children," she blurted out, then immediately looked uncomfortable.

I stared at her. Clearly, she hadn't meant to share that bit of info, and looking at her now, sophisticated and sexy in her black dress, you couldn't imagine her as anybody's mother, but for some strange reason I knew without a shred of doubt she would make a wonderful mother. I shook my head in surprise at that thought. Where the fuck had that come from, and what made me an expert on Lillian?

"And you? You're an only child, aren't you?" she countered, smoothly turning the tables on me.

"Yes," I replied.

She sipped her champagne and set the glass back down. "Did you ever long for siblings when you were growing up?"

I shook my head. "No." My voice was flat and unencouraging. I was unused to anyone probing into my private life.

My parents never had time for me when I was a kid. My father's first love had always been business, and my mother's was socializing and shopping. I always wondered why they bothered having a child, but I suppose it was something to do. In a way, I was glad they hadn't had another child to feel as unwanted and unloved as I had felt growing up. I'd never spoken about any of this to anyone and I wasn't about to start now.

I was relieved when the waiter returned with our food and I could move us on to more cheerful topics, like what I was going to do to her tonight.

"When we get back upstairs, I want you to get on the bed and open your legs as wide as you can for me. Can you do that?"

Her gaze bounced around the room, then she swallowed the food in her mouth, and nodded.

Chapter 18
Lillian

I barely ate my dinner while Max cleaned his plate.

I may be inexperienced, but I sure as hell knew what it meant to share a hotel suite with my boss.

How could he be so irritatingly relaxed? As soon as the question formed, the answer quickly followed. This was his lifestyle. There was no point in fooling myself that I was special. That I was the first woman he had flown by private jet to spend a weekend in a new city.

My spirits plummeted, but I quickly told myself to stop being silly. Wasn't I using him for sexual gratification too? I wasn't interested in Max beyond the satisfaction he could give me in bed. I knew what I was getting myself into when I laid down on his splendid bed and did what I did.

I sat with my legs squeezed tightly together to ease the ache that had taken permanent residence between my naked legs.

"Isn't the steak to your liking?" Max asked innocently.

I longed to wipe that smug look off his face. He knew exactly what was bothering me. To look cool and collected, I affected a serenity I did not feel. Languidly, I lifted up my wine glass and brought it to my lips. I took a sip and welcomed the rich and complex taste of the red wine he had ordered to go with our steaks. All the while I never took my gaze off Max's all-knowing eyes.

"The steak is fine. I'm not that hungry."

His eyes glittered in the soft lighting of the restaurant. "If you prefer, we can leave. Go back up to our suite..."

Part of me wanted to leave the restaurant and go back to our suite, but a part of me was petrified. I knew how much he wanted me; I saw it in his eyes. But what if I didn't live up to his expectations?

I wasn't worried about him not living up to my expectations. After all, I'd already had two previews on his office desk. It was my own performance I was worried about. Contrary to what most people assumed when they looked at me, I wasn't sophisticated at all. I'd only had one boyfriend in my entire life.

That was my big secret.

I'd only ever had sex with one man.

Not even Maggie knew this.

"No, I'm waiting for dessert," I lied.

I chugged another two glasses of wine which did help calm my nerves a bit. By the time I had played around with my sumptuous Faberge egg-shaped chocolate pudding covered in a shimmering edible gold leaf and filled with champagne jelly and pretended to drink my coffee, I'd managed to convince myself that I was ready for anything and everything that he could throw at me. I stood up and swayed slightly. He regarded me with watchful eyes.

Maybe I was tipsier than I thought.

As we walked out of the restaurant, he took my hand in an unexpectedly sweet gesture. It surprised me, but also made me feel a little less slutty. I mean, what decent woman agreed to a no-strings night of torrid sex with her boss?

He let go of my hand to call the elevator, and I felt the loss of it as if all warmth had left my body. I folded my arms across my chest and tried to ignore the warning bells going off in my head. I tried not to think about tomorrow or the day after, but those thoughts refused to be pushed away. What if he fired me after this? I needed this job desperately to keep up with my mom's mortgage payments. I didn't want to admit it before, but my savings were really dwindling fast.

I pushed all those niggling worries away.

For one night, just tonight, I wanted to have fun, and after that, Mr. Frost and I could go back to our roles as boss and personal assistant. For this one night, I was going to pretend to be his date, which was easy to do in an anonymous city. Besides, I'd had my chance to say no earlier this evening when he first told me I was coming with him as his fuck toy.

We didn't speak as we strolled down the corridor. Our feet were so silent on the thick carpet I could hear the blood pounding in my temples.

Then, he opened our door and waited for me to enter first. For a second, I stood at the threshold. This is it, Lillian. This is your last chance to escape. I glanced sideways at him. He was watching me and his eyes were so incredibly beautiful I felt a strange tingling at the pit of my stomach. I'd never met a man with such stunning eyes. The wine was singing in my veins. I had to have him. No matter what. Consequences be damned.

I took a step forward and entered the suite. He followed me into the room. Suddenly, we were standing in the middle, facing each other.

My thighs trembled. I swallowed hard and cleared my throat. "Mr. Frost," I began and could have kicked myself. Where did that come from?

But it seemed to please him. A mocking smile pulled at the corners of his lips. "I like it when you call me Mr. Frost, especially when you're begging me to fuck you."

A delicious shudder shot through me. I was powerless to resist him. Almost against my will, I started to undress for him. I unzipped the dress and let it drop to the floor. He looked at my chest. "I need everything off."

I undid my bra and allowed my breasts to pop out. My chest heaved making my breasts undulate with the rhythm of my breathing.

"You are so fucking sexy," Max growled, as he hungrily devoured me with his eyes. He undid the first two buttons on his shirt, then he pulled it over his head and tossed it to the floor.

Naked and shameless, I watched him undress. His boxer briefs were the last to go, but as he straightened, I gasped at the sight of his cock. Wow! So huge and entwined with angry, pulsating veins, it was almost intimidating.

I hadn't intended to be honest, but the words just left my mouth. "You're nearly as big as a twelve-inch Subway sandwich."

He grinned. "Don't worry, all pussies love Subway sandwiches. Especially when I feed it in one go"

"I've never been with someone so big," I whispered in awe. "Is it going to hurt?"

He smiled slowly. "Don't you know? Pleasure is the flower of pain."

He wrapped a hand around his thick shaft and gave it a few strokes. I'd never imagined that it would be this insanely hot watching a man handle his cock.

On a whim, I decided to give him a little show similar to the one he had just given me. Before I could change my mind, I moved my hands to my breasts and circled my nipples.

His cock jerked.

I teased my nipples and as they hardened, a moan escaped my lips. I'd never done anything like that before.

"Get on the bed," he ordered.

I did as he asked, and remembering what he'd said during dinner, spread my legs as far as they could go.

"I like a woman who listens to instructions," he said as he joined me on the bed and braced his hands on either side of my inner thighs. He looked at my pussy as if he was a spider about to consume its prey.

Holding me still, he licked and sucked me into delirium. I felt my body tremble in his hands and before too long, I was ready to burst and yet he still had me in his mouth, devouring me.

Sticky cream gushed out of me and flowed down my legs. I moaned and fisted the sheets. "Please... please... please..." I begged.

I felt like screaming at him to give me release, but I knew from what he had done to me all day, that he wanted me to suffer. He enjoyed watching me suffer at his hands. I let my head drop backwards and groaned. Just when I was about to topple over the edge, he pulled away again, his glistening mouth leaving my pussy throbbing with frustration.

The sound of tearing plastic filled the air.

My body was ready for him. He positioned himself between my legs and I felt his hardness at the entrance to my pussy. He paused and stared at me. He looked as if he was memorizing the moment and filing it away in his mind: that night he joined his PA in an act of copulation in a hotel in South Carolina.

"Please," I raised my hips and showed him my hot wet pussy.

I was shaking with excitement, ready to be taken, ready for anything to come. He rubbed the head of his wonderful, big, angry cock against the velvet lips of my pussy several times then pressed in gently.

“Ohhh,” I moaned as I felt the thick column enter me, and the tight walls of my sex stretching unbearably around the foreign shape that was inexorably pushing itself into my heated interior.

I could see my breasts shaking, and below them, between my thighs, the hard, tanned body of the man who was panting harshly, primal desire burning in his eyes, and his mouth growling with possessive delight, as he watched his massive cock enter my body.

Then he stopped.

I knew what he was doing. He was giving my pussy time to accustom itself and preparing my interior for what was about to happen. He was basking in this moment of trembling anticipation as he looked at my body with unholy excitement.

Pleasure is the flower of pain.

I gripped the sheets tightly, as tightly as I could.

A second later, he pushed his hips forward in one powerful and decisive move and pierced right into me.

My mouth opened in a silent scream of shock and pain, even as his mouth opened in a triumphant snarl. He immediately began to move his hips steadily back and forth, each time pushing, penetrating a little deeper into my tender slit. The sensations and impulses experienced in my body and brain sent me into a state of ecstatic stupor. With each thrust, his huge cock fucked my pussy in a way it had never been.

It evoked an uninhibited cry of intense pleasure within me, but it seemed as if he was completely out of control as if he was driven by a frenzy of desire.

As my body began to accommodate his intruder cock, he picked pace and fucked me even harder, methodically ramming into me with deep, powerful thrusts. Like a copulating animal, he pounded mercilessly into me.

With lustful greed, he swooped down and took one juicy nipple in his mouth. Like a starving animal, he clamped his teeth on the delicate breast, biting one then the other. Again and again. All the while his hips kept pushing rhythmically, constantly fucking my tight sex. As soon as my muscles began to clench at my approaching orgasm, he wrapped his mouth around my stiff nipple and sucked hard at the swollen shape.

It was surreal.

My boss on top of me, fucking me as if I was an inanimate doll, while his lustful mouth sucked on my breasts. My body felt as if I didn't own it. As if it belonged to him. As if I had left the gates of reality and this was nothing but a dream. I even had the impression I was copulating not with a man, but with a strange wild beast.

I felt my jerking body start to shake powerfully with pleasure. Waves of heat washed over me as he continued to batter my pussy relentlessly. He didn't stop even for a second, bringing me closer to yet another climax that I couldn't contain or control.

Waves of juices flowed out of me, as his massive shaft slid in and out. Then suddenly, just as I stood at the crest of my climax, things happened all at once. He bit hard on my nipple, much harder than before and he drove his full length into my pussy until his pubic bone rubbed against my clit.

My body was shaken by an orgasm of such extraordinary intensity it felt as if I was free falling. I screamed. He held his penis deep inside my climaxing body and ran his tongue over my breasts, cupping them tightly in his hands, until a guttural noise escaped his mouth and he shuddered and found his own release. My muscles clenched around his cock, milking him.

His cock was still deep inside me but unmoving. I could feel each throb of his penis, the swollen head pressing against my inner walls. I wrapped my legs around him, pulling him deeper into me. It felt as if he had already become part of me.

Chapter 19
Max

With a towel hanging low on my hips, I pushed the bathroom door open and stepped into our room. I'd left Lillian sound asleep, but now she was awake, her eyes ogling me. She raised her gaze to my face before quickly looking away as if she'd been caught with her hand in the cookie jar. Biting her bottom lip, she wrapped the sheet around herself and rushed past me to the bathroom.

It had been tempting to pull her to me when I woke up, but I was worried that things were happening too fast. It was my habit to keep women at bay with my rules of self-preservation, like getting out of bed as soon as I woke up. If I lingered, it could give the woman the idea that what we had was more. Never a good thing.

But with her, I wanted to linger...

I grabbed a bathrobe from the hotel closet and placed an order for breakfast. I couldn't be bothered shouting out to her to ask what she wanted so I ordered everything they had. The sound of the shower brought images of joining a naked Lillian in the shower.

I felt myself go hard.

I was going to ignore the itch, but what the hell? I slipped on a condom, went back to the bathroom, and slid the door open.

She whirled around, "Oh."

"Don't worry. This won't take long," I said. Grabbing her hips, I pushed into her wonderfully hot pussy. I'd fucked her so many times during the night and early morning hours she must be swollen and tender, but she pushed her ass back and welcomed me in.

I came quickly and withdrew from her body. I knew she hadn't climaxed, but that was a good thing. It would keep her on her toes for later. I planned to fuck her many, many more times before our trip was over. I left her to finish her shower and went back to the bedroom.

Drying my hair with a towel, I settled down in the small seating area with my laptop and threw myself into work. I checked my stocks, then skimmed through the financial headlines before moving to the Jed Burner documents.

The company he was working for was a well-known, expensive electrical goods brand. It hadn't been as popular three years ago as it is now and that was solely a result of Jed Burner's leadership. If I knew him well, he was probably restless having achieved what he had set out to, and even though he didn't know it yet, he was ready for the next challenge.

Chris had assembled a confidential document for him with all the information he needed about the company we had made a bid for. Hopefully, the challenge would be enough to sway him. Men like Jed Burner lived off that kind of adrenaline, needing doses of it every so often.

I worked until the bathroom door opened.

Lillian emerged with her fair hair wet and her face scrubbed clean, making her look more innocent than she usually did. My eyes dropped to take in the rest of her. Even covered by a huge towel, her curves were visible and very, very enticing. If I had not ordered food, she would have been breakfast.

"Good morning," she said, moving to the door.

At that moment, a knock came on the door. Lillian looked at me questioningly.

"Room service. I ordered breakfast," I explained briefly, as I headed towards the main living area. I opened the door and a uniformed server wheeled in a trolley.

The scent of bacon, eggs, waffles and croissants filled the room as he arranged the dishes on the dining table.

Lillian crossed her arms. "All *that* for two people?"

"Think of it as a food adventure," I suggested.

The server left and she moved to the table and proceeded to pour both of us a fresh cup of coffee. The sight of Lillian in a bathrobe, barefoot and with wet hair did something strange to me. It made me happy! In fact, I felt so foolishly happy I had to shake my head at my own silliness.

"What will you do while I have lunch with Jed?" I asked as I filled my plate with food.

She told me she had booked a day tour to visit sights in North Carolina. Not my thing, but she made it sound enticing.

My phone vibrated with a message and I picked it up.

Chris had sent photos of male models parading different tuxedos with a question.

Which one do you like?

I didn't know I was frowning until Lillian asked me if anything was wrong.

"Nothing's wrong. Chris has sent me a bunch of photos of tuxedos to choose from, but I'm always terrible at picking clothes. That's why I have a stylist who shops for all my clothes. From suits, shirts, ties, and even socks. Made my life a whole lot easier the day I hired her."

"Why is Chris sending you photos of tuxedos to choose from?"

"He's getting married and he's asked me to be the best man. This is part of it, I suppose," I muttered.

"Can I take a look?"

I handed my phone to her and she peered down at the screen, her brow creased in concentration. Her face looked so fresh and clean. So fuckable.

She handed my phone back to me. "The dark grey in the second photo is extra special."

I looked at the second suit and nodded. "Yeah, I like it too." I typed a reply to Chris, then set my phone back on the table and looked at Lillian.

"Thank you. You've saved my life. I hate choosing clothes."

To my surprise, she laughed. She had never laughed before. I stared at her with fascination. "My mom did all my dad's clothes shopping. I doubt he ever picked out a shirt for himself in all the years they were married."

Her voice carried the warmth and love she felt for her family. She even looked different. It made me wonder about her. I knew hardly anything about her. And suddenly I was curious, intensely curious about her. I wanted to know everything there was to know.

"What?" she asked. "Why are you looking at me like that?"

I said the first thing that came into my head. "I was wondering if you'd like to do some shopping. Take my credit card and buy yourself something sexy to wear for tonight."

Her expression became inscrutable, then she dropped her gaze, and all the warmth that had animated her face when she was talking about her family was gone. When she looked up, the calm, unflappable mask she wore in the office was back.

"It's okay. I already have something sexy to wear tonight."

I couldn't understand it. Women loved it when I offered them my credit card. Getting it back was usually the problem.

"Well, get some underwear then. I keep ripping them."

"Why? Why do you want me to use your credit card?" Her voice was cold.

The question confused me. What the hell had offended her? I shrugged. "I want to buy you something."

Of course, I wasn't doing it from the goodness of my heart. Generosity ensured that when I ended the relationship, a woman would not feel used or at least less used. If anything, she would feel clever having left with something of value.

I'd never seen her solemn blue eyes look so distant and

sad. "I don't need expensive gifts from you."

She pushed her chair back and walked to the second bedroom where all her clothes were. I was gobsmacked. No one had ever reacted like that when I offered them free money. I didn't know how to react in turn. She returned a few minutes later, dressed.

"All the best for your meeting with Jed Burner." Without a smile or hint of friendliness, she turned around and left, shutting the door firmly behind her.

"I'll be damned," I said aloud.

I pushed her out of my mind, determined to get some work done. It worked somewhat, though it felt like war, with Lillian pushing into my mind and me forcing her out. It didn't help that her scent was everywhere, disrupting me and creating a longing for her.

I was glad when it was time to get ready for my meeting with Jed Burner. As I dressed, I couldn't help but wonder what Lillian was doing at that very moment.

Jed Burner was already at the restaurant when I got there and he stood when he spotted me crossing the room. We shook hands.

As we ate, I quizzed him about his current job and how he had managed to turn it around that fast. It felt good to be free from the thoughts of Lillian.

"The kind of questions you're asking are making me think you have an interesting offer?" Jed said as he tucked into swordfish and grilled potatoes.

I smiled. "I might have."

Then I told him about the company that Chris and I were snooping around, and why we thought it was a winner with the right CEO. I looked at him pointedly.

"You are that CEO."

He didn't respond immediately, but when he did, he made the hairs at the back of my neck stand.

"That's funny," he said slowly. "I've just been offered the exact same deal."

I felt my eyes narrowing. One thing I knew about Jed was that he told it straight. "By whom?"

He shook his head. "I don't know. The offer was made anonymously through an agency.

"When was this?"

"Yesterday. I said a tentative yes, but I'm not into underhand stuff so I'll be doing some research of my own."

"Yesterday," I said quietly. There was zero chance it was a coincidence. Someone else had front run us and yet only Chris and I knew. A little voice in my head said, "And Lillian."

Lillian knew.

She had typed up the letter for Jed. She had seen the file Chris drew up and my notes on the company. Suddenly, all the pieces of the jigsaw fell into place. Finally, I understood why she had not quit even though I had treated her far worse than the others. Even her scandalous behavior on my bed made perfect sense now. The little Matahari had been sent to seduce me and steal my business secrets, but the billion-dollar question was, who did she work for?

Jed wore an expression of regret. "I'm sorry you came all this way for nothing."

I thought about Lillian lying on the hotel bed, her legs wide open, her eyes wanton and desperate, and her pink, dripping pussy throbbing for my cock.

"I'm not," I said softly.

Chapter 20
Lillian

"The maiden felt the kisses, blushed and,
lifting her timid eyes up to the light, saw
the sky and her lover at the same time."
Pygmalion in the "Metamorphoses"

I was determined to enjoy myself and not think about the insulting way he offered me the use of his credit card to do a spot of shopping. It didn't take a genius to figure out it was a thing he did with women. A guilt assuager. It let him off the hook when he'd had enough of the unsuspecting women.

But I hated the fact that he believed he needed to do it with me. I wasn't one of those women he could buy off with an afternoon of shopping.

I knew what I was getting into when I agreed to go for a dirty weekend with him. I didn't need to spend his money to feel good about myself.

The tour was fun. I got to ride in a city bus and explore the city along with other tourists. Then I had lunch in a cafeteria at a brewery and made a couple of new friends with whom I exchanged numbers.

It could have been even more fun if my anger didn't keep flaring up. His offer had cheapened the weekend and made it less special. Less enjoyable. It did nothing for my self-esteem either. No woman wanted to feel she was another one in the zillion faceless women he'd slept with.

The tour lasted another two hours after lunch and at four, I hailed a cab to take me back to the hotel.

In the cab I gave myself a stern talking to.

The weekend was meant to be fun, but it wasn't going to be enjoyable if I didn't let go of my anger. What did it matter if he thought he could buy me off with some expensive clothes? It was not personal. That was how he was. The important thing was that I'd said no.

The best thing to do was to erase it from my mind and focus on having as great a time as I could. I rarely got to do crazy things like take off for the weekend. And definitely not with a sexy, intriguing man like him. When would such an opportunity ever come again?

Probably never.

I pushed the door open to find him lying on the bed reading a newspaper and wearing nothing more than a pair of boxer briefs. He looked so delicious lying there. Against my will, memories of the previous night filled my mind.

My anger had dissipated and all I wanted to do was drape my body over his very enticing one. Plus, I'd missed him. I'd been determined to have a good time, and I had, but

I'd felt his absence, knowing it would have been doubly fun with him.

He looked at me over the top of the newspapers, I knew straight away. Something was different. His eyes, his body, and even the air around him throbbed with something new. "I've been thinking of you and look what you've done to me." He moved the newspapers and I saw the impressive bulge in his briefs. I still found it hard to believe that all of him had fit inside me.

In spite of myself, I felt a thrill run through my body.

"Come and sit on my cock," he said, his voice quiet and silky.

"Let me have a shower first. I feel dirty."

He put the newspaper down. "I like dirty girls. Come here."

I shook my head and, turning away, fled towards the bathroom. I was desperate for a shower to wash down the cling of sweat on my skin. There was also something about him that seemed almost dangerous. I needed time to process this new aspect of him.

But before I could even reach the door, a vise-like grip encircled my wrist. I was whirled around and pulled forward so fast my body slammed into him. I could feel his hard cock digging into my flesh. I looked up at him, shocked. His gorgeous eyes were cold and hard. Why was he so angry? Surely not because I had refused to use his credit card?

"That was not an invitation," he said quietly. "It was an order. You disobeyed a direct order, Miss Hudson. Do you know what happens to disobedient staff?"

Speechlessly, I stared up at him.

"They get punished."

I couldn't understand the change in him. I opened my mouth to answer him, but he put his finger on my lips. "Don't bother," he advised. "Take all your clothes off."

He stepped away and watched me. I began to take my clothes off. There was an air of stillness about him. The stillness of a predator before it pounced on its prey. When I took my panties off, he held his hand out so I put them into his palm. He crushed them in his fist.

"Open your mouth," he commanded.

When I obeyed, he stuffed my panties into my mouth. Then he reached behind my head and released my hairband. Gently, he fluffed my hair and arranged it around my shoulders.

"You look mesmerizing like this. I like how your hair flows like liquid gold," he said, his voice almost awed.

I stared at him, unable to believe the change in him.

"Now, go to the bed and lie face down on the edge of it. Ass in the air."

I could feel my heart beating hard and fast as I walked past him and did as he instructed.

Of course, I knew why I was being asked to lie with my ass in the air, but it was still a shock when the first blow came. My head jerked violently and I gasped through the gag, but he held me down with a hand on the back of my neck. The other was swiftly brought down across my exposed ass.

The slaps turned my screams wordless.

My hands were gripping the bedclothes so hard my

knuckles showed white. After the sixth or seventh strike, I was quietly sobbing, my struggles weak. He should have stopped then, but he continued, landing blows harder and harder. He was trying to make me scream. Trying to make me beg and ask him to stop. Tell him it was enough punishment.

But I refused.

He kept going. The blows fell on my bottom, on my thighs, between my legs on my sex, each time worse and worse. It felt like he was shredding my skin. It hurt so, so much. When the pain was so excruciating, I felt unable to even breathe, he stopped.

He moved the strands of hair away from my face and took the gag out of my mouth. "Are you a slut, Lillian?"

Tears were pouring down my face. "No," I whispered hoarsely.

"You must be. Otherwise, you wouldn't have masturbated on my bed. You wouldn't have come to work without your underwear, you wouldn't have agreed to a dirty weekend with your boss, and you definitely wouldn't be wet between your legs now."

He slipped his fingers between my pussy lips. Shame crippled me, but I couldn't control my reaction. I was dripping wet. Even now, the feelings racing inside me felt alive. Ravenous. To my horror, my body craved his touch. I wanted more. I wanted not just his fingers on my sex, but his big strong cock deep inside me.

He brought his glistening fingers to his mouth and slipped them between his lips. Then he inserted them into my soaking sex again. This time they were relentless. Pushing in and out, making squishing sounds. The grip of my control was going. He was forcing pleasure into me, but so effortlessly.

I whimpered, my hips shuddering, and my body writhed. I pulsed against him, desperate for release.

Suddenly, he withdrew his fingers.

"Stand up," he ordered.

Chapter 21
Max

https://www.youtube.com/watch?v=Qq4j1LtCdww

I watched her get to her feet unsteadily. She could barely stand. Her ass was bright red. It must have stung like hell.

"Turn around." My voice was thick and guttural.

She obeyed, moving slowly. Her face was tear-stained, but her eyes glittered defiantly. My God, she was even more beautiful like this.

"Go to the window. Stand with your legs apart and place your palms on the glass above your head."

She gasped.

I smiled. "I know. Anyone who looks out of their window will be able to see me fucking you."

She stood there, her eyes enormous, staring at me.

"Do you need another lesson in obedience, Miss Hudson?"

She shook her head, then walked over to the window and stood as I had instructed. There was something so erotic about the way she was standing there that I felt rage in my belly. The rage was so intense, I did something I'd never done in my life.

I went to her and, roughly tilting her hips, I entered her raw.

"Good girl," I gritted through clenched teeth. "Just enjoy it." Suddenly and without warning, I plunged into her, balls deep. My body slapping against her burning skin, making her yelp in pain.

I was so furious with her, that I didn't care whether I hurt her. I just kept thrusting and thrusting. Taking my pleasure. My head felt as if it was ablaze, tingles of fire ran up and down my spine. I grabbed a fistful of her hair and turned her so I could see her profile. I wanted to see her break.

Her mouth was open and she was panting.

The faster and harder I slammed into her the more she moaned. Her pussy clenched my cock tightly. I knew she was about to climax. "If you dare to come, I'm going to fuck your ass," I snarled.

She froze in shock, but the muscles of her pussy spasmed with excitement. Her eyes, filled with some nameless emotion, swiveled in my direction. "So many vile things I could do to you," I relished.

"Then do it," she spat back, a crazy glint in her eyes.

It was as if the world had stopped and the only thing that mattered was making her submit. Using my hand in her ear as leverage, I thrust into her harder and faster. She shook all over. Was it fear, pain, or pleasure? I didn't know or care.

Like an animal, I just rocked my body back and forth into her.

It was a pit I was travelling into, a dark pit, but I didn't stop. I went deeper and deeper until I came. The release was so intense it hurt, I felt as if I'd been hit by lightning. My body buckled and my vision went black as waves rolled and spread beneath my skin. As if from a distance, I heard myself roar.

I was wet all over with sweat as I pulled out of her.

She collapsed to the ground in a heap. I lifted her into my arms and carried her to the bed. When I laid her down, she winced. I looked down at her. I had watched the tape of her masturbating so many times. I wanted to watch her again. I opened her legs. Her pussy was swollen and wet. My seed was seeping out of it.

"Have you come?"

Her eyes were enormous with hurt. She shook her head.

"Play with yourself."

Her hand moved slowly towards her pussy. With her fingers, she circled her clit. Two strokes later she came, explosively, her body arching, her mouth open in a frozen cry, and her juices gushing out of her.

It was irrational. It was madness, but I couldn't stop myself. I knelt down and gently, meticulously licked her slit clean.

She was a traitor.

She was an enemy.

But she was my traitor. My enemy.

She belonged to me. I felt as if I couldn't let her go. Her sweet pussy was mine. All mine. Only mine.

My head vibrated with the sound of her cries and breathless sobs as I made her climax again.

Chapter 22
Lillian

His strong arms wrapped around me. Nobody had held me like this before. I couldn't control my sobs anymore, my ass felt as if scalding hot water had been poured over it. I felt so exhausted as if I'd run a marathon, but I didn't want him to let me go.

He stroked my hair, while his other arm held me tight.

I felt safe somehow and I fell asleep. When I awakened it was dark outside and I was alone. I got out of bed and went to the bathroom. In the mirror, there was a wild-eyed, naked stranger. I turned around and looked at my bottom. It was bright red and there were bruises in the shape of his finger on my hips and thighs.

I stood under a warm shower. My mind felt numb. I couldn't think. Afterwards, I towel dried myself and slipped into a fluffy white bathrobe before I ventured out into the suite. He was nowhere to be seen, but there was a message for me on the table.

Dress up. We're going out for dinner

Max

I blow-dried my hair and got into the dress I'd chosen so carefully for this trip. It was long and simple, but it had a plunging back that went all the way down to my waist. As I was applying lipstick, I heard him enter the suite. He came and stood behind me. I had to marvel at how breathtakingly handsome he looked.

He stared at my reflection with unsmiling eyes, but that vicious fury was absent. I didn't know where it had come from and I didn't know where it had departed to, but I was glad it was gone.

His fingers brushed the naked skin on my back and I shivered.

"You look beautiful," he murmured.

I felt myself blush. "Thank you."

"But something's missing."

I frowned. He dipped his hand into his jacket pocket and fished out a necklace with blue jewels. His fingers brushed the back of my neck as he fastened it. "That's better."

I opened my mouth to protest, but he shook his head. "If you don't want it, give it away or bin it, I don't care."

I reached up and touched the beautiful stones. It was obviously a very expensive piece. Had I just become his mistress? A week ago, I would have reacted angrily, been insulted even. How dare anyone treat me as if I could be bought with a few trinkets, but it seemed as if he had a free pass with me. He could get away with anything. I realized I could be his mistress. If he asked, I would say yes.

"Ready to go?"

I took a deep breath and nodded.

One thing for sure, no matter what happened after this, as long as I lived, I would never forget this weekend away with him.

As we walked across the foyer, his phone rang. "Excuse me a minute," he said and moved away to take the call. My stomach clenched. If it was work, why did he move away? It must be a woman? But would he really care about how I felt if it was another woman? He wouldn't. It bothered me, but I pretended a nonchalance I did not feel and carried on walking.

"Hey, it is you, isn't it?" a man's voice called from behind me.

I turned around and didn't recognize him. He was an overweight man in his mid-forties. He looked like one of those salespeople who roamed the country selling their wares.

"Sorry," I said politely.

He leaned closer, his dark eyes knowing and lascivious. "I saw you at the window. You were getting fucked..."

He wanted to embarrass me, but I felt no shame. Not one shred of it. I regarded him calmly. "Yeah?"

He licked his lips, a vulgar gesture. "Yeah. I haven't seen a woman get fucked like that in a long, long time. I mean, he really destroyed you. How much do you charge?"

My voice was cold. "You can't afford me, but if you have nothing better to do later tonight, you can look out of your window and see me get fucked like that again."

His eyes bulged. "Look, why don't you come around to my room, after he's done with you? I promise I'll make it worth your while."

I took a leaf out of Mrs. Frost's book and let my gaze travel disdainfully down the length of his obese body before I brought it back to his eyes. "Thanks for the offer, but I'll have to pass."

I turned away from him and continued walking towards the restaurant.

"If you change your mind, I'm in room 716."

"What did he want?" Max asked, falling into step next to me.

"He wanted me to know he saw me at the window."

Max stopped abruptly. "What did you say?"

I stopped too and looked at him. There was a strange expression in his eyes. They were so hostile they were scary. "I told him to look out of his window later this evening if he wanted to see me get fucked like that again."

He scowled. "You told him that?"

I nodded and carried on walking.

He caught up with me and we walked in silence. Once we were seated, and the food was ordered, Max leaned back against his chair. I looked at him probingly. There was something almost indolent about him, but it was fake. He was actually tense. He tapped his fingers on the white table cloth and said invitingly, "Tell me about your day. I want to know exactly what you got up to."

I was amazed. Other than sexually he'd never shown the slightest bit of interest in the mundane things I got up to. But the attention must have been real because when a waiter came by with the bottle of Petrus 1995, he was so irritated with the interruption, he very nearly swatted the poor guy away like a fly even before he had even properly filled our glasses.

I took a sip of the perfectly chilled wine and shrugged. I didn't want to bore him. A tour on a tourist bus was almost certainly not his thing. "It was a tour of the city from a bus. You'd have been bored."

He leaned forward. "But did you enjoy it?"

The intense curiosity in his eyes was unnerving and exhilarating. "Yes. I did."

"Hmmm... I've never done anything like that," he said thoughtfully. "I always fly in and out of cities until they all blend together."

"I suppose you're not on holiday. You're working."

"Yes. So... did you see everything you wanted to?"

I'd only had half a glass of wine, but it must have gone to my head because I could have sworn he seemed to be so much warmer and kinder.

"I didn't get to see the waterfalls," I found myself saying, a wistful note in my voice. I suddenly remembered my parents taking my sister and me to theme parks all over the country. I hadn't thought of my childhood in such a long time. My mother's financial problems had crowded out all the old good memories I had of my parents.

He leaned forward. "What's the matter?"

"Nothing." I shook my head and reached for my glass of wine.

"Tell me about your family?" he invited softly.

My eyes widened. "My family? Why do you want to know?"

He shrugged. "Just curious about you. If I remember correctly, you told my mother that your dad had passed away and your family consisted of your mother and your older sister who was married with twins."

I stared at him astonished. He had remembered that throwaway bit of information!

"Do you miss your dad?" he asked gently.

Memories of my father came flooding back and I had to swallow the hard lump in my throat. "Yes, I miss him very much. None of this mess would have happened if he was still alive." As the words left my mouth, I knew I shouldn't have said that. The last thing I wanted to talk about was my private life or to relive that nightmare again.

"What mess?" Max asked. His voice was so full of warmth and caring I felt confused by the change in his character.

"Nothing."

"It's obviously not nothing. Tell me. I'm a good listener and I've been known to solve a few problems in my time," he said, his tone friendly and encouraging. I'd never heard him speak like this before.

"Okay." I took a sip of wine and inhaled deeply. I'd never discussed the situation with anyone apart from my sister, of course, but even with her, I'd just skimmed the surface as she had been angry with my mother for a long time.

"After my father died, my mother got married to a man whose great dream had always been to own a restaurant. He roped her in on his dream and to help him, she remortgaged our childhood home. It did well at first, but after the initial excitement died down, people moved on to other newer establishments."

Max nodded. "It's the nature of that business. You have to have something special that will keep them coming back."

"Unfortunately, Henry didn't have that special something. To keep the restaurant afloat she took out a loan on top of remortgaging the house. Both my sister and I tried to convince her to stop throwing away good money after bad, but Henry was adamant he just needed time to turn things around and my mother just went along with it."

It took a moment to realize that the voice coming out of me was throbbing with fury. I'd never before expressed my anger over the whole situation. I'd tried to be kind and understanding so as not to upset my mother more. But the truth was, I carried a lot of anger. Henry had no right to come into my mother's life and turn it completely upside down, in fact, getting very close to destroying it.

"A lot of people make that mistake," Max said quietly while softly caressing my hand.

"So he took his own life, leaving Mom with the loans and a huge mortgage that she couldn't make the payments on," I said bitterly. "My sister and I have tried to convince her to sell the big house and buy a smaller place, but she won't hear of it. Says all her memories are in that house."

"So how does your mother manage?" Max asked.

I lifted my wine glass and drained it. "She's got a job... and I help out where I can." I was careful with my words. I didn't want to tell Max that I was the one who paid my mother's mortgage. She wasn't there listening to the conversation, but it felt like betrayal saying that.

He refilled my glass without waiting for the waiter to do it and smiled an almost fatherly smile. "A job? What kind of job?"

I reached for my glass and took a big gulp. I suddenly

felt nervous. This interrogation, no matter how gentle it was, I didn't know how to handle it. "She works as an assistant at a dentist."

He nodded slowly. "I see. Basically, you're saddled with paying her mortgage."

I swallowed hard. I really didn't want to make my mother look bad, but I couldn't lie outright. "For the moment."

He looked grim. "What about your sister? Can't she help?"

"She's a stay-at-home mom," I explained quickly. "She decided to raise her kids herself rather than send them to day care. I think it was the right decision." Max had not criticized my sister's decision, but I couldn't stop defending her. Old habits, I guess.

"Is your salary enough to pay both your bills?" He looked so concerned I was touched.

I nodded and reached again for the wine. "Yes, I think I'll be able to manage."

"Good, good. It's rather lucky then, that you found this job. How did you come across it, Lillian?"

"Maggie, my best friend, is the owner of the recruitment agency your company is using."

"I see. I've never met Maggie, but I believe we have a long history of her agency sending me PAs that never work out... until you." His eyes narrowed. "What did she tell you about me?"

The wine on an empty stomach had gone straight to my head and I was feeling quite light-headed. I answered without caution. "That you're a tyrant and I wouldn't last a month," I babbled.

Suddenly, he looked forbidding and distant, reminding me of the way he usually was, but I couldn't stop my tongue from wagging on.

"We actually took a bet about it. She believed I couldn't last a whole month and I thought I could." I covered my mouth with my hand as soon as the words were out. Shit. Was I going to get Maggie's agency in trouble with my drunken confessions?

"You won't get angry with her, will you?"

He laughed indulgently. "Of course not. To be honest I have a feeling you'll win that bet." He was silent for a few seconds. "So, you really need this job, huh?"

I was honest. "Yes."

"And you thought sleeping with the boss would help you keep it?"

I felt as if the rug had been pulled out from under me. I decided to be honest. I'd come this far I might as well jump in with both feet.

"No," I said clearly. "I slept with you because I couldn't not. Every cell in my body was begging me to do it. You are my drug."

Chapter 23
Lillian

I didn't know whether he believed me or not, because the food arrived. He looked annoyed as if the delicious food was an interruption. I dug my fork into my West Australian rock lobster topped with winter black truffles and imported white stilton cheese, and seasoned with Laeso salt, and was stunned by how mouthwateringly opulent it was.

The meal passed in a haze of alcohol and indescribably delicious food. When the meal was finished, I stood and began walking towards the entrance. Three tables away I could see the fat salesman. He was watching me avidly. I lifted my chin and walked on. Max was just behind me.

Suddenly, I heard a pig-like squeal of horror. I turned around and saw Max standing over the man. He had poured a glass of red wine over the man's head. The shocked man was spluttering with impotent rage.

"Send me the dry-cleaning bill," Max sneered, dropping the empty glass into his plate of half-eaten food. Then he walked on and hooked my hand through his elbow.

"Good show. Thanks," I said, looking straight ahead.

"My pleasure," he said coolly.

We had to share the elevator with another couple and neither of us said anything. On our floor we got out and walked silently to our suite. He opened the door, walked straight to the master bedroom, and shut the curtains. Then he turned to look at me.

"Sorry," he said softly.

I couldn't believe my ears. He was apologizing to me. "Don't be. I wanted to do it."

"Why?"

I shrugged. "I've only ever been with one man and he was a nice guy with a deep and wonderful knowledge of art, history, and literature, but he was not too much into sex. Twice a week with him on top if I was lucky. Nobody had ever sucked my pussy, spanked me, or asked me to stand at a window until you came along. I'm here to tell you that I'm up for it all. Everything. I want to do it all with you."

"Are you on the pill?"

"Yes."

"Hmm..." He walked over to me, and I couldn't understand why it would be, but I thought I saw sadness in his eyes. He whispered something, but I didn't catch the entire sentence except the words, 'if only.' Then he dropped to his knees and through my dress kissed the mound of my sex. He inhaled my scent as if it was life-giving oxygen.

I clawed my hands into his thick hair.

"I can't get enough of the smell and taste of your pussy," he said, getting to his feet. "But first let me take this dress off. I don't want to ruin it. I like it on you."

He turned me around, unzipped my dress, and carefully draped it over the back of a cream armchair by the fireplace. He reached around my back, released the hook of my bra and flung it backwards. Next, he hooked his fingers into the waistband of my panties and pulled it downwards.

"Keep your high heels on," he instructed.

I stood in front of him naked but for my high heels. He lowered his face until it was only inches away from my glistening slit. Using the tip of his tongue, he flicked my clit. I moaned and, clutching his head in a vise-like grip, mindlessly ground my sex against his mouth. He let me use his mouth in that way.

As my movements became more frenzied and my groans deeper, he pushed his fingers into my wet center and fucked me with them. It was rough and quick.

"I'm going to come," I warned, as I came apart and gushed into his mouth.

Painstakingly, he licked my sex and thighs until I stopped trembling. Then he carried me to the bed and dropped me on it. Hungrily, he watched my breasts bounce. Then he pushed my legs up against his chest, pausing to stare at my pussy, gleaming with arousal juices.

"You're so fucking sexy," he said, as he undressed. All the while his eyes were glued to my exposed pussy. When he was naked, he ran a sole finger up and down my slick folds. He found my clit and teased it until I thought I would faint with pleasure.

Then... and only then... did he pounce.

His enormous cock festooned with pulsating veins plunged in. As easily as if it had been made especially for me. The fit was perfect. But something was different. It was instantly clear that he had been holding himself back all this time. He was a different man now. This man had no control. He was an animal. A caveman.

A caveman giving in to a primal need.

His sweat dripped down my body as he fucked me like a man possessed. It was like a dream. I didn't want it to end. Ever.

But no matter how much I tried to hold on to the sensations, the onslaught came. Rushing towards me. Impossible to stop. I had no choice but to give in to that rush of pure pleasure. My whimpers filled the room as I wrapped my legs tightly around him and cried out his name.

Watching me come brought his own orgasm. It felt good to take his hot seed and to watch him above me, lose it. Here in this hotel room, on this anonymous hotel bed, he was mine. All mine. Tonight, he had no thoughts about his business or the other women he slept with.

It was only me. Me. And me.

He was still buried in me. I didn't want him to withdraw so I grabbed his hips and pulled him in.

"You feel so good inside me," I said. "I wish I could fall asleep with you still deep in me."

"You're not sleeping tonight, Lillian," he said softly. "I'm fucking you every way I know how. By the time dawn comes, you'll need a shower badly."

"Do your worst," I dared.

And he did.

All night long.

If I slept at all it was only fitfully, until I was awakened by a tongue slipping into my mouth or my pussy. He filled my mouth, my belly, and my womb with his seed.

I loved it all.

He behaved like a man who thought tomorrow was not going to come for him. Everything he wanted he must take tonight, for tomorrow it would become mist in the morning sun.

Chapter 24
Max

I never slept all night.

When the luminous dial of the clock showed it was 6.00 a.m. I woke her up again.

"Have you really only been with one man?" I asked.

"Yes, but don't worry," she said with a little laugh. "I'm not going to demand that you put a ring on it. I ask for nothing, except a weekend of sex and more sex.

I wanted to shake her. How could she give this all up for some money to pay her mother's mortgage? This was special. You had to live many lifetimes to find something like this. We could have been so fucking great together.

"So, do you do this a lot?" she asked, her voice casual.

"What?"

"Treat all your women to romantic weekends away."

I was so furious I flipped her soft alluring body face down. I ran my hands over her curves, stopping to knead her round ass before sliding my hand between the still-red cheeks. She was dripping wet and ready for me.

"Is this how you wake up every morning?" I growled, sliding a finger into her wet center.

"No," she admitted, her voice husky with desire and sleep.

I pushed my hard cock into her until I was balls deep and began to thrust.

Her cries filled the room and when she came, it was loud enough to wake the dead. My own orgasm quickly followed. Afterwards, I did something I never did with a woman. I gathered her close to me and held her tightly.

"You smell like a whore house. Time for a shower, Lillian."

Chapter 25
Lillian

I'd never showered with a man before.

Both Dan and I had small showers in our apartments, and even if we had, Dan would probably have turned the other way and started talking about the French Revolution or something. I had no idea what an intimate experience it was.

As Max soaped me, teasing my sensitive points, I stood still and pretended to be unaware of just what he was doing.

But God, how I loved his height and his muscular build. He made me feel protected as if nothing bad could happen to me when he was around.

I shook my head, dislodging the dangerous thoughts from my mind. Max had made it very clear what this was. Sex with no attachments. Allowing myself to fantasize that it was anything more than what it was -the fastest route to heartbreak. I wasn't going to allow that to happen.

Max turned me so I was facing away from him. His hands kneaded my shoulders, gently massaging and caressing me before they moved down to my ass. I was a curvy woman and I'd always thought my ass was too big, but Max seemed to love it. As he kneaded my ass cheeks, he made hungry sounds at the back of his throat.

He turned me to face him, took me into his arms, and in the hot mist gave me a bone-tingling kiss.

"I fantasized about fucking you in the shower," he murmured. "Hell, I even jerked off thinking of you."

"You did?" I asked, intrigued. Somehow, I couldn't visualize cold-eyed Max, his large hand wrapped around his large cock while he imagined fucking me in the shower.

"I did."

"When was this?"

"Not long after we met," he admitted, his hands roaming over my body, leaving heat everywhere he touched.

I palmed his chest, rubbing my hands lightly over his nipples. "How were you fucking me?" I asked in a voice that sounded like a purr. I'd never thought of myself as a seductive person, but Max made me feel like a sex kitten.

"You were bent over," he said.

"Like this?" I asked, bending over slightly, my hands braced on the wall. I wasn't familiar with this new person I was becoming, but I loved her confidence.

"Yes, but your ass was higher and your legs were spread further apart," Max said, his hands skimming over my ass and hips. He nudged my legs with his knees, adjusting me until he found the right angle to penetrate me.

Hot water rained down on our bodies as his cock drove into me. An odd cry escaped me. My powers of speech had gone. All I could think of was the wild sensations coursing through my body each time Max slammed into me. When it was over, Max pulled out of me and turned me around to rinse me under the water.

I looked at him. God, he was beautiful. Never in a million years would I have dreamed of having a man like him. *But he's not yours*, a mocking voice said in my head. We dried ourselves in those huge fluffy hotel towels, and then we stood in front of the mirror and brushed our teeth.

I looked at Max from the corner of my eyes, and felt a pang of sadness. I wanted this for myself. A man to call my own, to wake up to every morning, and partake in this simple routine. My thoughts surprised me, but the weekend had opened up my eyes to how it could be with a person whom you were in perfect sync with.

I put the toothbrush into the glass and turned to him. "What are we doing today?"

"Breakfast, waterfall, then catching our flight back."

My eyes widened with surprise and delight. "Did you really say waterfall?"

Max's features softened. "Yes."

I grinned at him. "Oh wow! Thank you."

He cocked his head to one side and contemplated me for a few seconds before he spoke. "Apart from waterfalls, what else does Lillian love? What gets her eyes sparkling?"

"I'm not one of those mysterious women whose personality slowly and tantalizingly emerges over time. I just love dancing. Though, I haven't been to a concert in a long time."

"Why is that?" Max asked, his gaze trained on me as if he didn't want to miss a word I said. It was flattering and it could go to a person's head.

"I guess I've been so caught up in sorting out my mother's problems, that there's been no space for fun."

"I'll take you one day...soon," he promised.

My little heart leaped with joy and I beamed happily at him.

"I have to warn you though, I'm no dancer and I'll definitely step on your feet," he added with a laugh.

"I promise there's nothing to it. Just move any way you want. That's what I do," I said cheerfully.

"It's a date," Max assured softly.

My heart was so full of joy it felt as if it would burst with happiness, but my head knew the truth. I was his PA. And as his employee, I was way out of his league. There was no way I should dream of anything serious happening between us.

As I dressed, I made a mental list of why I shouldn't be interested in Max.

One: He was my boss, and I knew that those relationships always ended in tears. The stories I'd heard over the years.

Two: as good as Max was in bed, he was a cold machine.

Maybe, two wasn't quite true though.

The weekend had shown me a glimpse of Max that made me revise my first impression of him. Inside his gruff exterior there was a passionate and caring human being. And of course, one heck of a lover. He had made me feel things that I was sure I would never experience with another man. Max had spoiled me for all other men and set me up for disappointment in the future. Of that, I was sure.

Still, I didn't want to be hopeful that he would be a different man when we were back in the office. I should prepare myself for grumpy, bad-tempered, arrogant Mr. Frost to show up.

I pulled my hair into a hair tie and gazed at my reflection. My eyes were shining and I looked happy. I'd never seen myself look so happy before.

Chapter 26
Lillian

After a breakfast of scrambled eggs, bacon, toast, and strong coffee, we made our way out to the rental car waiting by the front steps of the hotel. To my surprise, he opened the passenger door for me, waited until I got in, and closed it before he went around to the driver's side.

We used the GPS to find our way to the waterfalls and were lucky to find a parking space close to the entrance. Together we walked down the steep steps that led to the waterfall. The roar of the water rushing down to crash over the rocks below filled the clean-smelling air.

Eventually the waterfall came into view and Max and I stared, struck by its massive size and the incredible amount of water that was gushing down like a white curtain.

"Wow," I whispered, moving closer to the edge of the rock platform we were standing on.

"Don't wander too close to the edge, Lillian love. Those who fall into the plunge pool can only be retrieved by divers long after they've expired."

Instinctively, I stepped back and turned slowly to look at Max. His eyes were expressionless, but his warning had sounded like he was robotically reciting a line he'd read somewhere... or a veiled threat that had nothing to do with the waterfall.

His gaze never left my eyes. "That's better," he said softly. "Stay close to me and nothing bad will happen."

Again, I had the impression he was talking about something completely different.

"Is everything okay, Max?"

He smiled, but it didn't reach his eyes. "Everything is just fine."

"Do you want me to take a picture of you two lovebirds?" a kind tiny woman with pure white hair asked.

I was still confused by the strange vibes I was getting from Max, and I didn't want to embarrass the little old lady by correcting her assumption that we were lovebirds, so I gave her my phone. She took a couple of photos.

"A kiss?" she urged with a cheeky smile.

Max pulled me into his arms and gave me a full kiss without a care about who was watching. I couldn't help it. The moment his lips touched mine I lost myself in his kiss. I forgot the little old lady, the waterfall, and the other people milling around us. I threw my hands around his neck and kissed him back with everything I had.

Whistles and cheers brought me back to earth and I pulled away, but I was unembarrassed. I took my phone back and thanked the stranger. She had unknowingly given me more memories to remember the weekend by.

We followed the walking trail, and it took us behind the waterfalls to a series of caves, where I took more photos. As we watched the water cascade down from inside the caves, Max snaked his hand around my waist.

"I'm a convert," Max said. "Waterfalls are amazing."

I gave a low bow. "My work here is done."

Max's rumbling laugh warmed me inside. I liked making him laugh.

"What do you like doing in your free time?" I asked curiously.

"Work," Max said without missing a beat. "I love my work and it's what I do for fun."

"Are you serious?" I asked.

"Yes. I gave everything up to build what I have and no one is going to take it away from me." His tone was suddenly tight and a little muscle in his jaw pulsed angrily with some emotion.

It was a bizarre answer to a light and teasing question, but I decided to let it drop. Perhaps he had competitors who were trying to steal his business.

Afterwards, he bought us bottles of water, and we sat on the benches that faced the waterfalls.

"How come you didn't insist on glass bottles?" I teased.

He shrugged. "I only behave like a diva when I am in New York."

I laughed. "Why are you so horrible to your PAs?"

He didn't take his eyes off the waterfall. "I've never had one good PA before you."

I smiled at him, glad he thought I was good at my job, and glad that he had enjoyed the morning. We were leaving in the next two hours and soon it was time to drive back to the hotel.

"I'll never forget this weekend," I said, a little smile playing on my lips.

"Me too," he agreed, but his voice was strangely and inexplicably sad.

Chapter 27
Max

I spoke to Chris last night and by early this morning he'd already arranged an exhaustive sweep of the entire building for bugs and surveillance devices. They found two bugs in my office, one under the table where the cleaners never got to, and another inside the phone. There were none in Lillian's office area.

Chris had also spoken with the Security staff who remained steadfast in their assertion that no one, other than the cleaners who had been with the company for almost five years, had been allowed into my office while Lillian or I were not around.

Combined with the timing of Lillian's arrival, the evidence pointed to her being the mole.

But despite the damning findings, I found it almost impossible to believe she could be that good an actress. There was just nothing about her that raised any red flags for me, and I was good, brilliant actually, at spotting liars and scammers.

Maybe I was fooled because I didn't want to believe she

was treacherous. Blinded by her sex appeal, I let my dick do the thinking for me. Even now I was refusing to believe it because I didn't want to give her up.

It was a shock to suddenly realize she was the first woman I'd ever wanted to keep.

"When is the bachelor party?" Lillian asked, intruding into my dark introspection.

I turned my gaze away from the airplane window and looked at her. Her face was completely innocent of any kind of guilt. If this was an act, she was wasted working as a PA. She should find her way to Hollywood. She was certainly good enough to win an Oscar.

"Bachelor party?" I echoed.

"For Chris's wedding."

I shrugged. "He never mentioned it."

"It's part of the best man's duties," she explained calmly.

I grimaced. "Is he expecting me to throw a bachelor's party?"

She nodded and tried not to react though it was pretty obvious she thought I was the most clueless person she had ever come across.

To be honest, I didn't give two fucks about the bachelor party. Chris's wedding was the last thing on my mind. What I needed to sort out as a matter of urgency was to find a way out of the fucking bear pit I'd let myself fall into.

The plan had seemed like a good idea. In one weekend, Lillian would be out of my system. Except, she wasn't. I wanted to fuck her right now, here on the plane. It had never happened before. Even now that I knew she was almost certainly poison. That confused the shit out of me.

"You don't know where to start, do you?" she asked gently.

"Not really."

"It's okay. I'll help you out," she said, a teasing smile playing about her sweet mouth. "I'll make you look like the most competent best man in the world."

With that little tease, my cock roared to life and began to pulse painfully for her. My own lack of self-control irritated me. It was almost as if I was addicted to her scent, her taste, her body.

I nodded curtly… and her smile died.

As I turned away from that dying smile all kinds of unwanted and foreign feelings slammed into me. Protective feelings. Like the type I felt when that idiot came to tell her he saw her at the window. The kind of sensations I'd never felt for a woman, especially after what should have been an uncomplicated, no-strings-attached, dirty weekend.

I didn't like or want these unfamiliar feelings.

I pushed them away violently and stared moodily at the white clouds. Even if there wasn't the issue of her being a traitor, I didn't want to have feelings for any woman. No thank you. I liked my life just as it was.

Business came first, second, and third.

"I'm sorry, I didn't mean to offend or upset you. I was just trying to help."

I swung my gaze back to Lillian, and the expression of hurt on her white face made my stomach tighten in knots. For fuck's sake! No matter how much I told myself she was no good, one wounded look from her and I wanted to punch myself.

I had no control over my hand when it reached out and

touched a strand of her silky blonde hair, or my fingers when they trailed over the smooth flesh of her cheek. Only when my finger touched her trembling mouth did I realize what I was doing. I dropped my hand as if I had been burned by fire.

I took control of myself. I had two choices.

I could just confront her now, threaten to involve the police and scare her enough to make her confess. There was a good possibility though she didn't really know who had hired her. It could have been a middleman making the transaction for some powerful entity. Which meant the opportunity to find out who my enemy/competitor would be lost.

The second option would be to pretend that nothing was amiss until I could smoke out the real identity of the person who had planted bugs.

There was no contest. The second option won hands down.

"I'm not upset with you, Lillian," I said. "In fact, I'd very much appreciate it if you could help. I wouldn't know where to start. I'll text Chris and ask him if he wants a party. He is unpredictable."

I quickly texted Chris.

He answered seconds later.

Hell yes!!

"Well, looks like he wants one," I said, showing her the text.

Lillian laughed. "Of course, he does. What man doesn't?"

I wouldn't. I'd rather work than get plastered in a strip club in Vegas.

"You do know the rest of the best man's duties? Like the best man has to make a speech?"

"Yeah, I got that much. What else?"

"Look after the rings."

"I can do that."

"Help the groom get ready for the ceremony."

"I'm good with that. The hardest job is the bachelor's party, but I have the best PA helping out, don't I?"

Her eyes twinkled. "You do."

I stared at her. Still unable to believe she could be pretending. To stop myself from giving the game away, I opened my laptop and forced myself to do some work.

We arrived home an hour and a half later. My driver was waiting for us and after stowing the luggage, he drove us home. The air in the car was suddenly tense as if neither of us knew how to behave now that we were back home. I told myself I was glad the fantasy was over, and I knew the truth, but who was I kidding? I hated it. It had been amazing to be living in my fool's paradise.

I missed it. I craved it.

The car came to a stop in front of Lillian's apartment building. I jumped out and opened her door before the driver could. She flashed me a smile.

"Should I go back to calling you Mr. Frost?"

I shook my head. "No."

Then I took her weekend bag from the driver and walked her to the building entrance. "Thank you for an unforgettable weekend."

An expression of sorrow crossed her features, but it was gone in a flash.

"I had fun too." She smiled but it wasn't the natural smile that I'd gotten used to. It seemed forced.

At that moment I knew. I couldn't pretend nothing was wrong. My head was completely fucked. I needed space from her to think this out. Get my priorities in order. The more I stayed around her, the more involved I was becoming. The idea that one weekend with her would cure me was terrible. It was like pouring oil on fire to put it out.

I handed her the luggage and took a step back. "I won't see you tomorrow because I'm away for a week?"

Her eyebrows rose. "But I have booked all kinds of appointments for you next week."

"This is an emergency. Family stuff."

"Oh!" Her face showed her confusion. "Do you want me to reschedule your meetings for the week after?"

"Yes, rebook everything except the Sanderson meeting. I can attend that via Zoom."

She looked up at me. She seemed so authentic and warm, not a trace of pretentiousness or fakeness about her. Her beautiful eyes brimmed with sincerity... or a very good impression of it.

"Is there anything else I can do to help?"

I shook my head. "Not for the moment. I'll contact you if I need anything else."

She shifted her weight from one foot to another awkwardly. Deliberately, I said nothing. Let her make all the moves.

"Okay. In that case, goodbye and have a good week," she said finally.

"Goodbye, Lillian."

She turned and unlocked the door. Without another glance at me, she pushed the door open and stepped in.

The memory of the first time I'd fucked her with my fingers popped into my mind. It had been insanely hot knowing that she wanted me to stop, but her body betrayed her and she asked for more and more.

Then I'd stopped when she'd been on the verge of coming, and her face...

I wanted to catch the closing door and go in with her. The craving was so strong I had to clench my fists to stop myself. I strode to the car, my head a total mess. Yes, I needed a little time away from her. I had become too involved. Sleeping with her was definitely a mistake. A big mistake.

One I planned to correct.

I had to stop being this weak-willed addict. I had to go back to the person I was before she appeared outside my office in her tight pencil skirt.

Chapter 28
Lillian

The buzzer downstairs rang, and I ran to let Maggie through the entrance door. I'd invited her over because I needed to talk to someone about Max. For the last two hours since I'd been home, I kept replaying the weekend, ending with the cold goodbye from him.

Not even a kiss or a hug.

He'd handed me my weekend bag as if my usefulness had ended.

It had hurt even though all along I'd known what I was getting into when I agreed to a weekend away with him. I hated that I'd allowed him to get to me so much.

I'd even cried in the shower.

Over a man. And worse, my boss.

How was it that some women were able to have friends with benefits and when it was time to move on, they did, without a backward glance?

I unlocked the door and Maggie appeared bearing a big box of pizza and a brown bag. She looked wholesome and cheerful with her strawberry blonde hair pulled back in a ponytail.

"You look exhausted," she noted.

"Thanks," I said in a dry tone.

"No, I meant it in the best way possible. You look as though you used the weekend for the purpose it was intended for - lots of sex..."

My chest constricted as an image of Max sprawled in bed filled my mind. I pushed it away, knowing it would bring tears to my eyes. "I thought weekends were for rest and relaxation."

Maggie groaned dramatically. "Please... I'm already so bored. Both my boyfriend, who won't marry me, and my best friend were away and I had nothing to do but binge Netflix. If it sounds like I'm whining, it's because I am. I was hoping you, at least, got some action with a stranger at the hotel bar."

I laughed uncomfortably. "A stranger at the hotel bar?"

"No? Shame." She fished out a bottle of Merlot from the bag. "Never mind, I come bearing gifts."

I raised an eyebrow. "On a Sunday?" Still, I led the way to the kitchen and set the wine glasses on the island while Maggie got the wine opener from the drawer.

"Don't bother messing about with fancy glasses. Get the mugs out."

Minutes later, we were settled in with our mugs filled almost to the top with wine and munching on our favorite pepperoni pizza.

"If you look so hollow and wasted, and it wasn't a stranger at the bar, then I'm guessing the weekend was a nightmare. It was, wasn't it? I knew he would work you to the ground. I'll let the bet pass if you want to quit."

I hadn't planned on how much to tell Maggie about the weekend, but a sob burst out of me and I dropped the pizza back into the box.

"Lillian, what is it? What happened? Did he hurt you?" Maggie cried.

I wiped the tears with the back of my hand and fought to get control of my emotions. "No, he didn't hurt me." My voice did not sound like me at all. It sounded feeble, but I wasn't the vulnerable type. I was strong and I always kept my emotions in check.

"What then? What happened?" Maggie asked worriedly.

I reached for my wine and took a huge gulp, then set it back down. "I slept with him."

Her eyes widened and she let out a shriek of disbelief. "No. No way. Not Frost."

I nodded miserably.

"No! You did not," she gasped.

"I did. And not just once... the whole weekend."

"Oh my God." Maggie stared at me as if I had turned into someone she didn't know. That made two of us. "Was he any good?"

The question was so unexpected; a fit of giggles came over me. "Very. I never knew sex could be like that."

"Fuck, Lillian. What's going on? You're not the type of woman who would sleep with her boss. And Frost of all people. You didn't do it to win the bet, did you?"

"Are you crazy? Of course not. You know me. I don't care about winning like you do."

"Alright. Start from the beginning. I want to hear everything. How did it start?"

I told her most of it, leaving out a few details which Maggie picked on right away, and begged me to tell her. She sounded so fascinated by the whole thing that I stopped feeling like a complete slut for sleeping with my boss.

"In one week, you've had more excitement than I've had all of my life," Maggie said. "I don't understand the tears. Sounds like the experience surpassed your expectations."

I bit my lower lip, embarrassingly close to tears again. I was such a fool. Why had I allowed myself to think that when we got back, Max and I would continue with our affair? I should have known and prepared for the end when we were on the plane. He had already started being distant, but I'd chosen to ignore what my eyes were seeing.

Max had already moved on.

"I fell for him, Maggie" I admitted, shamefaced.

"What!" she exclaimed. "You can't fall for someone in one weekend?"

I'd never been with a man who made me feel special just with a look or a touch. I couldn't believe that I was entertaining such tender thoughts about a man whom I'd believed to be a complete asshole. But I'd gotten a peak into the real man behind the gruff grumpy façade, and he was nothing like the jerk everyone thought he was.

I remembered the way he looked at me, as if I was precious and listened to everything I said, as if every word mattered. Then I made myself recall the cold way he'd said goodbye, and I no longer knew which one was the real Max.

"I can't believe I fell for him, but I did," I repeated in a daze.

Maggie gripped my hand. "No, you did not. Your problem is you haven't been with a man in such a long time you now think you have feelings for Frost just because he made you feel good in bed. Believe me, it's all physical. It's easy to confuse great sex with feelings. Those don't come easily. You'll be fine as long as you remember it was just great sex."

Her words penetrated the thick fog in my brain.

"You're right. I don't have feelings for Max. I guess I was so taken by his skills between the sheets, I thought it was more."

"There you go," Maggie said, shaking her head in awe. "I still can't believe that swine invited you on a dirty weekend and you said yes."

A sense of sadness crept back into my chest. "It was the greatest weekend I've ever had."

She looked solemn. "Would you go again if he asked you to?"

Every cell in my body screamed yes, but I shook my head firmly.

"No. It was exhilarating and so pleasurable it was addictive, but you're right it was only sex. Max is my boss and he's not interested in a relationship."

"As long as you remember that, you'll be fine. He's never been linked for any length of time to a woman in all the years that I've known him. That should tell you something."

But something did happen between us.

I pushed the thought away. It was the kind of dangerous

thinking that could get my heart broken. I'd gotten a glimpse of the kind of pain that Maximus Frost could inflict on me... if I let him.

I smiled at her. "Let's talk about something else. Like your soon-to-be fiancé."

"Oh, him..."

Maggie and I polished off the bottle of Merlot.

Hours later, as I walked her to the door, my steps were a little wobbly. I was probably going to regret drinking so much in the morning, but I was really glad that Maggie had come.

She had snapped me out of my melancholy mood and made me see the weekend for what it had been. I cleaned up, drank a glass of water and headed to bed.

Chapter 29
Max
https://www.youtube.com/watch?v=4zAThXFOy2c&t=78s

I parked the car and walked to the front of the building.

It was 3.00 a.m. The only sign of life was a couple on the other side of the street, clearly intoxicated, their slurred voices and laughter breaking the silence of the night. I pressed the buzzer next to the Hudson name tag and waited.

It was late.

Maybe she wouldn't answer. Maybe that was the best-case scenario. This was a stupid idea, anyway. Disgusted with myself, I turned away from the door.

"Max?" she called sleepily through the intercom.

I snapped to attention. "Are you alone?"

"Yeah, I'm alone. Come on up."

The buzzer sounded and I pushed the door open. I was too hyped up to wait for the elevator. I ran up the stairs three at a time. Within a few minutes I was on Lillian's floor.

I walked down the corridor towards her open door.

She stood at the doorway with an uncertain look on her face... and a nightgown that was too short... for eyes other than mine. The thought of another man looking at her incensed me.

Why? Why did it have to be her?

She took one look at my face and backed away. I kicked the door shut behind me.

"Sorry to come so late," I said, not sorry at all.

"Have you been drinking?" she asked.

"Yes, but not so much that I don't know what I'm doing."

"You said goodbye..."

I slipped a hand around her and pulled her soft, warm body against mine. "I did, but I realized the weekend is not over, Lillian. In a few hours it will be, but not yet. We'll party until dawn comes."

"I'm glad you came," she whispered. "Shall I make us some coffee?"

"No. I have other things in mind."

She held my gaze. "What things?"

"Wild, scandalous things."

I dipped my hands under her nightshirt and cupped her breasts. They were soft and supple, fitting perfectly into my palms. I gently kneaded them, feeling her nipples harden beneath my touch. She let out a soft moan and I slid my hand down her stomach, feeling the heat between her legs.

The whiskey had blurred the lines between reality and fantasy. She looked like a merciful angel. I paid no attention to the fact that the bible is full of angels of destruction. I trailed kisses along the elegant curve of her neck.

"I got into bed to sleep, but all I could think about was my Lillian and what I wanted to do to her."

"I wish I was your Lillian," she said with a sad smile.

I had called her my Lillian unthinkingly. Hadn't meant to. Of course, she wasn't mine. The thought filled me with a new rage. I swooped down on her mouth and kissed her hungrily. Her smell made me dizzy.

"Take me in your mouth, angel, make me forget," I commanded huskily.

"Forget what?" she asked.

My mind was a buzzing mess of static. I didn't answer her, just guided her head downwards towards my crotch. I watched her unzip my jeans and pull my erect cock out. Greedily, I watched my cock smoothly disappear into her gorgeous face.

It was a beautiful, beautiful sight.

I face fucked my angel of destruction. I was rough. I watched her gag. I watched the tears come in her eyes. And when I came, I held her head tightly and shot my seed deep into her throat. I filled her belly with it, but through all of it, I could see in her eyes that she knew. She knew the real power lay with her. It was me who had lost control.

She was the mighty one.

She was the angel of destruction.

And her job was almost done.

Afterwards, I lifted her into my arms and carried her to her bed. It was a small bed. Rickety and quite uncomfortable, but there I gave her the best orgasm she'd ever had. Multiple times she screamed my name. When the waves died away, she looked at me in wonder.

"I cried for you in the shower," she whispered. Her eyes were still wild with lust and her beautiful face was flushed.

Oh, Lillian, Lillian. If only I could believe your sweet lies.

I lowered my head, took one of her nipples into my mouth and sucked it gently. Lillian arched her back, pushing her breasts further into my mouth. How could a woman have captivated me so completely? Lillian had me completely under her spell.

"Max, please," she pleaded.

"You're irresistible when you beg," I said, burying my whole cock, every last inch, into her hot, wet slit.

She wrapped her hands and her legs around me. "Harder," she moaned.

My breath became drawn out and ragged as I slammed into her. My climax was like hot lava. The pleasure was so immense it burned me. We lay in her narrow bed intertwined, our breathing hard.

"I'm so glad you're here. I've loved waking up with you in bed. You made me feel safe and warm." Her voice was heavy with sleep.

I watched her until she fell into a deep slumber, then I got dressed and left. Dawn was filtering through the curtains as I closed her door.

The weekend was over.

Chapter 30
Lillian

I walked into the office the following morning at ten minutes to eight. My headache was increasing in intensity so I made myself a strong cup of black coffee and carried it to my desk. As I walked past Max's closed door, I felt a pang of desolation hit me.

I put the coffee down on my table and I went into his office. His desk was clear of all papers. I went and sat in his chair, closed my eyes, and remembered that day I had sat on this desk with my legs wide open and allowed him to do whatever he wanted with me.

"Oh, Max," I whispered.

Maggie was wrong.

It was not just sex.

I felt him deep inside my body. He was like an unexpressed pain because I knew I could not have him. Perhaps no woman could. No matter how deep our sexual connection was, one thing was clear, he didn't allow me into his head. When I thought back to our conversations, he had hardly revealed anything about himself.

The phone rang and I picked it up.

"Is my son there?" Mrs. Frost's haughty voice demanded.

My spine straightened. "Uh... no. He's not here, Mrs. Frost."

"Where is here?"

"I don't know. He didn't say."

"I recognize your voice... where do I know you from?"

"Um... we met the last time you were in New York. We had dinner together."

"Lillian?"

"Yes."

"What are you doing in his office while he isn't there?"

"I'm his PA."

"You work for him?" she asked incredulously.

I closed my eyes. "Yes."

"And you sleep with him?"

"Yes."

"It's completely inappropriate behavior. I would have thought my son would know better," she said disapprovingly.

"Would you like me to pass on a message if he calls?" I asked politely.

"Yes. Tell him to call me. Tell him I'm disappointed in him."

Then the line went dead. Ouch!

I leaned back against the leather chair and swiveled around.

Well, that was that.

* * *

At lunchtime, my sister texted me that she would be at Mom's place and asked if we could meet there for coffee. I said yes, glad to have something to do after work. The less time I spent with my own thoughts the better.

I drove straight to my mother's house and found that my sister was already there. I raised an eyebrow in surprise. Rose was never early for anything. I parked my car and headed to the front door. Rose answered the door, her face breaking into a wide grin.

"Hello stranger," she said as we hugged each other.

"You're wearing perfume. That's a huge change. Usually, you smell of bread and spices."

"And dirty diapers," she added, wrinkling her nose.

I laughed. "Never that." I followed her into the house to the kitchen where Mom was nursing a mug of coffee.

She smiled when she saw us. "It's been so long since I saw you two girls together. It reminds me of when you were little and I would dress you in similar outfits."

"Yeah, please don't remind me of that. We hated it, didn't we, Lillian?" Rose said, sliding onto a stool.

"Well, you hated it. I didn't mind." I served myself some coffee and sat down with my mother and sister.

"How was your trip to North Carolina?" my mother asked.

I tried to keep a neutral face as I told them how productive it had been for the company, and how my boss and I had bonded professionally. All the while, an ache wedged itself in the middle of my chest and sat there, refusing to move or melt away.

Damn Max Frost.

Chapter 31
Max

It had been one hell of a week... and it wasn't over yet.

Pure torture. Keeping my need for Lillian reigned in when all I wanted to do was go back to her apartment and fuck her senseless, or until her wobbly bed broke. I kept thinking of the way she was at the beginning, cool as a cucumber, unflappable, her eyes more serene than a frozen blue lake... until I put her on my desk and opened her legs.

But I'd promised myself to keep away, and no matter how hard it was, that was what I did. The distance did help and I managed to clear my head enough to come up with a workable plan of how to trap my competitor. I realized that whoever was behind the bugs was an amateur.

Only someone who didn't have any real business sense would try to copy another businessman's idea in such a way. Also, the fact that they had moved so quickly on the idea showed they had done no research of their own and had relied solely on Chris's findings. Who did that?

But something also told me this was personal.

Whoever it was knew me.

It could even be someone seeking revenge.

I planned to go back to work as if nothing had happened and let the bugs pick up my conversations with Chris. The conversations would signal my intention to acquire a company that we had, in reality, already acquired recently through a shell company. The moment the people behind the bugs tried to acquire that company they would show their hand.

And then I would find out exactly where Lillian came in.

The plan was simple, but the execution would not be.

When I arrived at work, Lillian was not in. I glanced at her chair and realized that I hated seeing it empty. She brought life and animation to that dead space. The day she left would indeed be a sad day.

I had barely sat down and turned on my computer when I heard her come in. I couldn't stop my legs from jumping up and walking over to the door.

"Good morning," I said.

She whirled around. As our gazes met her cheeks flushed and she flashed me a huge smile. She was happy to see me. It was impossible not to see that. No matter whether she was a spy or not that smile was real. I would stake my life on it.

"You're back. I thought you were away for the whole week," the beauty said.

My heart thumped rapidly, foolishly as if I was face to face with my latest crush. I disliked myself at that moment.

My gaze dropped to her lips and I found myself longing for their softness against mine. I caught myself. *Hold on there, son. This is not how we're playing this. Either I controlled myself for a few days and got this done, or I ruin it all by allowing myself to act like a lovesick teen.*

I forced myself to calm down and summoned grumpy Max. It was not too hard to do.

"I sorted my problem out quicker than I anticipated. Can we go over my updated schedule?" I asked coldly.

She flinched, taken aback at the sharpness in my voice. I saw her swallow hard as hurt squeezed her chest.

"Of course," she mumbled. Grabbing her iPad, she followed me to my office. Her perfume teased my senses as she trailed after me. My gaze moved to her breasts and I remembered the firm feel of her flesh underneath me. Against my will, an ache formed between my legs and I cursed my body for its disloyalty.

She sat down and pretended to be busy with her iPad.

"I'm ready," she said, her sexy voice, curling around me and heating my blood.

No woman had ever affected me the way she did. I cleared my throat and forced myself to focus on my schedule. Thankfully, the years of pure self-discipline took over and I became the professional who had grown this company into what it was today. When we were done, I dismissed her and turned my attention to my computer screen. For a few seconds, she stood undecided, but I played my part so well, that she incorrectly assumed I had forgotten she was still in my office.

She was nearly in tears as she hurried out. I had to

clench my hands into fists to stop myself from going after her.

I stared out of the window. I was so aware of the bugs. Of someone listening to everything I was saying. My door opened suddenly and I turned to see Lillian enter.

"Look, Max," she began. "I know what we had was just one weekend and I understand it's finished and we've both moved on, but..."

A little flame burst to life in my cold heart. "But what?"

"But I had a really good time with you and I wanted to return the favor. I got us tickets for a concert."

I stared at her. How could she possibly be my enemy?

She walked towards me in her white shirt and unbelievably erotic pencil skirt. "Here," she said, holding out two scraps of printed paper.

Our hands brushed and awareness spread through my body, settling in my cock. I looked down at the papers. Tickets to a Bruno Mars concert.

"I'd like us to go together," she said, her voice tight. I could feel the tension in her body as she waited for my reaction.

"Okay," I heard myself say.

A slow smile spread across her face. "Thank you,"

I stared at her for too long. "I'll pick you up at six."

"That's perfect," she said, her features growing so soft, that it practically made me want to growl with happiness.

She left, leaving a hint of her signature honey and lavender scent behind.

Chapter 32
Max

https://www.youtube.com/watch?v=dElRVQFqj-k
-marry you-

I rang Lillian's buzzer.

"Come on up," she said breathlessly.

I pushed the door open and made for the elevator. It was an ancient thing. I would have classed it under the dangerous category. I shifted my weight from one foot to the other, willing it to move faster. As soon as the doors creaked open, I was out.

"Hi," Lillian said, opening the door.

I took a sharp breath at the sight of her. I know it was a concert and some girls even wore bikini tops to these events, but that silver dress she had squeezed into should have been illegal.

"You look... edible," I said, my voice husky, revealing my uncontrollable desire.

"Good. That's exactly how I wanted to look," she said with a smile. "Come in. I only need to grab my purse and I'm ready."

I followed her in. The last time I was too jacked up to notice anything. Now, I looked around her living room while she went to the bedroom. She had a small bookshelf and I went to it and perused her tastes in books. A set of hardbacks about the French Revolution. That was a surprise. I opened one and found out some man called Dan had given the books to her.

Hope you find the contents of the pages as exciting as I did.

With all my love, Dan.

I hated Dan instantly and violently. If he had been standing in front of me then I'd have punched him in the jaw. Warning bells went off in my head, but for once, I didn't want to heed them. It would have been very satisfying to punch the pretentious idiot's teeth in. See how much he enjoyed the French Revolution then.

I shoved the book back into its place and turned away to look around me. The room was small, but feminine and cozy. I looked for signs of hidden wealth, but there were none. She was poor and it showed. That must have been why it was so easy to buy her.

Lillian returned a minute later carrying a clutch bag and a soft shawl around her shoulders. "I'm ready."

I couldn't stop staring at her. She looked so beautiful.

"What's up?" she asked.

"Nothing."

"So why are you staring at me as if I've grown a horn?"

How ironic. It was me who'd grown a horn from just looking at her. "I changed the tickets," I said, handing them out to her.

She looked down at them. "What? These are VIP tickets? How could you even buy them at the last minute?" she exclaimed, her eyes shining.

It was exactly the reaction I had been hoping for. I looked her in the eye and said, "Everything and everyone can be bought for the right price."

I watched her intently for any kind of guilty reaction, but there was none when she asked. "Oh dear. Are we talking a lot of money here?"

I nodded. "You don't want to know."

"I do want to know unless they cost more than I earn in a month. That'll just spoil the concert for me."

"In that case, we should leave."

She gasped. "Oh!"

I opened the door for her and shut it after us. It could have been awkward in the elevator but surprisingly enough, it wasn't. That old chemistry sizzled and crackled between us. If I had a choice, I'd have hit the elevator to take us back up to her apartment, the concert forgotten.

Outside, my driver was already waiting with the passenger door open for her.

"I thought we'd have a light dinner before the concert. There's a nice restaurant near the venue," I said.

"Sounds great," she said happily.

The hostess led us to our table and a waiter brought us the menus.

"I'm not sure I can eat anything," Lillian whispered. "I'm full just from sheer excitement."

"Eat. It'll be a long night for you."

The waiter returned and we gave him our orders. Lillian ordered a shrimp, lobster and black butter concoction, while I went for the roasted duck breast with pea and wild garlic velouté sauce. I sat back in my chair, my gaze on Lillian.

"How is your mom doing?" I asked. The more I could get her to talk, the more chance that she would accidentally reveal something I could use. Even the smallest thing could be helpful. "Have you tried again to convince her to sell the house and get something smaller?"

Lillian grew solemn. "No. I'm a coward when it comes to my mom. I hate causing her distress. I had the perfect opportunity to ask her when my sister was there, but it was such a nice evening and we hadn't been together in months so I just let it go."

I nodded. "Understandable ...Tell me about your sister."

She cheered up and regaled me with stories about her, her husband and children. Nothing I could use, but to my surprise I enjoyed listening to her talk. Some time ago I would have dismissed such talk as chatter or gossip. Ultimately uninteresting.

She stared at her empty plate in surprise. "I can't believe I ate all that. Goes to show how important good company is." Her cheeks reddened as if she had just realized what she had said. We were both treading carefully. Friends with a past.

"Thank you. I... like your company too," I said.

"Good," she said softly.

I paid the bill, and we left shortly after. Outside, the air was cool and the sky a gorgeous deep blue streaked with wavy orange lines.

We weren't the only ones walking to the arena. Couples, groups of friends, and even solo concertgoers strolled along the walking path. It felt good to be anonymous. I was used to commanding respect or curiosity wherever I went. Being a regular guy out on a date with a beautiful woman was different and exhilarating.

Simple was the word.

It dawned on me that this is what I'd craved from the women I'd dated in the past. Simplicity. Enjoying something as simple as taking a walk.

"Come on," Lillian said, pointing to a long, slow-moving queue. "The queue to enter the arena is that way."

"The VIP entrance is over here," I said, nodding towards a queue that was short and moving quickly.

We showed our tickets at the entrance and entered the huge arena. The noise from the crowd was incredible, but it was the energy that struck me. Everyone was hyped up and I realized I was too.

The VIP section was close to the stage, and when the band came roaring on stage, they were so close, you could almost reach out and touch them. The crowd went wild when Bruno grabbed the mic, welcomed us to the show, and immediately began to sing, *Marry me.*

Lillian turned to me, her face alive and bouncing with excitement. "It's one of my favorite songs," she shouted, and grabbing my hands urged me to dance with her. I was a terrible dancer, but she didn't seem to care. She was so wonderfully lost in her favorite song it was captivating.

"Cuz it's a beautiful night, we're looking for something dumb to do," she happily screamed out the lyrics, as she twirled, and gyrated around me, willing me to enter her state of joyful abandon.

I didn't even attempt to resist such sweeping enthusiasm. I dipped my toe in, but in seconds she had pulled me in head first.

I forgot I was Maximus Frost: billionaire, grumpy, difficult, arrogant, impossible-to-please, founder and CEO of Frost Inc. I moved my body to match my fallen angel. To my astonishment, I instantly began to relish the unnatural experience.

And I enjoyed myself in a way I hadn't in years.

If Chris could have seen me, he would have sworn I had a twin. There was simply no way the man gyrating and twisting around the blonde beauty was me.

Chapter 33
Lillian

https://www.youtube.com/watch?v=ekzHIouo8Q4
-when I was your man-

I was covered in sweat by the time the band played the last number, but I didn't care. All that mattered was that I was in Max's arms even if it would only be for the three minutes of the soft ballad, *When I was your man.*

His sweat, intermingled with his cologne, was intoxicating.

I looked into his eyes and the sound of the music faded away as did the crowd that surrounded us. The only thing I was aware of was the feel of Max's strong arms around me. He held me tight, my body pressed against his and I couldn't tell where mine began and his ended.

I wished we could stay like that forever.

I hadn't had anything alcoholic to drink, but I felt high on life and arousal. Every nerve cell in my body was awake, attuned to each movement that Max made. I craved his naked skin on mine. I wanted to be alone with him.

The song came to an end, signaling the end of the concert.

"I have backstage passes if you want to meet Bruno."

I looked into his gorgeously translucent eyes. "I don't want to meet him. I want to leave."

"Okay," he agreed easily.

I never thought I would be relieved to leave a concert, but I was. My body was gripped by a physical ache that intensified between my legs. Being outside in the fresh air helped, but I was consumed by the thought of being in Max's arms. There was no room in my brain for anything else.

"Did you enjoy the concert?" he asked, his voice gruff.

"It was the best concert I've ever been to." It was true, not because of the singer, but the company.

"I enjoyed myself too, more than I thought I would," he confessed.

"Maybe we can go to another concert," I said hopefully.

"Maybe," he conceded.

Joy coursed through me. If he wanted to go to another concert with me, it meant that he saw me in his future. At least in the near future. I was happy with that. It was crazy and insane, but I wanted Max Frost as my lover. Not a one-time thing. I wanted to enjoy what we'd had in North Carolina for as long as I could.

When it ended, I would deal with it then.

We got into the car and as we drove away, tension came over me. What if he dropped me off at my apartment and said goodbye? Did I have the guts to ask him in for a drink?

Then I remembered that I did not have a drink in my apartment. I inwardly cursed myself. I couldn't offer him dinner either as we'd already eaten. I should have planned it better. I didn't want the night to end just yet.

My problem was solved a few minutes later.

"Want to come to my place for a drink?" Max said. "It would be a shame to end the evening so early."

It was before ten o'clock, hardly so early, but we both needed an excuse. "I'd love that."

We got to his gate and at the press of a button in his car, the gates slid open. My heart thumped wildly in my chest and the need between my legs intensified. I pressed my legs together but that didn't help one bit.

Max parked the car.

"I remember the last time I was here," I said as I got out.

"I can't forget it," he said, offering his hand to me.

I took it and sparks flew between us. His eyes flashed and I was sure he'd felt it too. The physical attraction between us was so hot, it could have lit a fire.

Max pushed the door open and his dogs ran to him excitedly, their short tails wagging. How different they were the last time I saw them, snarling so ferociously they were salivating.

He scratched their heads. "This is Tomo and Tyson. Want to say hello?"

I held back. "If they promise not to bite my hand off."

He turned his face towards me. "They are highly trained and incredibly loyal. They'd bite their own paws off before they bite the hand of a friend of mine."

I moved forward and offered the back of my hand for them to sniff. When they had sniffed it, I knelt and rubbed their shiny necks. They eyed me curiously, but neutrally. No hostility and no affection. "They're stunning dogs."

"Yes, that they are. Stunning."

"I could do with a shower," Max said, his eyes boring into mine. "Feel like one?"

I was dying to say yes. "I don't have fresh clothes to change into."

"You can wear one of my shirts until Dana brings you some stuff."

I rose to my feet. "Dana?"

"My personal shopper. I think I told you about her. She has excellent taste."

"But at this time of the night?"

"That should be no problem for her. She has access to clothing shops at all hours of the day. Part of the service." He scrolled through his phone, tapped the screen, and put it to his ear. "Dana, are you able to bring some women's clothes over? I'll also require a sports bra, a tracksuit, and running shoes as well." He paused to listen to her reply. Then held out his phone to me. "Give her your sizes and color preferences."

I took the phone from him and gave Dana, who was very friendly, my measurements, then I ended the call and gave the phone back to him.

I looked sideways at him. "Why do I need a sports bra and running shoes?"

"We're going running at dawn."

I smiled at the wonderful thought of running in the early morning with him. "Okay."

I followed him up the stairs, both dogs keeping up with us.

"Stay," Max instructed, giving each dog a treat. Both dogs immediately sat down and began to eat their little morsels with surprising delicacy. He shut his bedroom door and his eyes moved over my body.

My nipples pushed against the material of my dress, aching to be touched. I knew that he could see them.

Chapter 34
Lillian

We moved at the same time, and within seconds, our clothes were on the floor and we were moving against each other. Max's hands and mouth were everywhere. On my aching breasts, my ass, and the sodden slit between my legs.

I moved my lips to his jawline, peppering kisses along the sexily rough skin. Max cupped the back of my head and brought my mouth to his.

He devoured me with his mouth.

I moaned into him and pressed my sticky body against his, needing to feel his skin next to mine. Heat whipped through me as our tongues tangled together. He broke the kiss and cupped my breasts. Pressing them together, he nipped each nipple.

"What about the shower?" I croaked.

"Yeah, the shower." He wrapped his arms around my knees and picked me up. Throwing me over his shoulder, as if I was a bag of potatoes, he carried me to the shower. I screamed with indignant laughter. He set me down in the tiled cubicle and switched on the water. It was one of those rain shower heads. And it was freezing cold. I yelped and tried to escape, but he held me tightly.

"What the hell?" I gasped.

"Just wait," he said, his eyes boring into mine.

My skin was full of goose pimples, but I couldn't stop staring at his eyes. There was something intriguing in them. Something mysterious. Something I didn't understand, even though I wanted to, so badly. It was as if I was a rabbit hypnotized by a snake. Any moment it would consume me, but I didn't care.

The water became warm then hot, but I never stopped staring at him.

"Good?" he asked softly.

I nodded. He was right, the extremes from cold to heat made the water feel as sensuous as flowing silk, far more delicious than any shower I'd ever taken.

Slowly, he lowered his head, cupping my ass with his large hands, and licked at my sex.

It drove me insane.

He looked up at me. "I think I became addicted to your pussy the very first time I ate you out at the office. Do you remember?"

"How could I forget? I couldn't believe that I was letting my new boss..." my words faded off.

Max grinned. "It was the hottest thing I'd ever done."

The next thing I knew Max had found my clit and wrapped his tongue around it. My body turned to liquid. He began to suck, the way only he knew how to. The beginnings of a climax started in my belly, increasing until it reached a crescendo.

"I'm going to come," I whimpered.

Max pushed a finger in and fucked me rapidly with it. I came apart, seeing stars as my body shook and trembled.

"Open your eyes," Max ordered. "I want to look into your eyes as I fuck you."

I opened my eyes and a moment of intense intimacy passed between us, making me shiver with emotion. His eyes were dark with desire and something else. If I was given to fancies, I would call it possession. He looked at me as if he wanted to claim me as his own.

It felt as if we belonged to each other. Like two parts of a puzzle. It was surreal and crazy and I desperately wanted to hold on to it.

I let out a cry of pleasure and clung to his shoulders. As I got closer to orgasm, I dug into his skin, but as soon as I realized I might bruise him, I loosened my hold.

"Don't hold back. I don't care if you hurt me," he growled. "I like knowing what I'm doing to you."

I had never been with a man whose desire for me was so obvious and so deep. It made me feel like the most beautiful woman on earth.

I came a second time, this one was drawn out and sweet. I purred like a cat and raised my hips to him.

"I need this as badly as I need air," Max growled moments before he came.

A glow spread through my body and I immediately cautioned myself. I shouldn't read too much into his words. It was probably just sex talk. Maybe he said that to all the women he had sex with.

That thought brought a wave of jealousy within me that shook me by its strength. I imagined Max whispering loving words to a faceless woman and I came down from the high I'd been feeling.

His hands softly caressing my ass brought me back to the present, and I wanted to laugh at my ridiculousness. Here I was feeling jealous when I had no right to feel jealous at all. Max had not promised anything. I had no permanent claim on him.

Chapter 35
Max

"How much did this bed cost?" she asked.

I frowned. "What?"

"I wanted to know how much your bed cost?"

I stared at her curiously. What a strange question. "I don't know. I paid a total price for the interior design and never looked at the detailed breakdown."

"Oh. So you didn't choose it."

"Yes, I did. I was given a choice of five different types of beds and I went for this one, but the price was never discussed."

"I see," she murmured.

"Why do you ask?"

"No reason."

"Tell me. Why is this information important to you?"

She took her phone out, scrolled through it and showed me a picture of a mood board that had the same bed as mine on it."

"I don't understand," I said.

"I chose the same bed as you on my 'dream house' board. Only, I knew I couldn't afford this bed so I was planning to get a carpenter to copy the headboard."

"But this bed is special because of the handmade mattress."

"Now that I have slept in it, I understand that," she conceded, her expression self-deprecating. "It is the natural mistake of poor people to miss the nuances of true luxury that are obvious to rich people."

"Tell you what... Let me buy it for you..."

She shook her head intently, a frown appearing on her forehead. "No, no, please don't. I wasn't trying to manipulate you into buying me a bed. I just wanted you to know we chose the same bed. It made me happy that we did."

Contemplatively, I caressed her curvy ass, squeezing and cupping her tightly. My enemy had chosen well. Not only did she play her part perfectly, she had the sexiest body of any woman I had ever met and I was utterly captivated by it. My cock, still buried inside her, started to stir.

She let out a soft laugh. "You're not serious."

"Do you blame my cock for being excited to be where it is?"

She laughed softly. "I like having your cock inside me. I wish I could fall asleep like this."

"I certainly won't be able to," I said, even though I loathed the idea of being kicked out. This was new to me. Wanting to fall asleep with my dick buried deep inside a woman. Shit. Who would have thought it could feel so perfect? So fucking right.

She shifted and my cock grew harder.

My hands moved to her hips and I rocked her up and

down. Her inner walls, slick with wetness clenched around my cock. Suddenly, a ringing sound interrupted us. Lillian tensed. She glanced back at me, her face apologetic.

"Sorry, but I have to check if it's my mom. If it's her I just have to say I'll call her back, and end the call, otherwise she'll sit and worry until I call her back."

"Go ahead," I invited.

She reached down to her bag, pulled out her phone, glanced at it and put it back into her purse.

"Not your mother?"

"No. It's just Dan."

Dan? The pansy who gave her the book about the French Revolution. The phone kept on ringing.

"Answer it," I said softly.

"It's okay. I'll call him back later."

"No, really. Answer it. Perhaps it's urgent."

I watched her closely as she took the call.

"Hey, what's up? Um... No... Not really. Well, I suppose I could do Wednesday lunch. Where? At the museum? Yeah, it'll be fine. Sure. That's good with me. Me too. Bye."

My whole body felt like it was on fire. She had just made a date with him while my cock was still buried inside her. "I hope you were not intending to meet up on Wednesday at lunchtime."

She looked at me blankly. "Why? What's happening then?"

"I have a lunch meeting and you're coming with me."

"Oh. I'll arrange a different date."

"I thought he was your ex," I heard myself grind out.

"He is. We're friends now. We decided we were never

meant to be lovers, just friends. He's a nice guy. You'll like him."

"I doubt it," I muttered.

"Max..."

"What?"

"Are you jealous?"

"Jealous? Of a man who gives a woman a book about the French Revolution?" I sneered, while rampaging jealousy ate me up from the inside.

Her mouth dropped open. "Oh my God! You so are." Then she began to laugh.

I pulled out of her, furious with myself and her. I was losing sight of what I was really supposed to be doing. I wasn't supposed to be falling deeper in lust with her. I was supposed to be tricking her into revealing who had hired her to plant the bugs. I rolled away from her and sat on the side of the bed. I wanted to hate her, but I couldn't. The harder I tried the more entangled I became in her silky web.

"Have you ever betrayed anyone, Lilian?" I asked.

She stopped laughing abruptly. "No."

I turned my head and stared at her. "Never?"

"Never."

She sat up, tossing her thick golden mane, and exposing her ripe full breasts to me. Instantly, the beast in me woke up.

"I want to fuck you while I look at your gorgeous ass," I said, my voice thick with strange emotions I'd never experienced before.

She got on her hands and knees and waited, while I moved behind her, my cock fully erect. I paused for a moment to admire her round beautiful ass. Instead of penetrating her like she expected me to, I spread her open, exposing her glistening pussy. Then I bent to lick the nectar made from sweet fruit. I couldn't get enough of her. I licked her again and again until she wriggled her hips with impatience.

When I took her, it was with a savagery I didn't know I was capable of. She moaned with pleasure while I held her hips firmly in place and slammed into her, watching her shapely ass as it jiggled with every thrust.

She didn't know it yet, but I was taking her away for the weekend to Connecticut. Together we were going to attend a tedious society party my mother was throwing.

My reason was simple.

I couldn't shake off the strong feeling that my competitor/enemy was known to me. Perhaps, just perhaps, Lillian would not be able to conceal her instinctive expression of recognition if she ever came face to face with the person or persons who hired her.

Chapter 36
Lillian

"You want to take me to your mother's house for the weekend?" I asked incredulously, as I pulled on the divinely soft turquoise tracksuit Dana had dropped off.

"Yes."

"So we'll be pretending I'm your girlfriend?"

"We wouldn't have to pretend very hard since we're going at it like rabbits," he quipped dryly from the bed.

"But your mother won't like it. She told me in no uncertain terms that she was disappointed you had hooked up with one of your staff."

"She'll get over it," he said callously.

I went to sit on the bed. "I'm not sure she will, Max. She sounded very sure of her disapproval."

"Leave my mother to me. She knows better than to cross me."

"It'll be awkward," I insisted.

"It won't be. I'll be there next to you the whole time."

I frowned. “But I have nothing I can wear to a society party.”

“Wear anything you want. You look good in everything, anyway” he dismissed simply.

I chewed my lower lip anxiously. Typical male. Easy for him to say. He could just pick up a black tux from the tens of black tuxedos in his walk-in closet and he would fit in anywhere. Not so for me. It was clear his mother thought I was not good enough for her son, I definitely didn’t want everyone else to think that too.

“Stop panicking. Just call Dana and ask her to come back with some cocktail dresses for you to choose from.”

I began to shake my head, but he stopped me with a stern raised finger.

“I have to attend Peter’s pre-wedding party, but it will be a working weekend so I’m picking up the bill.”

My shoulders slumped. No real point in trying to argue with him. The undeniable fact was I didn’t have anything suitable to wear to a society party, and the last thing I wanted to do was make a fool of myself by looking like I belonged in Max’s front office and not on his arm.

“So we’re going to drive down to Connecticut?”

“That’s the plan.”

“What time do we leave?”

“2.00 p.m.”

* * *

The next morning after an invigorating run and a delicious fifteen minutes in the shower together, I went downstairs to find Dana was back with a whole rack of gorgeous dresses she thought would suit me. Max was right, she did have an excellent fashion sense.

It was difficult, but I finally decided on an elegant off-the-shoulder black silk dress. It reminded me of Lady Diana's 'revenge dress'. Form-fitting and sexy, but in a classy way. Paired with the necklace Max had given me it would be the perfect look for a high-society function. Dana had also picked out a pair of matching crocodile skin high heels to complete the outfit.

After a quick lunch, Max's driver took me home so I could pack the rest of my stuff. It didn't take me long to get a small suitcase ready since it was only for one night. The plan was to be back by Sunday.

I was looking forward to the hour or so that Max and I would be alone in the car. There was something romantic and thrilling about being on a road trip with someone you fancied.

A whole hour of no interruptions, just me and Max.

I knew I was making the weekend out to be more than it was, and Max would be horrified if he knew, but I couldn't help the excitement building up over the trip.

True, I was nervous about sleeping in his parents' house, but Max had assured me his parents would have no problem with him bringing someone. Besides, there would be other guests staying overnight too. It didn't make me feel any better, but it did make me wonder how many women he had taken home for a weekend. I quickly stopped that thought, knowing I was only inflicting unnecessary pain on myself.

Rather than have Max come up, I made my way downstairs to wait for him a few minutes before we agreed to meet. I smiled when I spotted his car turning the corner. I loved that Max was a stickler for time, something we had in common.

He brought the car to a stop and slid out. He looked casually sexy in a white button-down shirt and chino pants. Like he'd stepped out of a magazine page.

"Nice outfit," he complimented, eyeing me up and down.

"This old thing," I said laughing and gesturing at the summer dress I had once, in the days before my mom got into financial troubles, spent nearly a quarter of my salary on. It was playful with a bow at the chest and it came up to my knees, showing off my legs.

Max drew me into his arms and ran hot kisses along my neck that made tingles run up my spine.

"You're a tease, Mr. Frost," I complained when he withdrew.

"That makes two of us," he said with a chuckle, as he took my bag and tossed it in the back seat. "Don't think I've forgotten that day when you came dressed to kill and told me, I could look but not touch."

"As if that ever stopped you," I shot back with a laugh and entered the car.

Sitting on his desk and opening my legs wide to show him my naked sex had been the most daring thing I'd ever done in my life, but it had been completely worth it.

Max entered the car, his scent dancing in the air. I sneaked a glance at him and met his gaze, which sent an electric current sizzling through me.

"Nothing stops me when I want something." Then he frowned suddenly and all the good feelings inside me evaporated.

"What's wrong?" I asked.

"Just someone walking over my grave," he said and smiled, but this time his smile didn't reach his eyes.

We drove in silence for a while.

"I've been thinking maybe I should sleep in a hotel?" I blurted out.

Max glanced at me. "Why?"

"I think your mother would appreciate it more."

He shook his head cynically. "Then you don't know my mother. She'd be horrified. How dare you behave as if her home is not good enough for you?"

"Oh, I never thought about it like that."

"Like I said, leave my mother to me. Besides, the whole point of taking you with me is to have you in my bed."

"Max," I exclaimed, shocked. "You're not planning on sharing a room with me in your parents' house?"

He laughed. "What a little Victorian maiden you turned out to be! If we didn't share a bedroom, I'd have to creep into your room in the dead of the night when everyone else had retired."

I laughed awkwardly. My mother wouldn't know where to look if I wanted to bring a man home to sleep for the night.

"Right. Us sharing a room would be normal at your home?"

"Us not sharing a room would be abnormal."

"It'll be nice to sleep holding you," I said weakly.

"Don't count on getting much sleep. I have plans for you... all night," he replied.

I grinned. "Really?"

He looked directly into my eyes. "Really."

I could feel the heat rushing through me. At that moment I wanted him to pull over and take me right there in the car. I needed to change the subject.

"How are the acquisition plans for La Zaire going?" I asked as I grasped for a topic that might interest him. I was also curious about that company. It had appeared on my desk as a well-researched complete file from Chris and was then never seen again.

His hands tightened on the wheel, and a strange tension came into his body. "It's going well. Just a few snags which I'm confident will be taken care of."

"That's good," I said and did not ask him to elaborate. I understood his cool tone and deliberately vague answer to mean he didn't want to talk about work. Which was fine by me.

I turned to look out the window.

There was something marvelous about leaving the skyscrapers behind and seeing the scenery give way to stretches of woods and open patches of land. I stretched, slipped my feet out of my shoes, rested them on the sun-warmed dashboard, and wriggled my toes.

"Did I tell you I also have a foot fetish?" he teased.

"Nope, but suck away," I said with a laugh. I was determined to enjoy this weekend.

Chapter 37
Lillian

The tall gates and long driveway should have alerted me that the house was going to be special, but I had no idea how special.

I'd seen luxurious homes, especially when I'd been called to my bosses' homes to bring in some urgent paperwork or something of that nature, but I'd never seen a home of the kind which stood in front of me.

His family home was a mansion.

A French-style stone mansion with hundreds of windows and a grand pillared entrance. Lush perfectly manicured formal gardens surrounded it.

A rift opened up between us.

Max was downright horrible to the people around him, mostly because they were slowing him down with their incompetence, but he never gave the impression he was not their equal. Or that he was better. He was so good at making people believe they were his equal that even after I met his mother and she had looked down her nose at me, I didn't truly realize how different both of them were from me.

I saw now that I was dealing with old money, the one percent, the elite ruling class of America. My yellow dress with its big playful bow felt silly now, and I wished I'd not worn it.

"Wow," I said my voice filled with awe. "*This* is where you grew up?"

"Yes," Max said in a flat voice. "Looks are deceiving. All this doesn't matter when there is very little love in the house. I'd have swapped it for caring parents."

My head whirled around at the bitterness in his voice. It was the first time Max had ever shown emotion about his family. My chest contracted as I imagined the little boy that Max was, roaming the hallways of this huge house, lonely and sad.

"Shall we?" he asked.

Nervously, I followed him out of the car and stood staring at the house as he fetched our bags from the back seat. He didn't speak as we walked to the front door and rang the bell. I found myself apprehensively shifting from one foot to another.

"Stop fidgeting. No one is going to bite you... other than me," Max teased.

I tried to smile back. He was about to say something else when the heavy door swung open, and a woman in a dark blue uniform, I assumed she must be the housekeeper, stood to one side, and invited us in.

"Welcome home, Master Frost."

"How are you, Rosella?" Max greeted.

"Very good," she said with a nod, then turned to me. "Welcome to Winterfell Manor, Miss Hudson."

"Thank you, Rosella."

She turned her attention to Max. "Your mother instructed me to prepare the Princess Anne room for you and Miss Hudson. She thought it would be quieter and more private than your old room. Would you like me to show you up?"

"Nah, we'll find our own way there. Thanks, Rosella."

"Shall I get some refreshments sent up for you and Miss Hudson?"

"Sure, why not?"

She nodded politely and withdrew quietly.

I wrinkled my nose. The interior of the house smelled of antiseptic, reminding me of a hospital.

"My mother has an obsession with germs," Max explained with a shrug.

I took in my surroundings. The hardwood flooring shone as if it had never been stepped on. Huge, museum-quality pieces of European art hung on the pristine walls, and everywhere there was gilt, gold, and wonderful priceless antiques.

"Maximus, you're here," Max's mother called, as she emerged from a doorway on the left. She was wearing pearls, a cream silk shirt neatly tucked into black jeans and skin-colored pumps. She air-kissed Max and fussed over him before turning to me, her expression changing. A cold, unfriendly stiffness slid over her features, making her face appear mask-like.

"Hello, Lillian," she greeted coolly, as she eyed my dress as if it was something I'd found in a jumble sale.

"Hello, Mrs. Frost. Thank you for having me," I said politely.

"You're welcome," she said crisply, then turned her

attention back to her son. "You don't have long to get ready before we have to leave for the party. Shall I send some refreshments up for you to have while you're getting ready?"

"Thanks, but Rosella has already seen to that," he said.

She nodded. "Your father wants a word with you. He is in the library. After you show Lillian up to the west wing, perhaps you'll go and see him."

"Of course."

"Good. I'll see you both later," she said, but she only looked at her son.

Max's mother had been somewhat friendly the first time we met, but that was before she knew I worked for Max. Once she'd established I wasn't in their class, she had become outrightly hostile.

I followed Max up a grand sweeping staircase and down a long wall-papered corridor with gilded light sconces. Finally, he opened a door to his left and we went in.

The room was beautiful with a huge ornate bed and tall windows that looked out to grasslands as far as the eye could see. There was an ancient oak tree in the distance.

"Did you climb that tree?" I asked.

"Yes."

I imagined Max climbing the tree as a child. I knew almost nothing about him.

"Make yourself at home. I'll just pop into the library and see what my dad wants," Max said from behind.

I turned around and my instinct was to run to him and tell him not to leave me, instead, I hugged myself and said, "Okay. See you soon."

He smiled and closed the door behind him.

Any other time, I would have been delighted with my surroundings and flopped on the bed. As it was, I felt unwanted and awkward. Max's mother hadn't even bothered to pretend she was pleased to have me. I wondered what was the real reason why she put us in this room. Probably because she didn't want her other guests mixing with me.

The whole weekend stretched out as an unbearable ordeal.

Chapter 38
Lillian

I unpacked, then ran a hot bath and hung my dress over the steam to make sure it didn't have any wrinkles in it. As I was unwrapping my shoes, there was a knock on the door. I opened it to a maid carrying a tray with finger sandwiches, a jug of orange juice and two glasses.

After she was gone, I stood at the window looking out at the stunning beauty eating a delicious cucumber sandwich and washing it down with a cool sip of sweet juice.

I decided not to let patronizing Mrs. Frost upset me. After all, it was only one night I'd be staying under her roof. And for one night I could hold my own. My armor was my Lady Diana's revenge dress and my classy crocodile skin shoes.

I hurried to the bathroom with my makeup kit. After washing my face, I spent the next half hour applying makeup and getting dressed. When I was ready I looked at my reflection critically in the long bathroom mirror. I was pleased to note I didn't look half-bad.

But it dawned on me that my looks didn't matter.

As far as Mrs. Frost was concerned, I was trash, and no amount of makeup, expensive clothes and shoes would change her mind, so I might as well forget about trying to impress any of them and just enjoy my time with Max.

The door opened and Max came in.

I walked to the bathroom door and to my surprise, realized that he must have gone to his old room and changed there because he was already dressed in his tux. And he looked magnificent.

I couldn't take my eyes off him.

His translucent gaze rippled down the lines of my body voraciously, with unhidden admiration. This was it, I told myself. This was all that was important to me. I didn't need anyone else's approval.

"You look amazing," he whispered.

With a laugh, I took a step back and said in a faux severe voice, "Don't you dare. I know what that look means, Max Frost. It took me more than half an hour to get myself looking like this."

He raised his hands in the air in mock surrender. "I won't touch you I promise, but it's tempting. Very tempting. Fortunately for you, my father is downstairs waiting to meet you."

New anxiety coiled itself like a snake in my stomach. I took a deep breath and reminded myself that it didn't matter what anyone else thought. The hungry look in Max's eyes a few seconds ago was enough.

"I'm looking forward to meeting him too," I said courteously. "But I have to say your mother didn't look too happy to see me here."

Max's features hardened. "I told you, leave her to me. Come and meet my father. His reception will be different."

"Why is that?"

"My father is deep. You will never know what he truly thinks of you. You know only that he is the most charming man you'll ever come across... until you feel the knife in your back."

"Well,' I gasped. "That's some introduction. I can't wait to meet your father."

He smiled.

I picked up my purse and walked towards him.

"By the way did I tell you how good you look?" I said as I passed by him.

He shut the door and fell into step beside me. "No. How good do I look?"

I touched his arm. "Good enough that I want to ride you for hours."

"Can you hold that thought until later tonight?"

"Yes," I replied serenely.

Max's father was a tall, heavy man with the same good looks as his son, but his eyes danced with humor and grace. Unlike his brusque son, he was charismatic in a way I had never encountered before. His eyes caressed you, not in a sexual way, but in a way that told you he thought you were not only the most beautiful woman in the room but also the most important. Even though Max had warned me what he was like, I felt myself automatically relaxing and liking him as we shook hands.

"It's a pleasure to meet you, Lillian," he drawled, holding my hand. "You must be a very special young lady seeing as Max brought you home. He has never brought anyone home before to my recollection."

Warmth spread over me but it didn't last. Max's mother strolled in saying, "Paige spent a night here."

"I'm not sure that counts, seeing as I wasn't home," Max pointed out.

"Well, you let a good one go, Maximus. She's a fine girl from a solid family, but she'll be at the party tonight so it's not too late. I spoke to her last night and I believe you still have a chance with her."

"Shouldn't we be leaving now?" Max asked, sounding irritated.

"Yes," his mother said. She inspected her husband, then Max, then shot me a cursory glance. "Let's go."

I hung on to Max's arm as we left the house, glad that we were using different cars. I only relaxed when we entered Max's car, away from his mother's cold gaze. Max had never mentioned any of his past girlfriends, but now I had a name for one. Paige.

"Tell me about the engagement party," I encouraged, to take my mind off obsessing about Paige. A woman who clearly had Mrs. Frost's approval. "Who is Peter getting married to?"

Max cleared his throat. "Her name is Ella, but to be perfectly honest I've never met her."

I gazed at his profile. "Why did you want to go to this party? Seems like you're not close friends anymore?"

He shrugged. "A man can change his mind about keeping in touch with his old friends."

"Yes, of course," I agreed, but that didn't sound like Max at all. He wasn't a needy person or someone who depended on other people for his entertainment. If I was pressed to pick between an introvert and an extrovert, I would say Max was an introvert. His need for people was very minimal but hey, I'd only known him for a few months, maybe he was a social butterfly sometimes.

I wasn't surprised that Peter's parents lived in a house as impressive as the Frost's home. At the front of the house, a valet took the car and Max and I followed the other guests through the massive home to the back garden where the party was being held.

His parents were just ahead of us, and we stood in line behind them to say hello to the hosts.

"How wonderful to see you. And you brought Max," Peter's mother crowed as she did the air-kissing thing on Max's mother.

We were pulled into the circle. When my turn came to be introduced, Max draped his arm around me and introduced me as his girlfriend. He said it so naturally, even I almost believed him. After that, nothing could bring me down from the high I was on.

Peter's fiancée, Ella, was a petite blonde, and she looked as if a strong wind could blow her away. She was quite friendly though, making me feel welcome. A waiter came by with a tray full of champagne flutes.

"I need to go to the restroom. Be back in a few," Max said, and slipped away.

I sipped my drink, and with great detachment watched the gathering of fine feathered birds around me.

Laughter broke out behind me and I looked around to

see a couple who had just walked in. The thing that stood out about them was that they were holding hands. Nobody else was doing that. They also seemed to have eyes only for each other. They also neither preened nor displayed the pretentious mannerisms of the other partygoers. I noticed their shining rings and concluded they must be newlyweds. They spoke with their heads so close they were almost touching.

Why did love come so easily to some people?

Ferocious longing and envy crept into me. Why couldn't I find someone who looked at me the way that man was looking at his woman? I desperately wanted to be Max's woman. I wanted Max to look at me like that.

The longing was so ferocious I had to look away.

I stared blankly at a moss-covered stone statue in the middle of a fountain. I'd long accepted that not everybody (basically me) would be lucky enough to find their soulmate so why did it bother me now? Especially when I was with Max for a weekend of excitement and passion.

Someone bumped into me and my glass was knocked out of my hand. I looked up and it was the woman I'd been watching and envying.

"Sorry. I'm so sorry," she apologized. "I wasn't looking where I was going. I hope I haven't ruined your lovely dress."

"No, you haven't. Don't worry. No harm done," I reassured her with a smile. I already liked her. She hadn't given herself a pompous accent or any airs and graces.

"Thank God. I'm Dahlia and this beast here is my husband, Zane."

I turned to look at the man and was shocked to see his

face properly. He wasn't anything like the rest of the pampered elitist guests of this party. He had a scar on one side of his face, but it was his eyes that held me spellbound.

They were the dangerous, merciless eyes of a killer. Yet, when they were turned towards Dahlia, they melted. He gazed at her as if he couldn't get enough of her.

"I'm Lillian. Nice to meet you both," I said.

"Yeah, same here," Dahlia said. "It's really nice to meet a normal person. Everyone here is so freaking snooty."

I laughed.

"Are you here alone?" Dahlia asked.

"No, I came with Max Frost," I said and glanced around to look for him. I spotted him talking to a woman. No one needed to tell me she was Paige.

Chapter 39
Max

"It's so nice to see you again, Max," Paige said, drawing me to one side, a little away from everybody. She had trimmed her blonde hair and become even thinner, a look that did not suit her at all. She kept her hand on my arm.

"Your mother told me you would be coming, but I could hardly believe it. What? Max at a party like this? No way," she said flirtatiously and moved too close to me.

I took a step back, which somehow caused her to lose her footing, and she started to fall forward. Instinctively, I caught her. As I righted her, I realized she was smiling, a secret victorious smile. She had let herself fall on purpose. Immediately, my gaze searched for Lillian.

She was staring at us, a look of unspeakable hurt on her face.

Frustration welled up inside me. I hated women who played games. I remembered now what I hated about Paige. She played games. All the fucking time.

All the way to the restrooms I'd endured people who

wanted to indulge in meaningless small talk about the people we had in common. People I cared little or nothing for. I'd grown up with the majority of these people, but I had a completely different outlook on life now. Almost all of them lived off their parents, or trust funds from their grand-parents.

It sickened me to see people wasting their lives in such a manner and I wanted no part of it. All I wanted to do was go back to Lillian. Away from this conniving little bitch.

I looked beyond her to where Lillian was standing with Zane and Dahlia, seemingly happy. I should have been glad they were keeping her company, but I found it hard to trust any man near Lillian. Let alone a man like Zane. He was not like the highly cultivated, ultimately weak hot- house-flower type of men at this party. Zane was electrifyingly virile. A killer. Even though I'd never seen a man get so crazy for a woman, as Zane had for Dahlia, I still felt threat-ened if he got too close to Lillian.

"Have a good night, Paige," I said through gritted teeth and started to make my way towards Lillian.

She locked eyes with me and began to walk towards me too. I'd never seen her look so lost and unhappy, like she was about to burst into tears. We stopped a foot away from each other.

"I've been waiting to dance with you," she whispered, her eyes enormous.

The band was playing so I took her hand and led her to the dancefloor. I held her tightly and we swayed to the beat. Slowly, I felt all the tension in her limbs evaporating. I nuzzled her neck as we danced, peppering kisses on her skin, and inhaling her scent, which oddly made me feel as if I'd finally come home.

"Are you okay?" I asked.

"Yeah." My fallen angel looked up at me, her face vulnerable and sad. "Did you want to go with Paige?"

I froze. "What? No. I came with you and I'm going back with you."

She nodded but looked unconvinced. "I'm contemplating whether or not to tell you about the conversation I had with your mother."

"Tell me," I commanded. I could feel my insides clenching. If she had said anything, anything at all to hurt Lillian...

"But I don't want to cause any trouble between the two of you."

"Tell me or I'll get it out of her and that won't be pretty."

She sighed. "Okay. She told me that you and Paige were in love for a very long time and she thinks that you're still carrying a torch for her."

I was too furious to speak. This kind of bullshit was exactly why I left Connecticut.

Lillian forced a smile, but it only made her look more wretched. "I told her not to concern herself with me as I wasn't a threat to the great love between you and Paige."

I took a deep breath. "This nonsense has gone on long enough. I never loved Paige and I only...it doesn't matter. It was a long time ago. I'm only interested in one woman here tonight. And that woman is you. Paige may be the woman my mother wants me to marry and start a family with, but it's certainly not the woman I want, and she knows better than to try and interfere in my life by telling you a bunch of lies. I'll have a word with her tomorrow."

"Please don't say anything to her. It'll only make her hate me more," Lillian begged worriedly. "Promise?"

I stared at her, still furious with my mother. "I can't not say anything, Lillian."

"Please just leave it. It's fine," she pleaded. "What we have is casual, we have no claim on each other, and I'll probably never see her again."

My mother needed someone to stop her in her fucking tracks, but at the same time, I didn't want to make Lillian more uncomfortable than she probably already was. I decided to tackle my mother when Lillian was out of my parents' home.

Lillian stayed in silent contemplation, and when she spoke it was almost to herself. "Strange how she seemed to really hate it that I was one of your staff. She called me a secretary as if it was a dirty word."

I looked down at her fair bent head and a memory came to mind, one that I'd long forgotten about. And suddenly, I knew why my mother was being so unreasonable.

"My mother's hatred is not personal, Lillian. It comes from the biggest humiliation of her life. My father was having an affair with his secretary, and while they were going to a hotel from a party he met with an accident. His secretary died on the spot and it became a big scandal. The newspapers carried the story and all her friends were whispering about it behind her back.

"I was twelve then, but I can still recall how incensed she was about the discovery of the affair rather than the actual affair. She was willing to accept my father's affairs as long as he was discreet about them."

"You've probably hit the nail on the head. Until she found out I was your assistant she was quite friendly," Lillian said. "After what happened to her, I guess she hates all secretaries and PAs."

We'd talked about my mother enough. I had an idea of how to make the rest of the night pleasurable for both of us.

Chapter 40
Lillian

He brought the car to a stop in front of his parents' house, killed the engine and turned to look at me, his face serious.

"You know me; I'm an asshole, but I don't play games. When I'm with someone, I'm with only that person. Okay?"

'A girl like Paige,' Max's mother had said, 'is from our class. Can't you see how well they look together?'

Once she had let me know that Max and Paige could have been the love affair of the century, she gleefully went on to advise me that Max was just using me. I understood perfectly what Max's mother was trying to drum into me. Of course, she was right: men had been sleeping with their secretaries for centuries and never married them, but it had hurt seeing Max and Paige draw so close to each other.

I shook my head, determined not to let that memory of Max grabbing her and holding her next to him bother me. I lifted my face to his. "I know, but you just looked like you were getting a bit... close to her."

"Looks can be deceiving."

I nodded. "Yeah, I know that too."

"Paige tripped and would have fallen if I'd not caught her. That was all that happened between us."

He hadn't pulled her to him, the little madam had fallen on him. A ray of happy sunshine pierced my heart. A small smile tugged at the corners of my mouth. "So you weren't being a total asshole."

He smiled back. "How much longer do you think this inquisition is going to last because this asshole is in heat?"

I giggled. "The things you say, Max, could make a woman fall for you."

A veil dropped over his eyes when I said that.

"That was a joke," I said quickly.

"Don't worry, I know," he said and opened his door.

I tiptoed after Max into the house trying to make as little noise as possible with my high heels. We had reached the middle of the staircase when I put my hand on his arm.

"I want to see your room."

"Now?"

I nodded.

"Why?"

"I don't know. I just want to take a peek into little Max's life. You can tell a lot about a man by looking at his childhood bedroom."

He shrugged. "Fine. I can fuck you anywhere."

He opened the door to his old room and switched on the light. In the glow of the yellow light, the room appeared to belong to another time. There were trophies in a glass case, aircraft models, and framed certificates of merit.

His mother had preserved it exactly as he had left it. No

wonder she did not want me to sleep in here. This was a shrine to the teenage Max. I turned to look at him.

"Your mother loves you very much, you know."

"Yes, but her kind of suffocating love makes her insufferable."

His face had become hard again. I hated seeing him like that. I decided to change the subject to something more playful. "Did you ever sneak girls in here?"

He chuckled. "Never. I was a late developer and when the hormonal urge to fuck as many girls as I could kicked in, I already had my own place."

"Smooth," I said and brought my mouth up to his. "So will I be the first girl you brought up to your room then?"

He grinned suddenly. "Yeah. You are."

"I like being the first girl you took up to your room," I whispered.

Something changed in his face. He cupped my cheeks with his large warm palms. "You're a witch, Lillian. A beautiful, blue-eyed witch. Bit by bit you've bewitched me and turned everything upside down. I'll never be able to come back to this room again without remembering you in it."

I felt like I was drowning.

His eyes had always reminded me of ice. If you're not careful, you could slip and hurt yourself badly. Now that ice had melted and become deep pools of water that I had already slipped and fallen into.

I took a deep breath and he captured my open mouth with his.

The kiss was like nothing we had ever shared before. This one was so passionate it liquefied me. It went on and on. My whole body felt as if it had turned to liquid and we had become one.

In the room where the youthful Max had once lived, reality began to drift away, and my unthinking body felt as if we would, could never be parted again.

Then he led me to his childhood bed and undressed me with care. Never before had he been so gentle. I stared at him, ravenously drank in the sight of him, and refused to believe he was not mine.

When he entered me, I called out his name.

"Max," I called again.

He covered my mouth with his and continued his slow thrusts. There was nothing in this spinning world but his body joined with mine, inside mine. We fit together so perfectly.

I could deny it no longer.

I was in love with Max. Probably had been for a long time.

The climax when it came was earth-shattering. When one was over another began. My body shook uncontrollably as it went on and on, the colors, the sensations, the indescribable pleasure until I thought it would never end. It would always be like this. He and I joined in ecstasy. Forever.

But it did come to an end. And I cried for its loss.

He looked deep into my eyes and looked confused. "What happened?" he asked, his voice hoarse.

"I don't know, but it was beautiful. Really beautiful, Max."

Chapter 41
Lillian

Revisiting Max's past had made the visit to Connecticut an eye-opener.

Now I understood why Max's mother hated me with such intensity. Now I could see her in a different light and it hurt less. I understood she had been taking her pain out on me. I reminded her of the most agonizing thing that had happened to her. To my surprise, I even felt sorry for her which was ironic. In the world's eyes she was celebrated as the much-envied woman who had it all. But in exchange, she had sacrificed having a loyal man and real friends. They, she had found, could not be bought.

So she had neither.

In a way, it was restful to be back at work. Max appeared to be busy with some secret private project that only he and Chris seemed to be privy to. Even stranger, he never asked me to come into his office for anything naughty. We had so much fun on his desk that I thought he would want to repeat, but he never seemed to want to.

I asked him once if he ever got serious with a woman and thought about settling down. His answer was instant.

Never.

It was like a knife in my heart. It was not easy being in love with someone who was not in love with you. It feels as if your heart is being torn to pieces in a bear's claws.

I was a fool for love, but I'd never felt for another man the way I felt for Max. One smile from him made my whole day exciting and meaningful. He was the salt and sugar in my food. Without him life was in grayscale. Black, white, and shades of gray.

No colors, no flavors.

I knew I was setting myself up for heartbreak, but right then, I was still quietly hopeful. I really was.

To keep me busy so I didn't obsess about what was going to happen to me if Max got bored and wanted to move on, I decided to put the finishing touches on the bachelor party invitation cards before sending them off to the men on Chris's list.

I had made sure it would be a night to remember. The rented limo would pick them up and take them to the Empire Steak House on 50th Street. They would then start their night with premium steak, chops, and a feast of seafood. Afterwards, I had booked them on a pub crawl until they eventually ended up at Madame Tussauds on 42nd Street where bartenders from Lady Blue would make them delectable signature cocktails while they gambled at the pop-up casino, or they could indulge in 'escape the room' games together with nun strippers.

To make sure the night would never be forgotten, I also hired a professional photographer who was going to set up his own photo booth with props. I had also made sure to equip them with a hangover recovery kit, each complete with electrolyte drinks, pain relievers and snacks.

An hour later I put my computer in sleep mode and, grabbing my purse, left the office. Rose had asked me out for lunch and when my sister asked, you went because she rarely did.

It was a beautiful day to be out walking. Rose and I had agreed to meet at Max's favorite deli a block from the office.

I wasn't expecting her to be there and she wasn't, so I got myself a cup of coffee and sat at a table for two in the small seating area of the deli and daydreamed about Max.

"Hey," Rose said, snapping her fingers in front of me. "You look so deep in thought. Are you okay?" She set her coffee on the table and sat down.

"I'm good," I said, not ready to admit to anyone, even Rose, that I was in love with my boss. It was cool to have a wild, passionate affair, but not so cool to fall in love and not have it requited. I'd look like an idiot. What was wrong with me to even imagine that a man like Max could fall in love with his assistant?

"Just thinking about work," I lied. "You had some news? What's going on?"

"Let's get some sandwiches first then I'll tell you all about it," Rose said and stood up. "Grilled chicken?"

I nodded. A few minutes later, she came back with the food.

"Come on then. I'm dying of curiosity," I urged.

Rose laughed. "I got a job. It's just an admin position at a pediatrician's office, but I'm so excited. I can't wait to dress up and go to work every day. Dylan is happy too because I'll get experience to help him out when he starts his clinic."

"I'm so happy for you, Rose," I said, grinning. She had dedicated herself to raising her girls for two years, and if she felt that it was time for something else, then I was happy for her.

"Thanks," she said. "I know it will make Mom happy too and then maybe we'll stop irritating each other so much."

"She means well," I said, dabbing the sides of my mouth with a napkin.

"I know. Doesn't make it less irritating though," Rose quipped and we both laughed.

"So you're on for this evening, right," she asked, referring to her idea to get Mom to move. She wanted her realtor to show Mom some cute small houses because she believed sometimes seeing something might work out better than just hearing about it. The truth was I didn't think Mom would ever be ready to move, but I didn't want to discourage my sister. At this point, I was ready to try anything.

"I don't know how successful we will be, but I'm in," I said, putting as much enthusiasm into my voice as I could.

Chapter 42
Lillian

We got to our Mom's place and Rose brought the car to a stop in the driveway.

"What did you tell her exactly?" I asked, feeling slightly nervous.

"The truth. That we're going to look at houses so that she can see what options there are," Rose said.

"Wow! I can't believe she agreed."

"Not readily. I became a pest and wore her down," Rose said.

The front door opened and our mother stepped out. She was still a beautiful woman and it was sad that she had drifted apart from her friends and kept to herself so much. Recovery was taking a long time, but maybe if she moved that would be the first step.

She wore an irritated look as she entered the car. "Good evening," she said crisply.

We swapped pleasantries, but I could tell she didn't want to talk. Rose and I exchanged a look. Although, I wasn't surprised she was in a lousy mood. Anything that involved selling the house did that to her. I felt like a complete ass for forcing her to look at houses. I considered asking Rose to forget about it, but before I could voice the thought, we had reached the real estate agent's office.

Rose killed the engine. "I'll just let Leanne know that we're here."

Mom sighed when the car door shut. I turned to face her.

"Are you okay?" I asked.

"I'm fine," she said. "How's the job going? Is the moody boss thawing?"

I laughed, but it didn't sound genuine even to my ears. Mom would have been horrified if she knew what was going on between my boss and me.

"It's going okay. I'm enjoying it."

Rose returned after a few minutes. "We'll follow her car."

A black Honda stopped in front of us and honked.

"That's her," Rose said and eased the car onto the road.

My mom perked up when we started talking about her grandchildren. Picking on Mom's change of mood, Rose regaled us with tales of what they were up to now.

I listened with half an ear as my mind drifted back to Max. I wondered if he was thinking about me and missing me even the tiniest bit. I knew now that Maggie was definitely wrong. Not only had I fallen for Max, I had fallen hard. What other reason was there to think about a man for every minute that you were awake? The only respite was when I was asleep or when we were together.

"Here we are," Rose said, pulling me back to the present. "What do you think at first glance, Mom?"

The cottage was surrounded by a pretty garden which meant a lovely view every morning. It had a small porch, but it was enough to put a rocking chair on. It was like stepping back in time, but in a good way.

"Oh wow! It's gorgeous," I said. "I wouldn't be surprised if Goldilocks's bears walked out."

"It is pretty and homely," my mother admitted in a grudging tone.

"Let's go see if the inside matches the outside," Rose said, and we all got out of the car.

Leanne came over and Rose did the introductions. We followed her into the cottage. It was just as charming inside, but it was hard to interpret my mother's thoughts. Considering her mood earlier, I wasn't too hopeful.

She didn't make any comments when we returned to the car and headed to the next cottage. Nor did she comment on any of the other two cottages that we were shown either. I could see the strain on Rose's face as she waited for a reaction. Mom gave nothing away until we went for dinner at a deli near the real estate agency.

We ordered our food and as we waited, the waitress served us coffee. I sipped on mine gratefully.

"Girls, if you have something to tell me, I'd rather you come right out and say it," Mom said suddenly. "I'm tired of looking at houses. It's not my hobby and I don't think it's yours either." She trained her eyes on me. "Is the mortgage too much of a strain? I can speak to the—"

"Mom, I don't have a problem helping with the mortgage," I said quickly, already regretting not discouraging Rose from pushing Mom too hard and fast.

"Mom, it's not about that," Rose protested. "It's about starting life afresh for you."

"I know," Mom said. "But I'm not ready." She looked relieved when the waitress brought our food to the table.

We dropped Mom off later, then Rose drove me home.

"That wasn't a successful day," she said.

"It doesn't look like it, but it was a good idea," I said. "Those cottages were gorgeous. Makes me want to live there myself."

"They were, weren't they?"

"Yeah. It was a good idea, but I think we should let it rest for now, okay?"

"Okay."

I kissed her cheek and pushed the door open. "Say hi to Dylan for me and kiss the girls. Tell them I love them."

"Will do," Rose said. "I bet Dylan can't wait for me to get home. Those kids can be exhausting."

I laughed and shut the door. The first thing I did when I entered my apartment was check if Max had texted me.

He had not.

Chapter 43
Lillian

At lunchtime, Max left to go for lunch with his mother while I left to meeet Maggie. I was pleased to catch up with her. So much had happened to me, it seemed like forever since she had come around bringing pizza and wine.

I took an Uber to the Mexican restaurant next to Maggie's office. Since I got there first, I ordered a bottle of cold water and sipped on it while I waited. My thoughts immediately meandered to Max and the lunch with his mother. Would she be trying to convince him that I was the wrong type of woman for him?

My insides contracted.

I told myself how silly I was being. Max was a grown man who did not depend on his mother to make decisions for him. And he had also clearly indicated he wanted nothing to do with Paige.

I was glad when Maggie appeared before I drove myself insane.

"You are glowing. Must be all the sex," Maggie teased as we hugged and kissed each other's cheeks.

I laughed. If only she knew how painful my situation had become.

Sipping on her water, she studied my face. "I hope I'll look like you after next weekend."

At that moment the server came to take our orders. I chose a chicken taco and Maggie went for the beef.

"What's going on next weekend?" I asked.

She leaned on the table and grinned at me. "Martin has invited me to go away for the weekend. I'm thinking of it as a dirty weekend."

I laughed and cocked my head to one side. "Maybe he wants to propose?"

Maggie shook her head decisively. "I don't want to ruin my dirty weekend waiting for him to propose. Besides, you've inspired me. I realize that I've let our sex life become too stale and boring. Right now I'll take a dirty weekend over a romantic one." She winked at me. "You know what else?"

I grinned. "What?"

"I've bought chocolate sauce, edible body paint, and sex toys for both of us. I'm intending to have lots and lots of fun."

I began to laugh. "Oh, what a treat Martin is in for."

"You bet. I've even booked a bedroom with a jacuzzi in it. I'm going to make it a weekend he'll never forget for the rest of his life. When he's old and can't get his dick up anymore, he'll be talking about this weekend."

I laughed.

Her absolute commitment to her dirty weekend and her

excitement meant she didn't question me too deeply about my weekend. I quickly glossed over the fact that Max's mom hated me and she didn't pick up on how hurt I was. She reassured me that in time Mrs. Frost would fall in love with me because, 'hell, what's not to love?'

I could have told her how deeply painful and agonizingly horrible my unrequited love for Max was, but I would only have ruined her lovely enthusiasm and joy.

Besides, I was afraid any sympathy from her would make me burst into tears.

I was happy for Maggie, really happy. It had been a long time since I'd seen her this thrilled about her relationship, and I told myself this lunch was going to be about Maggie, not me.

So I steered the conversation away from me towards her exciting weekend. Her infectious joy was contagious and even before the tacos arrived, I found myself rooting on her behalf.

Let her have the best weekend she'd ever had in her life, I prayed.

Back at the office, Max wasn't back yet and after brushing my teeth to get rid of the smell of tacos, I settled at my desk and got to work. Max walked in an hour later. He came to my desk and smiled down at me.

"What?" I asked.

He shrugged. "Nothing," he said, still smiling.

I let out a sigh of relief I hadn't realized I'd been holding. Deep down, I'd been afraid that he would be cold and distant when he came back from lunch with his mother.

"How was lunch?" I asked.

"It was fine," he said, and the smile was replaced by a

frown. Almost immediately he got into work mode and asked me to print some documents for him. He moved to his office door. "Also, Chris will be here in a few minutes. Let him come straight in." He had already opened his door when he paused and turned to face me. "I've nothing more for you to do and since I'm going out for a drink with Chris before the bachelor party, you can leave whenever you want."

"Fine," I said, and even before he had closed the door, I jumped into work mode as well.

Chris appeared half an hour later and we exchanged pleasantries.

"I keep forgetting to bring your invitation to our wedding," he said. "I have it though, and I promise I'll drop it off tomorrow. You won't know many people at the wedding and Max will be busy, so bring a friend to keep you company, eh?"

I laughed. "That's very kind of you, but you don't have to, you know."

"Jennifer and I are looking forward to getting to know you better."

I liked Chris and warmth spread through my body. I didn't want to overthink it, but if your lover's best friend and his bride wanted to know you better, it had to be good, right? Because eventually, we'd be going for a meal together, or something like that.

Chapter 44
Max

"Well, that's all of it then," Chris said loudly to make sure the surveillance equipment picked him up clearly. "I'm just about to crunch the last numbers before we move in. And we have to be fast because I think there are other interested parties. The price we've been quoted makes it a bigger steal than I realized. I am one hundred percent sure we can turn this company around in less than a year and double its value."

"In that case, don't waste any more time. We've lost the La Zaire account because you were dithering, we need this one," I said sternly.

Chris grinned but kept his voice serious. "On it, boss. I'll get it done by this week."

"Good. This is urgent. Give me a report by the end of the week."

Had to be careful not to overdo it. I felt we had thrown enough breadcrumbs over the last week for whoever was listening, so I made a hand gesture to Chris to indicate we should end the conversation.

Chris nodded. "You up for a drink before my bachelor party?"

"Sure, let's go."

We walked to the door together and passed Lillian's empty desk and chair. I always felt a strange sense of loss when I saw that. Soon it might become a permanent feature. Once we discovered who my competitor was, my little romance might be dead in the water.

My stomach felt like a tense knot in my body as we waited for the lift. Only once we were inside, did Chris speak.

"You think they'll go for it?"

"I hope so, the paranoia caused by those bugs is fucking killing me. My office feels like enemy territory. I have to check myself the whole time," I ground out.

"They'll put their foot wrong soon enough. As you said, they're amateurs and they won't see us coming. The net is set and waiting."

"Good."

The lift doors opened and we stepped out. "Shall we just go around the corner to the Bear Trap?" Chris asked.

"Sure, why not?" I muttered unenthusiastically.

Chris's hand shot out to grasp my elbow suddenly. "What's the matter, Max?"

I stopped walking and turned towards him. "Nothing. It's just this situation. It's got to me."

"No, it's not," he insisted. "It's something else, isn't it?"

I said nothing and he frowned. "It's not a woman..." He stared at me. "Oh my God!" Then he began to laugh uproariously. "It's a fucking woman. I can't believe it, the great Max Frost has fallen in love."

I shook my arm off. "Go to hell," I snarled and strode away fast.

He caught up. "Relax, man. It's something to be celebrated, not be mad about."

We got out of the building into the noise of the traffic.

"Do I know her?" he asked.

"It's Lillian, okay."

His jaw dropped with shock. "What?"

"See. Nothing to be celebrated," I said bitterly.

"She's not even your type."

"I don't have a type," I corrected wryly.

"Yes, you do. Jennifer calls them girls with sad fridges."

"What the hell does that even mean?"

"Skinny girls. Evolutionary freaks who have managed to overcome the basic instinct to eat and turned it into a fashion statement. Have you seen the inside of their fridges? Always almost empty."

He might have a point, but I was not in the mood. I shook my head in disgust and left him standing in front of the building as I headed towards the Bear Trap. A few seconds later he fell into step beside me. He was no longer laughing. In fact, he looked so somber I almost wanted to laugh.

He looked sideways at me. "We still think she's the mole, right?"

I sighed. "Yes, we do."

"Right." He was silent for a while. "What are you going to do, Max?"

"Nothing. The ball is in their court. We carry on as before."

"I mean with Lillian. Are you... er... sleeping with her."

"Yes."

"Jesus, what a mess?"

Yeah, a fucking mess. We came to a stop at the crosswalk with tens of other people.

"Um... you know, I invited her to the wedding, right?"

"Yes. Nothing has changed. She's arranging the bachelor party for you so it would be quite appropriate for you to invite her. We play the game exactly as we discussed. We don't do anything that could alert them to the fact that we are aware of their existence."

"Man, this is such a mess," Chris mumbled as we waited for the pedestrian lights to change.

Chapter 45
Lillian

I woke up at dawn to Max nuzzling the back of my neck. I'd shown him where I kept my spare key and he must have come directly from the bachelor party. Before I knew it, we were moving together in perfect rhythm.

I came first, crying out his name and holding his body tightly to mine. He came a few seconds later, growling as if words could not fully express the intensity of what he was experiencing.

He took two painkillers for his hangover and left soon after.

I stood at the window and watched him leave. Sometimes I was sure we were one being cut into two halves, and at other times he seemed to be a stranger. Sometimes, he looked at me as if he wanted to devour me whole, and other times he looked at me as if he hated me.

As he reached his car he turned and looked up at my window. I didn't wave and neither did he. For a while he simply stood there staring at me, then he turned and slid into the backseat of the car. He did not look up again as his chauffeur drove away.

I went back to bed and lay on the pillow he had rested his head on. His scent was faint, but if I closed my eyes, I could see it all again. How he had come last night. Drunk, angry, and sad at the same time. I could feel his blood pounding in his wrist when I caught it.

"Have you missed me?" he asked.

"Yes," I admitted.

"Show me how much."

I got naked and rode him. The whole time I was grinding my sex on top of him he watched me avidly, ravenously. When he touched my skin it was as if he couldn't believe I was real.

* * *

I got to work early. I had a couple of hours before he was due back from a meeting on the other side of town, so I was going through some emails and anticipating another quiet hour or so when I heard the elevator doors swish open. I looked up and was surprised to see the familiar super-thin woman strolling into my office.

Paige.

She narrowed her eyes as she tried to place me. Incredulous recognition came quickly. "You were with Max at Peter's engagement party, weren't you?"

"Hello, Paige," I said calmly while internally, a dead weight sat on my chest. What was she doing here? She belonged in Connecticut.

"Your Max's secretary?" she asked, looking pleased about that.

"Yes, I'm his personal assistant," I replied.

"How convenient," she said.

I refused to rise to the bait. I just looked at her blankly.

She frowned. "Well, can I go in?"

"He's not in and I'm not sure what time he'll be back," I said, glad that Max was out of the office.

"He didn't mention that he would be out when we met for lunch yesterday."

My surprise must have shown on my face because she looked like a cat that had got the cream.

"You didn't know about that, did you?" She gave a delighted little laugh. "I guess he doesn't tell you everything about his whereabouts."

Pain rumbled through me, even though I kept my face impassive. "Do you have a message for him?"

"Nope. I'll call him directly."

Her job was done so she turned around and sashayed out of the office.

Max had told me he was going to lunch with his mother. Instead, he had gone for lunch with Paige... and not mentioned it. How had that happened? Images of Paige and Max having a good time over lunch filled my mind. Stop that, I told myself, shaking the images away. There had to be a perfectly good reason why he had lunch with Paige.

Max Frost didn't play games.

He said so himself.

And I believed him.

If he'd had enough of us, he would have told me, not gone

behind my back. But a voice in my head planted small seeds of doubt inside me. *Do you really know Max? You have no friends in common apart from Maggie who was only an acquaintance.*

And she didn't have good things to say about him.

* * *

"Paige came by," I said casually when Max returned from his meeting.

He scowled. "Oh! Why didn't she call before coming?"

I stared at him. "I don't know. She said you hadn't mentioned you wouldn't be in when you had lunch together yesterday."

Max put his phone away slowly and met my gaze. I hadn't planned on asking him, but I really needed to know why he hadn't mentioned it. We may not have been dating seriously, but Max had assured me that while we were together that meant no other women.

He moved closer to my desk, a vicious look in his eyes. "I'm sorry I didn't mention it to you, but a quick question. Are you still going to meet Dan?"

My eyes widened with surprise. "Yes, but that is completely different."

"Why?" he thundered.

"Because Dan doesn't want me back and Paige obviously does."

"Dan doesn't want you back! Do me a favor, look in the fucking mirror. Of course, he wants you back. But he's such a little lily-livered pansy he doesn't know how to go about it."

"Dan and I are just friends," I defended.

"Paige and I are just friends too."

I stood. "All right. I won't go to meet Dan."

It was as if Max was a balloon and I had pricked him with a needle. He deflated in front of me. All the fight went out of him. He exhaled audibly.

"Meet Dan if you must. It doesn't matter anyway. I didn't agree to meet Paige for lunch. I was meant to be having lunch with my mother. Instead, I found Paige waiting because my mother had taken to bed with a migraine episode. It was a lie and it was irritating, but I stayed out of respect for my mother. It was not an enjoyable lunch."

"Why do you always have to come across as if you don't need anybody," I whispered.

His eyes glittered. "You want me to need you?"

I said nothing.

"Well, I don't need you. I don't need anyone."

I could tell by his tone that he meant every word. I swallowed hard. What a catastrophe to fall for a man who didn't share my dreams. It was better to know early, I told myself, even though it felt like a knife had been plunged into my chest.

He turned and retreated to his office.

Chapter 46
Lillian

The hard truth was Max had not mentioned a future with me. Not even once. He'd never once made any promises other than the intoxicatingly sweet words he whispered in my ear when we were having sex.

I pulled myself up short.

It was me who was changing the rules. I started this affair with the intention to enjoy the present, and yet here I was back to planning a future with him again.

I was glad when my mother rang and asked me to pass by her place for coffee. I needed to get out of my own head. Max hadn't texted me with new work by the time I left the office so I figured he must be really busy.

Not hearing from him made me sad.

Rose rang as I was closing up and asked me to pick her up on the way to Mom's. I texted her to come out to the car when I got to her place. My melancholy felt contagious and I didn't want to go in and say hello to the girls and Dylan when I was in such a lousy mood.

Rose noticed it as soon as she entered the car. "Tough day?" she asked, sympathy in her voice.

"Sort of," I said, not sure how to classify my day. I'd not told Rose about Max yet.

"Come on, out with it," she ordered.

"I think I'm in love with my boss."

"What?" she shouted, looking at me with a horrified expression.

I said nothing.

"Are you serious?"

I didn't look at her, I just nodded.

"So you're sleeping with your boss," she said slowly.

I took a deep breath. "Yes."

"Why, Lillian?"

"I couldn't help it. Like a moth to a flame, I was drawn to him."

"He's not married, is he?" she asked worriedly.

"No, he's not."

"Well, that's a relief."

"Not really," I said. "The relationship is very sexual. I don't think he's interested in a serious relationship."

"Lillian, just because the relationship is very sexual doesn't mean he's not interested in a serious relationship. But if you guys are to get serious, I don't think working in the same office is a good idea."

"Then there's Paige," I said, and the hurt came tumbling out from somewhere deep inside me. As words poured out of me, it made me realize what little chance I had with Max.

"And his mother was very quick to let me know how in love they had been," I finished.

"She was just being a jerk," Rose said loyally. "It wasn't

her place to tell you if Max did or did not have feelings for Paige. Listen. Relax. Stop overthinking this. What will be will be and stressing about it won't change anything."

"Easier said than done," I muttered.

"I know. Are you forgetting how many times Dylan and I broke things off and then got back together again?" she asked.

I laughed at the memory. Dylan had had serious commitment issues, and at times I'd doubted whether he was really interested in my sister in the long term. "And look at the two of you now."

"That's what I mean. It takes time for a couple to figure out what they want. Some people more than others. Does Max seem like a player to you?"

"I don't think so."

"Well, there you go then. Be patient. And give it a chance."

We got to my mother's place and as we got out of the car, I pulled Rose in for a quick hug. "Thank you. I feel a bit better."

"You're welcome," she said. "I'm glad we're friends not just sisters."

"Me too."

Rose knocked and moments later, Mom flung the door open. "My girls. What a treat."

I hadn't seen her in such a good mood in a long time and just seeing her like that lifted my own spirits.

"Hey, Mom," I said, hugging her close. She felt so tiny in my arms and an avalanche of love came over me as I held her.

We walked into the house, making for our favorite room. Mom already had coffee brewing and we sat around the kitchen island. When the coffee was ready, she poured it into three mugs and carried them to the island.

"Girls, I've been a stubborn old fool," she said with a solemn expression. "I understood why you wanted me to move, but I allowed my emotions to cloud my judgement."

"It's okay, Mom. We understand," I said quickly. With the wisdom that came from hindsight, I knew we had pushed her too hard. It reminded me of what Max had said. All she needed was time. "There's no rush for you to move. Honestly."

She rested her hand on mine. "It's sweet of you to say so, but it's time. I've been a burden to my girl for long enough. There's one particular cottage we saw that won't leave my mind. I think I'd like it there."

Rose and I exchanged a glance of amazement.

"Are you sure, Mom?" Rose asked. "The last thing we want is for you to feel ambushed. Like what we did last time. I'm sorry, it was my idea, not Lillian's."

"It was our idea. Both of us," I said.

My mother covered my hand with hers. "I remember when your father and I first saw this house. I was pregnant with you, Lillian, and Rose was just a toddler. I could visualize my girls playing in the backyard, growing up in a safe space. But you're both grown up now. And it's time. It's time to move on." Tears filled her eyes.

"Oh, Mom," I whispered.

She blinked hard. "It's okay. It's okay. I guess this place is my last link with your father. I miss him."

"We'll always carry his memory with us," Rose said.

Mom nodded. "I know. He's in my heart. Not in this house."

Chapter 47
Lillian

Max was distracted all week and there was some distance between us. I was to blame too. After the revelation that he had gone for lunch with Paige and not mentioned it, I found myself drawing back, keeping my distance. The wedding preparations kept Max occupied and a lot of evenings he was going over things with Chris and Jennifer.

Still, I was glad when the wedding weekend rolled around. I had invited Maggie to be my plus one and it would be an occasion for both of us to let loose and have fun. Instead of driving my car, I hired a cab and picked Maggie up.

"You look gorgeous," I said, admiring the pale yellow ruffle dress Maggie was wearing.

"Thanks. You look pretty hot yourself. The best man won't be able to resist you," she said with a wink.

"That's the plan." I'd bought a new dress for the occasion. A demure dress with a plunging neckline that stopped just about short of showing too much.

"I haven't been to a wedding in ages," Maggie said as she fastened her seatbelt. "I'm excited even though I've never set eyes on the groom or the bride."

"I've only met the groom, so we're both almost in the same boat," I said with a laugh. I was glad I'd invited Maggie. I had a feeling I was going to need her strong personality to get through this wedding.

"Listen, I've deposited a hundred dollars into your account."

"Why?"

"Because: a) you deserve to win. I never imagined you'd get this far. And... b) I should never have taken the bet. It was unethical of me. I'm ashamed of my unprofessional behavior. So please accept the money and let's never talk about it again, okay?"

I squeezed her hand. "Let's go to dinner somewhere nice with that money, huh?"

She grinned. "Deal."

The venue took us twenty minutes to get to so Maggie and I caught up with our news.

"How's your mom doing? Is she thawing?" she asked.

"Not yet."

Then I told her about Rose and her new job and how it had done wonders for her general happiness. I wished I could say the same for myself. I had a sense of foreboding as if I was waiting for something bad to happen. It reminded me of the period just before my mom finally confessed that she was in financial difficulties.

In my gut, I already knew something was wrong, but I refused to acknowledge it. I wanted it not to be true. In my gut, I already knew there was something very wrong with my relationship with Max. I just didn't know what it was.

We found the cocktail hour going on and as soon as we entered the ballroom, Max spotted us and came over. "Max, this is Maggie Childs. Maggie, Max Frost."

"We finally meet," Maggie said as she shook Max's hand warmly. "Thank you for all the business you've given us."

Max smiled distantly. "I have a feeling I'm the one who should be thanking you for putting up with me... and for bringing this little minx into my life."

"Come, let me introduce you to Jennifer." He took my hand in his and led us to where the bride and groom were standing.

The bride was a very pretty brunette. She beamed at us happily.

"I've heard so much about you, Lillian. And it's so great to finally meet you. The photos from the stag party are amazing. I absolutely adore them. Almost makes me wish I could have been there. We have to go out for a drink when all this is over," she gushed. Then she turned to Maggie. "You must come too. A girl can never have too many friends."

Chris had a huge smile on his face throughout. It was sweet and touching to see how in love with each other they were.

Then something peculiar happened.

Chris got a message on his phone. He looked at it, then turned to Max and said in an excited voice, "The fish has taken the bait."

A strange expression crossed Max's face, then his head whirled around to look at me. For a few seconds we stared at each other, and then he looked back to Chris and with a smile said, "That's good news. Very good news."

But his smile was sad as if it was not good news at all.

"Oh my God, I can't believe this. You two are talking about business on my wedding day," Jennifer complained.

Chris switched off his phone and put it away with a sheepish grin. "Phone? What phone? Business? What business? I'm getting married to the most beautiful woman on earth."

Jennifer smiled. "Quite right."

The wedding planner came hurrying towards us. "We're almost ready to start. Groom and best man over there. Jennifer, please come with me."

"I thought the groom wasn't supposed to see the bride before the ceremony," Maggie commented when we were alone. "I definitely wouldn't want Martin to see me until I walk down the aisle."

"I guess it depends on the couple. Maybe they're not so heavy on tradition," I said distractedly, my eyes on Max.

He looked so sexy in his tuxedo.

Soon the master of ceremony was asking us all to proceed to the garden where the official part of the wedding was taking place. Maggie and I sat in a strategic spot where we had a nice view of the front where the groom and bride would be exchanging their vows, but I only had eyes for Max.

"I don't care what you say. That man has fallen for you, Lillian," Maggie whispered to me as the ceremony progressed.

"Why do you say that?"

"He just gave you 'that' look."

I grew hot all over and fervently wished it was true. When the time came for the couple to exchange vows, Chris cried, reminding me that love did change a person. Max had said that Chris had been a die-hard in the bachelor world, but clearly meeting the right woman had changed his thoughts about marriage.

Could the same thing happen with Max?

Not while Paige is around, a little voice in my head mocked.

As we moved back to the reception, I found myself confiding in Maggie about Paige. I needed to let it out else I would go insane.

"I've learned not to jump to conclusions," Maggie said sagely. "And to trust the person I'm with unless they give me a reason not to. If Max said that his mother set him up, I would believe him."

"I want to so badly, but I'd hate to look like a fool. She's everything that I'm not. She belongs to their family circle."

"He's not in that circle anymore and he's taking you with him. If he wasn't, then I'd be worried. I saw how that man was looking at you in church. Give it a chance and stop letting fear get the better of you."

I inhaled deeply. "Okay. I hear you."

Chapter 48
Max

https://www.youtube.com/watch?v=luwAMFcc2f8

As soon as I had done my best man duties and danced with the matron of honor, I escaped. But Lillian was nowhere to be seen in the ballroom. I couldn't spot her anywhere in the crowded bar either. Surely, she hadn't left? Cursing under my breath, I weaved through the throng of people and made my way out.

Relief surged through me when I spotted her outside with Maggie.

"Are you leaving?" I asked when I joined them.

"Nope, she's not leaving. Just me," Maggie said with a smile. Then she turned to Lillian. "Thanks for inviting me. It was a beautiful ceremony."

"Thank you for coming and keeping me company," Lillian replied with a sweet smile.

I stared at her intently. Why couldn't I stop wanting

her? Just hearing that first contact had been made with the company we were using as bait had brought an avalanche of emotions. It was confusing and if I was honest, frightening. What should have been good news felt like bad news. I might lose her forever.

A car drove up and came to a stop in front of us.

"This is my ride," Maggie said and hugged Lillian. "Talk to you soon," she called and entered the cab.

It pulled away and I closed my arms around Lillian. "How about we make an escape too?" I asked, inhaling her sweet, intoxicating scent.

She laughed softly. "I'm not wearing any panties so that idea is very tempting, but I don't want to be responsible for the best man disappearing."

The thought of her sweet pussy being naked under that 'butter wouldn't melt in my mouth' coy dress made my cock hard instantly. She had no idea how much power she had over me.

I slanted my mouth over hers and kissed her savagely, thrusting my tongue into her mouth and swirling it around hers. I ran my hands over her curves. I didn't have the words to describe how I was feeling. But for now, she was mine. I broke away and stared into her eyes.

"You're mine, right?" I asked thickly.

She nodded. "Yes."

That was enough.

I crushed her mouth with mine and she melted against me. I had no idea what had come over me. All I knew was she was everything I had ever wanted in a woman, and no one was going to take her away from me. Tomorrow was coming, and fast, but right now... she was mine.

Some kids passing by, laughingly screamed, "Get a room."

"It's getting cold out here," she said huskily. "Let's go in and dance the night away."

She looked so fucking beautiful I felt my stomach clench. We made our way back onto the dance floor. The first person we ran into was Chris.

"I was coming to look for you," he said. "Jennifer is about to toss her bouquet and she wants Lillian there."

Lillian laughed. "There's no way I'm catching it when there are so many eager single women waiting."

Inside the ballroom, Chris and I stood together as his new wife tossed her flowers to the group of single women. The entire group swayed in the direction that the bouquet was flying to, but it bounced over someone's head and landed squarely in Lillian's hands. Shocked, she threw it back into the midst of the disappointed women. I never loved her as much as I did at that moment.

She turned to me still laughing, happy, her eyes shining and her cheeks rosy.

"Did you see that? I caught it then tossed it away. Who does that?"

I stared at her, mesmerized. "Yeah, I did. Who does that?"

"Come on. Let's dance."

She took my hand and pulled me to the dance floor. I felt like the unluckiest man on earth as I held her close to me and we moved to the soft ballad. Everything I wanted was within touching distance, but I couldn't have it.

Later, after all my best man duties were done, we headed for home.

Lillian stretched next to me and predictably, my cock stirred in response. "I wish you were on my lap right now."

"If I wasn't so scared of being arrested or us getting into an accident, I'd be on your lap right now."

I knew exactly what to do.

I drove to my garage parking and instead of getting out of the car, I pressed the button to push my seat back, leaving ample space between the steering wheel and my body, and undid my seatbelt.

"There's no risk of being arrested now or being in an accident," I drawled.

"You're so full of wicked, dirty ideas," she cooed, as she undid her seat belt and scrambled over to straddle me. She inched forward until she was seated directly on my hard heat.

"Have you ever been fucked in a car?" I asked, pushing her dress up until it bunched at her waist. She was not kidding. No underwear and her pussy and thighs were slick with her juices.

"Never, but I have a feeling I won't say the same thing tomorrow," she said.

Lillian unzipped her dress, and it fell off her body, exposing a red bra. I pushed down the cups of her bra, exposing her beautiful breasts to my eyes.

"Did you wear this dress for me?"

"Yes," she murmured. "I wanted you to want me. To think about..." Her voice trailed off.

"Fucking you?"

"Yes."

She thrust her chest forward and I bent forward to take a nipple into my mouth.

She moaned as I sucked on her nipples, moving from one to another. They pebbled in my mouth. She raked her fingers through my hair and rocked against my throbbing cock.

"I need you, Max," she moaned.

Needing no further invitation, I unzipped my pants and pulled out my cock. She slid down on my waiting cock. I growled as she eased down all the way, my engorged shaft stretching her, pushing against her tight walls.

She looked wild, bouncing on my cock, her lips slightly parted and her breasts bobbing with every thrust. I gripped her ass and bounced her faster, grinding up to fuck her even deeper.

Within minutes, Lillian came, her fingers digging into my shoulders. No woman had ever made me feel that good. I fought the onslaught of sensation until I couldn't anymore. My balls tightened and I thundered into her, pumping every drop of my cum deep inside her.

Afterwards, we made our way, laughing into the house. A shared shower later, we slipped into bed, but I couldn't fall asleep. My mind was abuzz with what would happen once we had unmasked my enemy.

"You can't sleep?" she whispered.

"I'm going to have to go away for a couple of days," I said.

A shadow came over her features, but it passed, replaced by a mischievous look. "In that case, I have a goodbye present for you."

My mood lifted. "I love goodbye presents."

She moved down between my legs. Her mouth was

heaven around my cock and soon I found myself plunging my cock deeper into her mouth.

She did things with her tongue that completely undid me, leaving me with bare seconds to utter a warning.

"I'm going to come, Lillian."

Her answer was to suck my cock harder.

Chapter 49
Max

https://www.youtube.com/watch?v=1Osyw6Svv8U

Chris was on honeymoon, but the investigator he had hired was already in the process of unravelling the identity of the owner/owners of the shell company that had made the first offer.

Tick tock, tick tock. I could feel time passing.

Soon I would know. And the beautiful life I had built on a bed of lies would tear and I would fall into the dark pit below.

On an impulse, I got into my car and drove to Connecticut. I needed the time alone. I picked up my sports car, put the top down, and blasted the music as I hit the freeway. But it didn't feel good. It felt strange. Nothing felt good without her. The more I told myself she was no good and I hated her, the more intensely I wanted her.

As I drove into the driveway of my parents' home, I

thought about the weekend I spent here with Lillian. I went upstairs to my room and I saw it with new eyes. I saw it with her inside it. On my bed.

I sat on the bed and stared out of the window and suddenly it occurred to me in a flash.

I was in love with her!

It was so shocking, that I refused to accept it. I pushed the thought away. No, that was not it. It was just lust. No more.

Slowly, I stood and went downstairs.

To my great surprise, my mother was in the rose garden. She was gardening, of all things.

"Hello, darling," she called.

"Since when did you start getting your hands dirty?" I asked.

She straightened up and waved with her gloved hands. "I'm not exactly getting my hands dirty." She looked at the rose bush she had been working on with a pensive look. "It's weird what old age does to you. You start to enjoy the oddest things."

"You're not old, Mother."

She shrugged and dropped the pruning snips she was holding. "Let's go in for a pot of tea."

I followed her into the music room, where Rosella came with a tray of tea and biscuits.

My mother delicately bit into a biscuit, then took a sip of tea. "How was lunch with Paige?"

"Good, we cleared the air between us and I think we both understand that we can only be friends," I said. "She said to tell you that she tried."

An expression of irritation came to her eyes. "Max,

what do you want? Paige is perfect for you. We've known her family for years and you've known each other from childhood. There won't be any nasty surprises down the road."

"I'm not interested in Paige, Mother. I never have been." I was surprised to note that my voice had no emotion in it. The deadness had a finality to it that succeeded in piercing my mother's stubborn constitution.

She sighed. "I had hoped..."

"I know," I said gently, "but when or if I do decide to get married, it will be a woman of my choice... not yours."

"You're surely not serious about that secretary of yours though, are you?" she asked unhappily.

"And if I am, will you stand in my way? Will you only be happy when I am as unhappy as you were in your marriage?"

I held her gaze until she shook her head in a defeated gesture. "No, I won't stand in your way."

"Thank you, Mother."

Her eyes took on a faraway look. "I've never told anyone this story, but your father was not my first choice."

I moved forward in my chair. My mother was not a sentimental person and she definitely wasn't given to reminiscing about her past so it was a rare thing when she opened up.

"I was in love with someone else." Her features softened and a slow smile pulled at her lips. "His name was Alvin and I couldn't wait to start my life with him. But my parents didn't want him because, well... his family was not wealthy. They were a different class.

"Those things were important then. Anyway, they

arranged for me to meet your father, who was their choice. Just one meeting, they said, and then I could refuse him if I didn't like the look of him. I knew he had a reputation for charming the birds out of the trees, but I thought I was immune. I thought my deep love for Alvin would protect me. So I met your father."

Her voice shook with sadness and regret as she continued, "And the rest, as they say, is history."

My mother had always come across as emotionless and even cold. I saw her in totally a different light now. She was a woman who wore a mask to cover up the disappointment of a life not well lived.

Tears brimmed in her eyes and I almost went forward and hugged her, but I knew that would have embarrassed her and made her uncomfortable so I remained where I was.

I picked up a biscuit and bit into it.

"These biscuits are delicious," I said, giving her a graceful way out of her moment of vulnerability.

She smiled gratefully at me. "They are homemade. Jacques bakes them. I'll get Rosella to pack some for you."

For a while there was silence, and then my mother spoke, her voice was forlorn. "I want you to be happy, Maximus. That's important. Very important to me."

"I am happy, Mother," I lied.

She appeared to believe me. When I finished my tea I stood and bade her goodbye. I had intended to stay the night, but I found I didn't want to sleep in my room without Lillian. I wanted to be back in the city, breathing the same air as her, as stupid as that sounded.

Chapter 50
Lillian

The office was too quiet and empty without Max. He'd asked me to take some time off too, but I preferred to work rather than sit alone in my apartment and drive myself crazy with my own runaway thoughts. Not that working was keeping my insecurities at bay. I tried to hold on to what Max had said.

That I was the one he wanted.

And over the next two days Mom, Rose, and I went to look at the cottage again and she confirmed that she indeed loved it. The next step was putting her home on the market after giving it a fresh coat of paint and getting it staged. I wanted to share the news with Max, but his phone was switched off.

On Wednesday, there was still no contact from Max, which had me worried. Even if he did not miss me or want to talk to me, he would have sent work through.

Desperate, I called Chris, but my call went straight to his voicemail. His playful recording said that he was on his honeymoon and unless it was a fire, he wasn't returning any calls.

Frustrated, I sat on my desk and contemplated driving to his place, but that seemed like overstepping boundaries since he had not bothered to call me at all in the last two days. He could still be in Connecticut for all I knew.

My next best option was to call his mother. I finally worked up the courage and found her number from Max's contacts list. She picked up on the first ring.

"Hello, Mrs. Frost, this is Lillian, Max's PA." It sounded so wrong to be so formal, but it was the truth. I was Max's assistant.

"Yes?" she said in a voice that was, to my surprise, not cold. It was not warm, but it was definitely not cold.

"He hasn't been to the office in three days... and I wondered if he was still in Connecticut." Silence followed and I rushed to fill it. "I'm just a little worried because he didn't send any work through and that's not like him at all."

"No, that's not like him. Well, he's not here," she said, her tone, anxious. "The last time I saw him was on Monday."

"Okay, thanks. I'll call you if I locate him," I said and hung up.

That had accomplished nothing. I closed up the office and decided to go to his place. I didn't care if he threw me out. I had to know if he was okay. I changed my mind several times on the way there, but I had never been a coward and I wasn't about to start now. Anyway, if I chickened out, the rest of my day and night would be ruined conjuring up all sorts of bad scenarios.

I ran into the first problem when I found his gate firmly

shut. I honked the horn, until to my relief, the gate slid open. I got out of the car and hurried to the front door. I rang the bell and waited. If he was home, it was likely that he was alone as he never had staff in the evenings.

I was about to ring the doorbell again when the door opened and Max stood there, pale and obviously unwell.

"What's wrong?" I blurted out, shocked by his appearance.

"It's just the flu. I need to sleep it off. I'll be fine," he said in a strained voice, then turned away and began to walk back into the house. I followed him to the living room where he stretched out on a couch. On the table, an untouched congealed meal of steak and mashed potatoes sat.

"When was the last time you ate?" I asked.

"My throat is sore... I've been sipping water," he said, keeping his eyes shut.

"Where's your housekeeper?"

"Told her not to come until tomorrow. Hate having people around when I'm not at my best."

I dropped my purse on the coffee table and folded my sleeves. Taking the plate of uneaten mashed potatoes and steak, I headed to the kitchen. What he needed was something easy to swallow, like soup. I rummaged through the freezer and found some homemade beef stock. There was a whole free-range chicken in the fridge. Then I gathered all the vegetables I could find and started dicing.

I left the soup to simmer on the stove and returned to the living room. "I'll help you up to your room. You'll be more comfortable there."

"No need to help me. I'm as strong as an ox," he said and began to walk up the stairs.

"Something smells good," he commented, as he passed by me.

"I'm making chicken and vegetable soup."

"It's not the soup. I think it might be you."

"I'm pretty sure it's the soup," I said firmly as I pulled back the covers of his bed. I waited while he climbed into bed.

"Have you ever had sex with a sick man?" he asked.

"No, and I don't intend to start now."

He grasped my hand. His hand was hot with fever. "But I want to have sex with you, Lillian."

"You're too ill to be thinking of sex," I said, hiding a smile.

"At least, stay with me," he grumbled.

"That I can do. I'm not going anywhere," I reassured softly.

"Good. Life's not the same without you."

He fell asleep as soon as I arranged the covers around him. I stood looking down at him, loving him so much it felt like my chest would explode.

When I returned downstairs, I called Max's mother.

"Have you found him?" she asked apprehensively.

"Yes. He's at home with the flu."

"Is he alright?"

"Yes, he'll be fine in a couple of days."

"Does he need a doctor?" she asked. The worry was evident in her voice and I realized despite what Max believed, his mother really did love him.

"I don't think so, but I'll stay the night, and I promise to call you if his situation changes."

"Yes, please do that."

Not wanting to wake Max up, I put the soup in the oven to keep it warm and watched a movie with the sound turned right down so I could hear him if he called. A couple of hours later, I carried a tray up to him. I pushed the door open and found Max writhing in his bed. Startled, I hurried to him and shook him awake. He looked disoriented at first.

"Why did you do that to me, Lillian?" he gasped, his eyes wild.

"I think you were having a nightmare," I said, noting that he was drenched in sweat.

"Yeah, it was just a nightmare," he said and sat up.

I went to the bathroom to wet a washcloth. Returning to the room, I gently wiped his face and neck. His temperature was still high, but so high it was a worry. I placed the tray on his lap and like a mother hen guarding her chick, I watched over him as he finished the soup.

"Thank you," he said.

"You're welcome."

"What time is it?"

"Nine."

"You're not leaving, are you?" he asked restlessly.

"No."

"That's good, but you don't want to catch what I've got. Sleep in the guest room."

I nodded and Max yawned and slid under the covers again. He closed his pretty eyes and I smiled at the sight. I kinda liked him this way. He seemed almost meek and kitten-like.

Friendly, at any rate.

I turned off the lights and carried his empty bowl downstairs. I ate a bowl as well, cleaned up, and headed upstairs to the guest room.

I checked on Max throughout the night and sometime in the early morning hours, he grabbed my hand and pulled me down on the bed next to him. "Don't go, Lillian. Please. There is so little time left," he whispered.

"What do you mean?" I asked.

"We don't have long," he muttered.

I touched his forehead. It was still hot, but not concerningly so. He couldn't be delirious. "Why don't we have long?"

He squeezed my hand desperately. "Because Chris will come back with the results soon."

Ah, something to do with his business. "We'll worry about that when it happens, okay. Just rest now," I consoled.

"I don't want to lose you," he mumbled.

"You won't. I'm right here." I curled myself around his feverish body, and eventually, we both fell asleep.

Chapter 51
Lillian

"That was a rough night," he said as we ate a breakfast of oatmeal at the dining table. It was more like brunch, as Max had slept in. But it had done him a world of good. The way he had grasped my hand earlier in bed and muttered nonsense worried me a little.

"You look a lot better now," I said, thinking it was my cue to leave.

"I might look better, but I still feel sickly," he said with an innocent expression.

"Ah yes, the man flu is a long-lasting thing," I mocked.

"Come and touch my forehead if you don't believe me."

"I believe you," I said with a laugh. I was playing along even though I knew I should leave.

The doorbell rang and I jumped.

"Probably some deliveries," Max guessed.

The housekeeper answered the door, but it wasn't a delivery. It was Mrs. Frost. Like a little hurricane, she came bustling into the sunny breakfast room where we were.

"Oh, Maximus, I was so worried about you," she cried. Going straight to him, she stood over him as her sharp eyes surveyed his face closely. "Has Lilian been taking care of you?"

"Mother, I'm quite capable of surviving a cold, but yes, Lillian has been taking care of me."

She turned to me. "Hello, Lillian. Thank you for taking care of Maximus."

I fought a giggle at her unrelenting use of his full first name. "It was a pleasure. Can I pour you a cup of coffee?"

"That would be nice, thank you," she said, sitting opposite her son.

I carried our bowls to the kitchen and rinsed them as the coffee brewed. It was awkward with Max's mother in the house, and it was tempting to just leave, but I wasn't going to go running off. I'd assured Max that I would stay and I would.

Max went back to bed and his mother joined me outside where I had decided to sun myself on the steps of the conservatory.

"Is there anything I can do for you, Mrs. Frost?" I asked, tensing.

"Marilyn," she said.

Wow, that was a turn-up for the books. "Okay, Marilyn it is."

She came to sit next to me and we sat quietly, watching the dogs as they raced around the grounds.

She cleared her throat. "I think I judged you too harshly and I haven't been very fair to you so I apologize. I'm protective when it comes to my son."

I felt myself thawing. "That's understandable."

"Obviously, Maximus cares a lot about you. Maybe you're what he needs in a woman. I just wanted to say, that I won't interfere in your relationship anymore, and if he decides to marry you, I'll welcome you into my family. You'll be the daughter I never had."

It was what I had longed to hear and yet, she was wrong again. Her son didn't want to marry me. "It's not serious between me and Max."

"You don't need to tell me that because you think that's what I want to hear."

"It's the truth. Max is very committed to his business, and I don't know if he'll ever marry me or anyone else."

She took a deep breath, her eyes set far on the horizon. "That's probably partly my fault. I haven't been the best mother, and that's a difficult admission to make. When I became pregnant, I was really hoping for a girl. Actually, I felt it in my bones. It was a girl. I was so sure. I even bought lovely pink baby grows. Then Maximus came along and... I... I just didn't know what to do with him."

I listened, fascinated and horrified in equal measures.

"I'm ashamed to say I was disappointed, and I was disappointed for a very long time. I couldn't give him the love he deserved."

"Why didn't you try again for a girl?" That was what most people did but then again, most people didn't feel so strongly about gender to the point of distancing themselves from a child they had borne.

She looked at me with a stricken expression. "What if I got another boy? I couldn't take that risk." She let out a long sigh. "I traumatized Maximum when he was a child and now I'm afraid it's too late to get close to him."

My heart went out to her. She really did love Max; she just didn't know how to relate to him. "Maybe you should start by calling him Max."

"Maximus is a beautiful name," she protested.

I bit my lip and shook my head.

Her eyes danced with amusement. "Is it very ghastly?"

I chuckled. It dawned on me that I had also judged her unfairly. People carried all sorts of burdens, and Marilyn was no exception just because she was wealthy.

"Let's just say it ranks up there with weird names."

"We should go shopping the next time I come to New York," she said. "Do the things I could have done with a daughter."

I didn't have the heart to tell her that I could be out of Max's life for good at any time. "That would be nice."

Chapter 52
Max

I felt I'd been in a fog the last three days, but even so, I was disgusted with myself when I looked in the mirror. I couldn't believe I'd almost given the game away last night. I had nearly unraveled all the good work Chris had done. They could so easily pull out and we'll never find who it was. After all this time of those bugs in my office driving me crazy.

Luckily, Lillian had not insisted and asked more questions.

I pulled on a pair of jogging pants and a white T-shirt and went downstairs.

Lillian and my mother were in the kitchen talking over coffee like old friends. It did something to me seeing them like that, but I dismissed that feeling as sentimentalism brought about by illness.

I sneaked a look at Lillian and warmth flooded me.

Not wanting to appear like a love-sick fool, I moved to the counter to pour myself a mug of coffee. I hadn't had coffee in days and I was craving it. I carried it to the kitchen island and stood drinking it.

"I must say you're looking a whole lot better after your little nap, Max," my mother noted.

I stared at her in disbelief. "That's the first time you've ever called me Max."

An embarrassed expression came over her features, then she shrugged as if it was no big deal. "Oh well. If that's the name you prefer..."

I grinned. "I've hated Maximus all my life, but it would be very weird if you stopped calling me that. You can keep calling me Maximus, Mother."

"Are you sure?"

"Yes. There are privileges to being my mother."

My mother flushed with quiet joy.

I turned to Lillian. "Did you sleep well?"

She smiled. "I did, thanks."

Her politeness reminded me of the early days when she became my PA.

"I'm going to leave now that I can see you're in good hands," my mother said, standing up. "I've booked a car to the airport. Should be here in ten minutes. I'll go get my things." She came and kissed me then left us alone.

"Can you manage some toast?" Lillian asked.

"That would be nice... um... thank you."

I would have given anything to know what she was thinking about as she toasted my bread. Just a week ago, I wouldn't have thought twice about going to stand behind her and wrapping her in my arms.

She brought the toast over and I proceeded to eat, my

appetite a lot better. Lillian's phone rang as I was eating and I could tell from her end of the conversation that she was speaking to Maggie. Then Lillian let out a shriek of excitement, jumped up, and as if unable to contain herself she did a little mad dance.

"Oh my God. Oh my God. I knew it. I knew it. Congratulations. I'm so happy for you," she sang, quite beside herself with joy.

"What was that all about?" I asked when she got off the phone

"Martin finally proposed."

I looked at her curiously. "Why are you doing the happy dance then?"

"I'm happy for her," she said simply.

Women were strange creatures. When Chris told me he was marrying Jennifer I was happy for him, but I was not so over the moon happy that I needed to break into a happy dance.

Her phone rang again. "It's my sister," she said as she swiped to answer.

"Hey, Rose," she said, then stiffened. "Is he okay? Okay, good. That's good. Of course, no problem, the only thing is that I'm not home. Hang on a second."

She put the call on hold and turned to me. "My brother-in-law has fractured his hand. Is it okay if my sister drops off the kids here for a few hours? Or should I meet them at my apartment?"

"Of course, it's okay for them to come here." I'd never been around children, but a part of me was looking forward to the experience if Lillian was going to be there as well.

She shot me a grateful smile and returned to her call. "That's fine. I'll send you the address."

She disconnected the call and grabbed my hand. "You could do with a shower. Let's go take one together. They'll be here soon."

We stripped our clothes and entered the bathroom. Lillian ran the shower until it was lovely and warm, and then she pulled me in.

"Tell me about your nieces," I invited as I soaped her down.

"Phoebe and Vera are two years old," she said, a soft look coming over her face. "And they're the sweetest kids you'll ever meet. My sister and Dylan have done a great job with them. Phoebe is curious and fearless while Vera is thoughtful. She likes to take her time before trying something new."

I could feel my cock start to unsicken and get hard as I spread the shower gel over Lillian's stomach. For some unfathomable, bizarre reason, I imagined her pregnant and a stirring came over me. Images of us together filled my mind.

If I had been alone, I would have laughed out loud at my mad thoughts. I still didn't even know if she was my enemy and I was already fantasizing about her pregnant with my babies.

Me, who had never had the urge to procreate.

"Are you sure you're okay about having a couple of two-year-olds in your house for a whole afternoon?" she asked as she soaped me. "They are well-behaved for kids, but they're still in their terrible twos and they will get into things."

"Very sure. I'm looking forward to it actually, plus I have something they'll love."

"What?"

"Tomo and Tyson. Kids love dogs, don't they?"

Lillian shook her head decisively. "Nope, the girls are not meeting your dogs. They're dangerous guard dogs. Who knows how they'll react to children?"

Chapter 53
Lillian

By the time Rose and Dylan arrived, Max had convinced me his dogs would be great with the girls, we had both climaxed, finished showering, and were decently dressed.

We went out to the car just as Rose stepped out. She wasn't focused on us because she was too busy taking in her surroundings. I remembered the first time I came here. It seemed so long ago and yet it wasn't.

The lush surroundings of his home had left me breathless. Max had created his own oasis. Within the compound, it was difficult to believe the city was only a short drive away.

Rose and I hugged, before she turned to Max and I introduced them. They were sizing each other up, but probably Rose more than Max.

"This is Max Frost," I said, having figured out before Rose arrived that the simplest introduction was best.

I turned to Max. "This is my older sister, Rose."

"Hello." Rose tucked strands of her white blonde hair

behind her ear, a gesture she adopted when she was in a thoughtful mood.

After that, we went around the passenger side to say hello to Dylan. His right hand was gripping his left one and he was obviously in pain, but trying hard to hide it.

I made another quick introduction.

Dylan nodded and tried to smile, but it came off like a grimace. Then Rose and I hurriedly got the girls out of the car while Max grabbed the girls' bag.

When their parents had driven off I took each of the girls' hands and led them into the house. They were too awestruck by new surroundings to fuss about their parents leaving and I was grateful for that.

"Doggie," Phoebe said, her hands on Tomo while Vera peered at the big dog from behind her sister.

Max and I laughed. Max was right. The dogs were infinitely gentle with the girls and they were a big hit with the girls. I suppose it was a natural thing with children and animals.

I glanced at Max's face. He had an expression of fascination as he watched the girls as if he had encountered an entirely different species. He had adopted that same expression ever since the girls arrived. True, a lot of people reacted that way to the twins, but it was nice to see it on Max as he hadn't seemed like the type to be interested in kids.

Feeling my eyes on him, he turned to me. "They're cute. Really cute. I can see why people love children."

I laughed. "You make it sound like a scientific experiment."

He laughed. "I've never spent any time with children, let alone twins, so yeah, it is a scientific experiment. Their personalities are obvious even at their young age."

"Oh yes. Phoebe is definitely the leader." I couldn't help but wonder what our kids would look like if we had some. A little boy who was a miniature of Max or a girl who looked like me. The thought brought a deep longing, almost like an ache in my chest.

"It must be an unbearable feeling to know that you're responsible for their lives," Max said.

"It's nothing once you've mastered the art of changing a dirty diaper," I joked. God. I'd fantasized about having children with a man who couldn't stomach the idea of being a father. Thank God he could not read my mind.

"Have you done it before?" he asked curiously.

"Yes. It's not pretty."

"I bet."

"They don't need that done, do they?" he asked worriedly.

I tried not to laugh. "Relax. They're potty-trained."

"Good. That's very good."

Soon after, we trooped back to the house. The girls were getting hungry and Vera needed to use the bathroom. I got some yogurt from the bag my sister had brought and served it to the children. Anyone looking at us would have thought that we were a family.

A pang came over me at the realization that it would never happen for us. I pushed those thoughts away knowing that I was only hurting myself. Then I made dinner and left Max to babysit.

As I worked, I kept an eye on them in case he got overwhelmed, but he seemed to be enjoying the novel experience. At one point, they all stood up to dance to a kid's show on TV. This was from a man who claimed he didn't know how to dance. He saw me laughing and wagged a finger at me.

"Your aunt thinks she can dance better than us," he told the girls and all three of them shot across the open plan space and came to pull me to the living room.

"Dance," Vera commanded bossily, pulling me into the circle.

"I'll get you for this," I swore. I was trying to sound fierce and serious, but laughter bubbled out of me. For the next ten minutes, we danced and made the same silly faces as the character on TV, making the girls double over with laughter.

Seeing Max being so childlike made my heart do little somersaults in my chest. It made me fall just a little more deeply in love with him, but who wouldn't fall for a man who could play with toddlers?

"Now can we have the hundred-dollar cookies?" Phoebe shouted.

I laughed. "Your mom told me you ate the last one a few days ago."

"Yeah, but Mom said, you got them from Uncle Max. Can we have some Uncle Max?" she insisted.

Max looked at me, puzzled and laughing.

"I gave them the box of cookies that Elizabeth brought for you. Remember? You didn't want them so I gave them to the girls. My sister called them the hundred-dollar cookies because the packaging looked so expensive."

"What?" he thundered suddenly.

His expression had changed to one of such serious intensity, I was shocked. "You wanted me to bin them," I blurted out defensively. "You didn't say I couldn't give them to my nieces and..."

He raised his hand to stop me from speaking. "Just a minute. Let me think."

I stared at him, astonished by the change in him.

He began to pace the floor, then stopped suddenly, and turned to me. "Who put the cookies in my office? Was it you?"

"No, she did."

"Did you go in with her?"

"No, she appeared to know her way around. I thought she was one of your girlfriends."

He came striding up to me, cupped my face with his palms, and kissed me on the lips. "You are a genius, Lillian Hudson."

"So can we have the cookies then?" Phoebe asked plaintively.

He turned to Phoebe. "You can have ten boxes."

Her eyes almost popped out of her face. She spread the fingers of both her hands out. "Ten boxes or ten cookies?"

"Ten boxes."

Both girls screamed with joy.

"Hang on a minute," I cautioned, confused, but happy because it appeared as if Max had made some sort of breakthrough. "Rose might have something to say about this."

"Look, I got to go to the office for a bit. Don't leave here until I get back," he said excitedly and sprinted up the stairs.

The kids fell asleep on the couch a couple of hours later and I covered them with soft blankets.

Rose and Dylan came back just as I finished cooking.

"Come in," I said, ushering them into the house.

"Where's Max?" Rose asked.

"He had to rush off to the office."

"Thank you so much for minding the girls," Rose said, taking in the sight of the girls sprawled out on the couch. "They must have had loads of fun to conk out like that," she added with a laugh.

"They did," I said. "They negotiated ten boxes of hundred-dollar cookies out of Max."

My sister's eyebrows flew upwards. "Right, that's it. I'm enrolling them in business school."

I laughed, not knowing that in a few hours, I would be crying my heart out.

Chapter 54
Max

I knew it was four in the morning where Chris was honeymooning, but I couldn't wait. I knew he'd want to know as soon as possible.

"What's up?" he asked sleepily.

"I know who it is," I said.

"Who?" he asked, all sleep gone from his voice.

"Elizabeth Bates."

"Who the fuck is she?"

"She's the daughter of Warren Bates. Ring any bells?"

"Warren Bates? Yeah, brilliant strategist and businessman. He came in with a few projects with us in the beginning. Didn't he just retire though?"

"Yup. And his daughter took over."

"But he was no enemy of ours, why would she target us?"

"He wasn't, but she apparently is."

"How did you figure it out?"

I gave a short laugh. "Lillian helped me. Elizabeth brought cookies to my office when she knew we all would be at the Stew Peters meeting. That was when she planted the bugs."

"Cookies? Why would she bring you cookies?"

I sighed. "We had a one-night stand. She thought it was going to be more, but for me, it was just a stupid mistake. Never should have mixed business and pleasure. It happened more than two years ago, but obviously she never forgave me. This could be her way of taking revenge, or maybe she thinks this is a good way to run a business."

"But I went through the visitor book for myself. She was never slotted in to see you."

"Yeah, I've looked. She popped into my office after an appointment with Ted Nugent, from Mergers and Acquisitions. So you would not have seen her name on my list of visitors."

"I see. Does this mean Lillian is off the hook?"

"Yes. Yes, she is." I felt so ecstatic I wanted to shout with joy.

"Oh, man. I'm so happy for you. But to be honest, I never thought it was her."

"I had a strong hunch it was not her too, but I had to be sure. I couldn't throw away a whole lifetime of work on a hunch no matter how strong it was."

"Yeah, I'd have done the same. What happens now?"

"I pay a visit to Elizabeth and make her an offer she can't refuse."

"Do you want me to get the guys in to remove the bugs?"

"I've already ripped the damn things out. They were driving me crazy. I hated knowing some creep was listening in."

He laughed. "This is great news, Max."

I heard Jennifer's voice in the background asking if everything was okay.

"Go back to bed, everything is perfectly fine, honey," Chris replied.

"I better let you go back to bed too. Speak to me when you get up."

"Great job, Max. Well done."

"All the credit goes to Lillian and her two wonderful little nieces," I said feeling on top of the world.

"Have you told Lillian how you feel about her?"

"Not yet."

"Not yet? Get off the phone now and go get her, man. Full throttle. No more ifs or buts."

"On it, boss. That's exactly what's next on the plan."

Chapter 55
Lillian

I was just putting away the washed dishes when Max came back. He looked almost as if he was vibrating with suppressed excitement.

"What's going on?" I asked curiously.

"Sit down and I'll tell you."

I sat down on the sofa and curled my feet under me while he perched on the edge of the sofa next to me.

He took a deep breath. "Okay. Let me start at the beginning. Soon after you arrived, we lost the La Zaire deal. Someone front-ran us and bought the company before we could, but the funny thing was they had also already anonymously contacted Jed Burner to ask him to run the company for them, exactly as we had planned to do. So we knew we had espionage in our organization. Chris did a sweep of our whole building and found out that both my office and phone were bugged."

I stared at him in amazement. So that's what happened to the La Zaire account.

"We planned to dangle another company we already

owned as bait to see if we could flush out the mole. Until today when the kids mentioned the cookies, I had completely forgotten that Elizabeth had brought them, or even connected her appearance with the spying. But now, I'm certain it is her. She knew I would be at a meeting because everybody in the industry attends it every year. She had the means and she had the motive. She just took over the company from her father."

I felt cold suddenly. Things were falling into place in my head. Things that didn't make sense were rapidly making sense. My voice sounded far away when I spoke.

"You're certain it's her now. Who did you think it was before today?"

He flinched. "You."

I blinked with hurt. "I see."

"I'm sorry. Everything pointed to you. You had the opportunity, you needed money, it happened just after you arrived. What else could I think?"

There were tears, an ocean of tears were waiting to fall, but they didn't because a rage I had never known swept through my body like wildfire.

"So the whole time you were fucking me and pretending to be interested in me, my life and my financial problems, in reality, you thought I was your enemy and you were trying to trap me into revealing myself as the mole."

He scowled. "No. Okay, yes. That's true, but I was-"

Before he could carry on, I sprang to my feet and started running for the door. He caught me by the arm. I didn't think. I just reacted. I swung my arm as far as it would go and slapped him. So hard the sound was like a clap of thunder. His head jerked sideways, and my hand left a white imprint on his cheek.

"Don't touch me," I yelled. "I can't believe you did that to me. How could you? I thought you were a difficult man, but a good man. I was wrong. You are a monster. A heartless cruel monster. You used me."

I pulled my hand out of his slack grip and ran from his home.

My eyes were so full of water I couldn't see properly and I had to stop my car by the side of the road, but I actually felt nothing. I was numb.

I looked at myself in the rearview mirror. My face was white with disbelief.

How could I have been so wrong, so blind about him? But it all made sense now. All of it. The way he blew hot and cold. The little odd questions. I cringed when I thought about the uninhibited way I responded to him sexually. I'd given him everything. I never held anything back.

And he had betrayed me. The betrayal was spectacular, so unexpected, so completely that I felt numb with shock.

I blinked and the tears that were pooling in my eyes ran down my face. I wiped them away with the back of my hand.

I couldn't go back to my apartment. I couldn't go anywhere where he'd been. I wanted to call Maggie, but I knew she was spending the day with Martin. I drove to my mother's place. Having coffee with my mother should help.

I saw Rose's car parked on the street and had to press my lips together to control the trembling. I was determined not to let my mother see what state I was in. I was going to pretend everything was okay until I could figure out what I was going to do.

I put the key in the door and entered.

My mother was sitting with Rose on the couch looking through old photograph albums she had unearthed while packing her stuff.

"There you are, honey. Come in, and see this. Remember this?" my mother asked, holding up an old photograph of the four of us on a beach holiday.

Rose and I were grinning at the camera, our scrawny ten and twelve-year-old bodies, and our hair wet from the ocean. I shifted my gaze to my dad and all of a sudden, a great wave of sadness came over me. I missed him so much. Missed his sound advice and his willingness to always listen.

"I remember that day," I said, my voice trembling. "God, I miss Dad."

Mom smiled mistily. "He would be so proud of you." She closed the album and put it in a crate.

A lump came to my throat. "Are you not going to take that with you?"

"Yes, this crate is coming with me."

I nodded.

Mom planned to put most of her furniture into storage and to sort them out at a later date. Sell the ones she didn't want to keep. She wanted to keep the furniture to a minimum in the new cottage and I agreed with her. There was something neat and healthy about lots of open spaces and natural light.

"I'm taking you for a drink," Rose said, staring at me

penetratingly. I'm sure the baby sister won't mind watching the girls for another hour or so."

"Yeah, why not." I hadn't thought it possible to be so consumed by thoughts of a man. He filled my brain and my thoughts like a virus.

Rose stood and came close to me. "What's going on? You look like crap," she whispered fiercely.

"Thanks," I said in a dry tone.

I got into my car and followed her, my mind finally and strangely quiet. It reminded me of the calm before the storm.

* * *

"Holly Hell," my sister gasped.

I sniffed. "I know. He used me, Rose. I was so stupid I never imagined."

Her head jerked back. "That's not what I meant at all. You're my sister and I love you to death, but hang on a minute."

"Oh my God! You're going to try and see it from his point of view, aren't you?" I asked incredulously.

"As a matter of fact, yes, I am. Look. Put yourself in his shoes. What would you have done?"

"I wouldn't have slept with me," I snapped.

"Even that is a credit to him and how deeply he must feel for you. He thought you were his enemy and he still couldn't help himself from sleeping with you. The man must have it really bad."

"Have you not listened to a word I said?" I asked

angrily. "He was sleeping with me because he was trying to find out if I was the leak."

"Bullshit," she said authoritatively. "He was already working on it. He didn't need you to accidentally slip up and confess at all. He slept with you because he desperately wanted to."

I leaned back and stared at my sister. "You're wrong."

"How hard did you slap him?" she asked curiously.

"So hard my hand is still stinging," I said.

She smiled. "Poor guy."

I glared at her. "Don't freaking pity him. He's a monster."

"You know he's not. He's one of the good guys. I like him. I like his house and I liked the way he looked at my little girls. He's a good guy."

"But it's over. I could never trust him again."

"I'm sorry, Lillian, but if I was him and I had to choose between a business that I'd spent the best part of life building and some come lately PA, I know which one I'm prioritizing. He had no choice. Don't you see that?"

She didn't understand. She didn't understand what had gone on between us. Of how deeply we had bonded and yet the whole time he'd kept this massive secret from me. I could never trust him again.

But God, how I missed him. I missed his laugh, his scent, even his grumpiness. Oh, to have those strong arms around me. The pain in my chest expanded with every thought.

We stayed for an hour, then Rose had to go.

That night, I fell into bed physically and mentally exhausted, but I couldn't sleep. Then the crying started and

I couldn't stop. I ugly cried, burying my head into the pillow.

Once, I'd vowed that whatever happened, I would never regret my affair with Max. Now, I wished we hadn't started it. It wasn't worth the unbearable pain I was feeling now.

Somehow, in the early morning hours, I managed to fall asleep and when the phone alarm woke me up the following morning, the first thing I saw was a message from Max.

I need to talk to you. Please, Lillian, it's important.

I did the only thing I could do. I blocked his number. That door must remain closed forever.

What he did was unforgivable.

Chapter 56
Max

I walked into Elizabeth Bates's outer office. Immediately her PA looked at me and asked if she could help.

"Not really," I said and strode past.

"Hey, you can't go in there," she wailed, but I'd already opened the door and walked in.

Elizabeth was on the phone, but when she saw me, she abruptly ended her phone call.

"I'm sorry, Miss Bates, but he barged through. Should I call Security?"

"No, that will be all, Susan."

Susan left and I went to sit opposite Elizabeth.

"I like what you've done with your father's office," I said.

"Thank you. What can I do for you?"

"You can sell La Zaire back to me for the price you bought it for."

For the first time she looked unsettled, but she didn't back down. "Why would I do that?"

"Because if you don't, you'll be selling it back to me for half the price next year."

She frowned. "Is that a threat?"

I smiled slowly. "No, it's a promise."

"What makes you think that would be the case?"

"Because I've locked Jed Burner into a ten-year contract with Frost Industries, and without him, you haven't got a hope in hell of turning that company around, especially when you'll have me as a competitor."

She looked at me defiantly. "I'm not selling. I don't need Jed. I can find someone else."

"The only reason you're sitting here and not in a police station is out of respect for your father. I like him, he's a fair man. We did good business together and I know he wouldn't want me to destroy his favorite daughter, but if you're smart you won't count on my benevolence lasting much longer.

She bristled. "I don't know what you're talking about."

I stood and walked to the window. The view was a sea of skyscrapers. Each one shining in the morning light.

"Your father built this company from nothing with his bare hands. He based it on honesty and hard work. If he knew what you've done, he would be embarrassed and ashamed. He'll tell you, you won't get far going the way you're going, but worse you'll ruin everything he's spent his whole life building."

I turned away from the window and looked at her.

"I'm the biggest fish in this pond, Elizabeth, and believe me, you don't want to cross me. We had a one-night stand that didn't work out, so fucking what? Get over it. Before I leave this office, you'll have to decide. Are you against me or are you with me? Once I walk out of here, there will be no second chances. You will have to reap the consequences of your decision whatever it may be."

She swiveled her chair around to face me. "Are you saying you will help me run my father's company?"

I laughed. God, she was naïve. "No, I'm not saying that. I'm saying, choose between me leaving you alone to run your business in peace, or prepare to be crushed under my heel like a cockroach."

She swallowed, then blurted out, "You can't bully me."

I walked over to where she was seated and stood over her. I could smell her fear.

"I have no more to say. Make your choice."

"No, I'm not making a choice. I'm not your secretary begging to be fucked on your table."

My smile turned nasty. She just did the one thing she shouldn't have done. She brought Lillian into the conversation.

"You've just made your choice." I began to walk away from her.

I had just touched the handle when she called. "Wait."

I turned around slowly and looked at her without pity. I remembered her under me. Panting, desperate, her small breasts jiggling, and I felt nothing but contempt.

"Look, I'm sorry, okay. I'm sorry. I shouldn't have done what I did. I'll sell La Zaire back to you at the price I bought it for. I'm sorry."

I nodded. "My lawyers will contact you."

"Thank you."

"Send my regards to your father."

Then I was gone.

I walked into the elevator and waited for the exhilaration to come. It didn't and my skin prickled with foreboding. My work was everything to me, if I couldn't derive joy from it, what did I have? Nothing. Without Lillian, everything was meaningless.

I sent Chris a text.

La Zaire is ours

His reply came in immediately.

Whoop! Whoop! Who's the master of this game? Well played, Max. Showed her who's boss.

I couldn't even answer him.

I headed to the office, feeling as if I was carrying the weight of the world on my shoulders. I didn't have the excuse of being unwell either. Lillian was the cause of my sour mood.

I tried to imagine my life without her. It stretched out like an endless desert. Desolate, empty, nothingness. True, I'd lived without her and I'd been pretty happy, but meeting her had been like having a door to an unimaginably wonderful room, cracked open. After giving me a quick peek inside, the door had been slammed shut.

In the brief time we had been together, Lillian had become a necessary part of my life. If I was to be brutally honest, I needed her. I loved her. That was it. I loved her. I was in love with her. She made everything in my life make sense. Life with Lillian was an adventure and I was determined to get her back.

No matter what, I wanted her back.

My phone vibrated. I looked at the screen.

"Hello, Mother."

"Hey, Maximus, I know you're going to complain, but I'm in town and I'd love to have dinner with you. Can you squeeze me in?"

"Sure," I said without feeling irritation. Something had shifted. Maybe it was the fact that she was really trying to bridge the distance between us.

"Oh, that was easy," she said, clearly pleased. "I expected to have to cajole you. I'm staying at The Supreme and I hear the food at their restaurant is great. Let's meet at six."

I was glad to have somewhere to go after work. My house, which was my sanctuary had become a mockery of something fleeting that I'd had before it had flown away. I arrived a few minutes before my mother. She was late, but it didn't matter. Nothing did any more. I used to be particular about people keeping time, but it didn't bother me now.

Chapter 57
Max

I sat brooding over a double shot of whisky, wondering where Lillian was. What if she was on a date? What if she had gone back to pansy Dan? The thought made me livid. I wanted to take a baseball bat to his bony knees.

"Must have been a rough day," my mother said.

I hadn't seen her approach and I stood up and she air-kissed my cheek.

"I'm fine."

The waiter brought the wine and poured it into our glasses.

"No, you're not. It's Lillian, isn't it?"

I slumped. I couldn't discuss Lillian with my mother. I just couldn't. "Can we please not talk about her?"

"No, we have to talk about her."

"I made a mistake many years ago and I won't let you make the same one. You're leaving right now. You're going to her home and you're going to tell her you love her.

Because she doesn't know that. And that will change everything."

I stared at my mother.

She smiled sadly and nodded. "I haven't been a good mother to you until today. Go now, my son. Go now and with both hands take what is yours."

"What about you?"

"I've reached the age where I can dine alone without anyone raising an eyebrow. Go, Maximus. You have nothing to lose and everything to gain. Go, make me proud. Soon it will be too late."

I stood and headed to her place, my heart pounding like crazy. I had to dry my palms every so often on my pants.

I rang her bell several times. No answer. The frustration inside me grew. I'd assumed that she would be home. I took out my phone and jabbed the screen until I got to Maggie's number.

"Do you know where Lillian is?" I asked when she answered her phone. I knew I was being rude, but the words were already out.

"Ask her yourself," she said equally curtly.

"I would, but she's blocked my number."

She chuckled. "She always was a bit dramatic."

"I'm standing outside her apartment, but she's not home. Can you help... please?"

"You know, if I didn't think you genuinely loved her, I would disconnect this call," Maggie said.

I fidgeted with impatience, but I kept my mouth shut.

"She's at her mother's house," she continued. "I'll text you the address. And hey... good luck."

I should have been practicing what to say to her, getting the words together, but I couldn't. All I could think of was how much I longed to see her. To hold her. To look into her eyes. To whisper sweet words into her ear and see a smile brighten up her face.

My GPS led me to a well-kept family home. I parked and hurried up to the front door and rang the bell. A woman opened the door. She bore a slight resemblance to Lillian.

"Hello, you must be Mrs. Hudson," I said quickly. "I'm Max Frost and I'm looking for Lillian."

She smiled. "Oh, Lillian's boss. Come in. I'll get her for you."

"Thanks, but I'll wait for her out here."

"Okay."

She left the door slightly ajar and disappeared into the interior of the house. A couple of minutes later, soft footsteps sounded, the door fully opened and Lillian stood there.

The sight of her took my breath away. Her hair was up in a ponytail and her face looked pure and beautiful. It was such a treat to be standing so close to her, inhaling her sweet scent and staring at her face, remembering every soft curve. I had missed her more than I'd thought it possible to miss someone.

But she kept one hand on the doorknob as if she was planning to slam the door in my face.

Pure fear speared through me. This woman held my future happiness in her hands. If she didn't want anything to do with me, I would be condemned to a life of misery. Like my mother. A sad life of watching other people live full lives while I became bitter with the knowledge I'd lost the one great love I'd found because I was such an idiot.

"What are you doing here?" she asked coldly.

The Lillian I knew would not have been so rude. "I'm missing something." I should have practiced a speech. Now, I was just blurting out whatever came to my mind.

"What?" she snapped.

I scrambled to find words that would floor her, but I couldn't. All I had was my raw truth. "I miss you, Lillian."

She folded her hands across her chest, a wary expression in her eyes. "Cut the flowery shit. You've got what you wanted. You've found out who your enemy is and your precious business is safe. What else do you want?"

"You. I want you."

"Yeah, I know you want me for sex. Go somewhere else because I'm not interested."

"I know I'm rude, aggressive, demanding, hostile, impossible to please, and completely lacking any kind of empathy towards my fellow humans, but I love you, Lillian."

Her jaw dropped and she stared at me incredulously. "What did you say?"

"I know I'm rude, aggressive, demand-"

"Not that part," she interrupted impatiently, "the last part."

"I'm in love with you, Lillian."

She took a step backwards as if my words were poison or dangerous to her. "When did you realize this?'

"When I went to Connecticut without you. I sat in my old room and knew that you're my source of joy... the woman who has my heart."

"You broke my heart, Max."

"I'm really so very sorry I hurt you, but whatever hurt I caused you I've suffered more."

"How can I ever trust you again?" she gasped.

"Because you know me. Even when I thought you were my enemy, I couldn't stay away from you."

"What would you have done if it had turned out that I was the leak?"

"I think I would have forgiven you. How can you punish a child for stealing bread to feed her mother?"

"So what now?"

"I want to marry you."

She let out a cry of delight. "You mean that?" Then her expression became sad.

"I love you too, Max, with all my heart, but what future is there for me if your first love is your business? Will you throw me under a bus every time you have to choose between your business and me?"

Strong emotions swirled inside of me and I felt my eyes mist. I loved this woman so damn much. "I want kids," I blurted out.

Her eyes widened. "Are you trying to bribe me?"

"Is it working?"

"Kind of."

"How big a family do you want?"

"Big," she whispered.

"Are ten kids enough for you?"

She shook her head and tears filled her eyes. "You'd have ten kids for me?"

I nodded vigorously. "I'd have a hundred kids if it would make you happy."

"I want four."

"I want whatever you want."

I couldn't stand the distance between us anymore. I tugged her hand and she crashed into me. I wrapped my arms around her and held her so tight she squealed.

When she drew back, she stared up into my eyes. "I love you. God, how much I love you. I've cried and cried thinking I'd lost you forever. Even now, I can hardly believe you're here." She cupped my face and looked at me with such love, it made me feel undeserving of that love.

"I'm so sorry. I was an ass. I promise to spend the rest of my life making it up to you."

"It's okay. I forgive you. All you need to do is love me."

"That I can definitely do," I said, covering her mouth with mine. Our tongues touched, familiar and exciting at the same time.

Lillian pressed her body to mine, showing me without words that she wanted me as much as I wanted her. Wanting a taste of every part of her, I moved from her mouth and nuzzled my way to her earlobe, biting it gently.

"Don't you think it's time we got on with making these ten babies?"

"Five," she corrected with a laugh.

"If we start tonight. That will be one down and four to go."

"Oh no. My mother!" Lillian cried with a groan.

"What about your mother?"

"I haven't told her about us. She still thinks you're my boss."

"So tell her," I said.

"Okay, but you have to wait out here for a few minutes while I tell her."

"I'll wait forever," I said.

She laughed. "I doubt that very much."

I sat down on the stone steps. She had no idea. No idea at all. I was here forever.

Chapter 58
Lillian

I wanted to cry and celebrate at the same time. I shut the door and felt as if I was walking on air. What if this was a dream? I pinched myself.

Ouch.

That had really happened.

Max loved me. I hadn't just been someone who just relieved an itch. I had meant something to him. Giddy joy filled me.

"I almost came looking for you." my mother said, concern on her face. "Is everything okay?"

I slid onto a stool and grinned at her. "Very okay. Mom. Um... there's something I need to tell you so please don't freak out."

"What is it?" she asked in a calm voice that took me by surprise. I expected her to panic the way she always did since Henry.

Remembering that Max was waiting outside, I ploughed on. "I guess I should have told you this a long time ago, but Max is not just my boss. We're kind of in a relationship."

"I figured that out," my mom said calmly, surprising me further.

"You knew?"

"Of course, I knew. That look on your face when you mentioned his name. I knew you were in love with him. I know my girls."

I laughed. "You're amazing, Mom. Anyway, he came by to tell me that he loves me and he wants us to be in a serious relationship."

She stood and hugged me. "I'm so happy for you. I can't tell you how many times I wanted to go find him and give him a good shake."

I laughed. "You don't even know what he looks like."

"You wouldn't understand. It's a Mom thing. You want to protect your children; however old they are."

"Thanks, Mom. I should have told you. I thought you'd be disappointed. You had such high standards when it came to your work."

A cheeky look came into her eyes. "How do you think I met your father? We worked in the same office in those early years. You could say he was my boss, though not directly," she said and burst into laughter at my expression.

I laughed. "You had an affair with your boss?"

Hands akimbo, she said, "He married me."

"Dad loved you so much," I said, remembering how my father had looked at my mother.

"So, are you going to invite Max in, or are you going to leave the poor man outside for the rest of the night?"

"I'm going to invite him in," I said and happily went out, almost unable to believe it was possible to feel as happy as I did. I flung the door open. Max looked up, and my heart expanded with love.

"Come, meet my Mom."

He got up and followed in.

Mom and Max took to each other immediately, and you'd not have believed that they had met less than an hour before. She regaled him with embarrassing stories about Rose and me growing up and Max encouraged her to reveal more.

He ended up staying for dinner.

We left at eight after dinner and a few glasses of wine. As fun as it had been, I couldn't wait to be alone with Max.

"Let's go to your apartment," Max said. "It's nearer and I'm not sure how long I can wait to see you naked. It feels like a lifetime ago that I opened your legs and ate you out."

I shivered at the intensity in his eyes and rested my hand on his thigh. That was what I had longed for, amongst other things. Knowing I could touch him whenever I wanted because I had a claim on him.

We got to my building and hurried out of the car. Holding hands we entered the elevator. Max didn't bother to wait for us to reach my apartment. He pulled me close and proceeded to kiss me passionately. Threading my hands through his thick, silky hair, I pressed my aching breasts against his chest.

Somehow we made it to my door. Max took my keys from my nerveless hand and unlocked the door. He kicked the door shut behind him. Then he pinned me to the wall, wedged his leg between mine and carried on kissing me. I found myself grinding against his leg, rubbing my pussy against his thigh, desperate for friction.

Clothes flew everywhere, and by the time we made it to the bedroom, we were both naked. I expected Max to fling me to the bed and take me urgently. Instead, he took a step back and let his gaze slide over me. It was a hungry look, but that wasn't what turned me to mush. It was the love that shimmered in his eyes. There was no guarded look, no protection, no self-preservation. It was out there for me to see.

"You're so beautiful," he whispered huskily.

Max took my hand and guided me to the bed. He draped his body over mine, traced my lower lip with his tongue and the rest of the world disappeared as...

He made love to me.

Chapter 59
Max

She walked around my desk and swiveled my chair around. Sitting on my lap she threw her arms around me. "You know I won't be your PA once the babies start coming, don't you?"

I nodded unhappily.

"Are you going to be nice to the poor thing?"

I rested my hands on her hips, loving the gentle swell. "Nice? Define nice." Her scent should have been sold in bottles. It was so fucking sexy, an aphrodisiac if I ever smelt one.

"You can't be rude and shout at them just because you feel like it," she said inching closer and spreading her legs.

My cock was surging to life at her nearness and flirty tone. I brought my hands to her thighs, caressing them. "What if she's no good?"

"I don't believe Maggie will send you anyone who is no good." I slipped a hand between her legs and came into contact with her soaking panties. I slipped my fingers under the edges and stroked her clit. "Can we worry about that when the time comes? That could be months, even years away."

"Oh yes," Lillian said, her breathing labored, her chest moving up and down.

I pinched her swollen clit and then slipped a finger inside. She cupped my face and kissed me, the sensations going all the way to my cock. She tasted of strawberry and lettuce. I loved it. Our tongues tangled together.

I slipped my finger in and out, then added a second one. Lillian moaned into my mouth. She didn't need to say a word. I knew she wanted me to fuck her faster.

My movements became more frantic as she neared her climax. As she came, she let out a muffled cry, but I kept on fucking her with my fingers until she was completely spent and slumped against me.

She rested a few minutes before she sat up. I slapped her lightly on her ass. "Up you go. Work calls."

She slid off my lap. "By the way. It's not months or even years away. Looks like it's just eight months away."

I grabbed her and pulled her back on top of me. "Oh, Lillian, Lillian..." I whispered. "You just made me the happiest man on earth."

"Tell me that when it's your turn to change the dirty diaper."

I began to laugh. And laugh. Life was so beautiful.

Epilogue

Lillian

"Your father would have given anything to walk you down the aisle," my mother said as she adjusted my veil.

"He'll be here in spirit," Rose said briskly. "We're not going to be sad today, so none of that emotional talk."

Rose had confided a few days earlier how guilty she felt that unlike her, I'd missed out on having our father walk me down the aisle. We'd had a good cry about it, but I'd made my peace with it a long time ago. Uncle Ralph was walking me down the aisle.

What really mattered was the man who was waiting for me at the end of it.

Max's parents had insisted on hosting the wedding at their home and we had agreed. They had the space for it and the garden was more beautiful than any venue we could have picked.

The door opened, and Maggie walked in looking gorgeous, with a small but noticeable bump and a glowing face. Marriage and pregnancy suited her. She and Martin had tied the knot three months earlier in a beach wedding in Maui that had been both beautiful and fun. I had acted as her maid of honor just as she was mine.

"How's Max?" I asked, my hand automatically resting on my own little bump. I'd sent her to the guest house where the groom and his groomsmen were getting ready.

She grinned. "That's the first thing he asked when he saw me. He's fine and he told me to tell you that he can't wait for you to be his wife."

Warmth engulfed me. I couldn't wait either. He was the man for me. My partner for life. The father of the babies we would have. Rose opened a bottle of champagne and poured the tiniest bit for all of us, then we toasted my marriage.

Outside, the guests had started to sit down on either side of the aisle. I'd opted for gold and cream as my theme, and the garden looked absolutely beautiful.

"It's almost time," Rose said. "The guys are making their way from the guest house."

In less than an hour, we would be husband and wife. My heart raced with excitement as my bridal party made our way from the main house to the back garden.

"I love you," Rose said, kissing me, then it was her turn to dance down the aisle as we had arranged.

It was relaxing to hear the guests chuckle at the dancing antics my bridesmaids were getting up to. Then it was my turn to walk down the aisle with my mother. Tears unexpectedly filled my eyes. Who would have thought that this moment would come? From this day forward, I would introduce Max as my husband.

"You ready, sweetheart?" my mother whispered to me.

I nodded. "I am. I love you, Mom."

"I love you too my girl," she said, her eyes brimming with tears.

I linked my arm through hers and together we made our way down the aisle as everyone oohed and ahhed. I smiled at everyone on either side of the aisle and when I met Marilyn's eyes, she blew me a kiss. I finally looked ahead and I saw Max, it was just the two of us.

He looked so handsome in a black tuxedo, satin white shirt and forest green tie. My chest tightened and my heart squeezed. I loved him with every fiber of my being. He was the man I had always dreamed of meeting but never imagined that I would. As I walked towards my future, I felt like the luckiest woman in the whole world.

We had chosen to say the traditional vows as they held a solemnity that appealed to Max and me. I tried to hold it together as Max said his vows, promising to love and cherish me till death do us part. I cried through my own vows, with Max doing his best to mop up my face. It was emotional and sweet, promising our love and devotion to each other in front of our friends and family, but I was glad when that part was over.

"You may kiss the bride," the smiling priest said.

Max stepped forward and cupped my face. "My soul mate," he said before his lips covered mine. He kissed me passionately until our guests started whistling and I laughingly broke the kiss. I stared into his eyes.

"My soul mate," I echoed.

I couldn't wait to begin our lives together as Mr. and Mrs. Frost.

That's all folks!

Coming Next...

Sweet Poison

Prologue

Cole

"Shall we try one more time, honey?"

My daughter chewed her bottom lip and nodded solemnly. "Okay."

"What is your name?"

She folded her little arms in front of her. "Anya Barrett."

Good. And your father's name?"

"Cole Barrett."

"Very good," I encouraged, with a smile. "And if anybody asks you where you come from?"

"Manhattan," she said clearly.

"Did you live in a big house with a housekeeper and maids or a small apartment?"

"A small apartment."

"What floor was the apartment?"

She looked upwards. "Mmm... Fifth floor."

"Have you ever had a chauffeur?" I threw at her suddenly.

"Nope"

"What about a gardener or a nanny?"

She shook her head decisively. "Never."

"Excellent. Why did your father want to move to Bison Ridge?"

"Because he wanted me to attend Bison Lodge Academy."

"Well done. Where did you go to school in Manhattan?"

"The Avenue Sc-," she began to say.

But I shook my head slightly, and she immediately covered her mouth with both hands and said, "Oops. Sorry, Daddy."

"It's okay," I reassured. "Try again."

"I was home-schooled."

I grinned at her. "That's better. What does your father do for a living?"

"He's an accountant. He files other people's taxes for them."

I nodded approvingly. "Next question, where is your mother?"

Her expression remained unchanged and her voice felt robotic. "My mother abandoned my father and me."

"And if anybody asks for more information about her, what will you say?"

"It's hard for me to talk about my mom. Can we talk about something else, please."

I touched her little nose with my finger. "Good answer. What about your grandparents? Where are they?"

She looked sideways at me. "They live in Miami?"

"Exactly. But don't look as if you're unsure. Try again. Say it naturally. You don't want to make anyone suspicious, do you?"

She shook her head vigorously. "No."

"Where do your grandparents live?"

"They live in Miami."

"That's better. I think that will be enough for tonight." I glanced at my watch. "Looks like it's your bedtime anyway."

"Will Mommy ever come back to see us?"

My heart broke for her. "I don't know, honey. She's busy with her new life. Maybe one day, when you're older you can go visit her, huh?"

"Daddy?"

"Yeah."

She looked down at a blue button on her dress. "I know Mommy is busy with her new life and she doesn't have time for us anymore, but will you check up on her sometimes and make sure she's alright."

I nodded. "I will. I promise. Now, bed."

"Daddy?"

"Yeah."

She took a deep breath. "When we go to the new town to start our new life, you won't leave me like Mommy did, will you?"

I looked intently into her big sad eyes. "Never. I will

never ever leave you, Anya. You're stuck with me for the rest of your life."

She grinned. "Good. Um... one last thing, Daddy."

"What?"

"Can I take my butterfly shoes with us? They're my favorite. I don't think I can bear to leave them behind."

"Darling, we can't take anything from this life with us. Nothing that will remind us, or trip us up. Remember we're not supposed to be rich. You didn't go to an expensive preschool and you've never owned any designer gear."

"What about if I scuff my shoes so that no one can see that they're expensive?"

Looking at her hopeful face made me feel incredibly sad. It was wrong and it was dangerous to make concessions now, but I couldn't say no to her. It was such a tiny thing what she was asking. "All right. You can bring the shoes with you. You don't have to scuff it, but if anybody asks, they're fakes from Hong Kong, okay? We bought them at a market."

"Okay, I'll tell everybody they're fakes from Hong Kong," she repeated beaming with innocent joy.

"And now, it's really bedtime. Go brush your teeth and get into your PJs and I'll come to read you a story and kiss you goodnight."

"Okay." She scrambled off the sofa and ran off, pigtails flying. I heard her running up the stairs, her butterfly shoes clacking on the specially imported marble slabs of the staircase.

I didn't know if the child could pull it off. I hoped and prayed she wouldn't slip up, but if she did, I was ready... for the river of blood that would flow.

Coming Next...

Sweet Poison is a Mafia romance.
Please pre-order here:
Sweet Poison

In the meantime if you're curious about Zane and Dahlia or you just want to slip into the Mafia vibe check out:
You Don't Own Me

About the Author

If you wish to leave a review for this book
please do so here:
Boss From Hell

Please click on this link to receive news of my latest releases and great giveaways.
http://bit.ly/10e9WdE

and remember
I **LOVE** hearing from readers so by all means come and say hello here:

Also by Georgia Le Carre

Owned

42 Days

Besotted

Seduce Me

Love's Sacrifice

Masquerade

Pretty Wicked (novella)

Disfigured Love

Hypnotized

Crystal Jake 1,2&3

Sexy Beast

Wounded Beast

Beautiful Beast

Dirty Aristocrat

You Don't Own Me 1 & 2

You Don't Know Me

Blind Reader Wanted

Redemption

The Heir

Blackmailed By The Beast

Submitting To The Billionaire

The Bad Boy Wants Me

Nanny & The Beast

His Frozen Heart

The Man In The Mirror

A Kiss Stolen

Can't Let Her Go

Highest Bidder

Saving Della Ray

Nice Day For A White Wedding

With This Ring

With This Secret

Saint & Sinner

Bodyguard Beast

Beauty & The Beast

The Other Side of Midnight

The Russian Billionaire

CEO's Revenge

Mine To Possess

Heat Of The Moment